NON SANZ DROICT.

Willliam Shakespeare

MEASURE
for
MEASURE

**With New Dramatic Criticism
and an Updated Bibliography**

Edited by S. Nagarajan

The Signet Classic Shakespeare
GENERAL EDITOR: SYLVAN BARNET

A SIGNET CLASSIC

SIGNET CLASSIC
Published by the Penguin Group
Penguin Books USA Inc., 375 Hudson Street,
New York, New York 10014, U.S.A.
Penguin Books Ltd, 27 Wrights Lane,
London W8 5TZ, England
Penguin Books Australia Ltd, Ringwood,
Victoria, Australia
Penguin Books Canada Ltd, 10 Alcorn Avenue,
Toronto, Ontario, Canada M4V 3B2
Penguin Books (N.Z.) Ltd, 182–190 Wairau Road,
Auckland 10, New Zealand

Penguin Books Ltd, Registered Offices:
Harmondsworth, Middlesex, England

Published by Signet Classic, an imprint of Dutton Signet,
a division of Penguin Books USA Inc.

First Signet Classic Printing, June, 1964
26 25 24

Ⓒ REGISTERED TRADEMARK—MARCA REGISTRADA

Library of Congress Catalog Card Number: 88-61100

Printed in the United States of America

Contents

Shakespeare: Prefatory Remarks

Between the record of his baptism in Stratford on 26 April 1564 and the record of his burial in Stratford on 25 April 1616, some forty documents name Shakespeare, and many others name his parents, his children, and his grandchildren. More facts are known about William Shakespeare than about any other playwright of the period except Ben Jonson. The facts should, however, be distinguished from the legends. The latter, inevitably more engaging and better known, tell us that the Stratford boy killed a calf in high style, poached deer and rabbits, and was forced to flee to London, where he held horses outside a playhouse. These traditions are only traditions; they may be true, but no evidence supports them, and it is well to stick to the facts.

Mary Arden, the dramatist's mother, was the daughter of a substantial landowner; about 1557 she married John Shakespeare, who was a glove-maker and trader in various farm commodities. In 1557 John Shakespeare was a member of the Council (the governing body of Stratford), in 1558 a constable of the borough, in 1561 one of the two town chamberlains, in 1565 an alderman (entitling him to the appellation "Mr."), in 1568 high bailiff—the town's highest political office, equivalent to mayor. After 1577, for an unknown reason he drops out of local politics. The birthday of William Shakespeare, the eldest son of this locally prominent man, is unrecorded; but the Stratford parish register records that the infant was baptized on 26 April 1564. (It is quite possible that he was born on 23 April, but this date has probably been assigned by tradition because it is the date on which, fifty-two years later, he died.) The attendance records of the Stratford grammar school of the period are not extant, but it is reasonable to assume that the son of a local official attended the school and received substantial training in Latin. The masters of the school from Shakespeare's seventh to fifteenth years held Oxford degrees; the Elizabethan curriculum excluded mathematics and the natural sciences but taught a good deal of Latin rhetoric, logic, and literature. On 27 November 1582 a marriage license was issued to Shakespeare and Anne Hathaway, eight years his senior. The couple had a child in May, 1583. Perhaps the marriage was necessary, but perhaps the couple had earlier engaged in a formal "troth plight" which would render their children legitimate even if no further ceremony were performed. In 1585 Anne Hathaway bore Shakespeare twins.

That Shakespeare was born is excellent; that he married and had children is pleasant; but that we know nothing about his departure from Stratford to London, or about the beginning of his theatrical career, is lamentable and must be admitted. We would gladly sacrifice details about his children's baptism for details about his earliest days on the stage. Perhaps the poaching episode is true (but it is first reported almost a century after Shakespeare's death), or perhaps he first left Stratford to be a schoolteacher, as another tradition holds; perhaps he was moved by

> Such wind as scatters young men through the world,
> To seek their fortunes further than at home
> Where small experience grows.

In 1592, thanks to the cantankerousness of Robert Greene, a rival playwright and a pamphleteer, we have our first reference, a snarling one, to Shakespeare as an actor and playwright. Greene warns those of his own educated friends who wrote for the theater against an actor who has presumed to turn playwright:

> There is an upstart crow, beautified with our feathers, that with his *tiger's heart wrapped in a player's hide*

supposes he is as well able to bombast out a blank verse as the best of you, and being an absolute Johannes-factotum is in his own conceit the only Shake-scene in a country.

The reference to the player, as well as the allusion to Aesop's crow (who strutted in borrowed plumage, as an actor struts in fine words not his own), makes it clear that by this date Shakespeare had both acted and written. That Shakespeare is meant is indicated not only by "Shake-scene" but by the parody of a line from one of Shakespeare's plays, *3 Henry VI:* "O, tiger's heart wrapped in a woman's hide." If Shakespeare in 1592 was prominent enough to be attacked by an envious dramatist, he probably had served an apprenticeship in the theater for at least a few years.

In any case, by 1592 Shakespeare had acted and written, and there are a number of subsequent references to him as an actor: documents indicate that in 1598 he is a "principal comedian," in 1603 a "principal tragedian," in 1608 he is one of the "men players." The profession of actor was not for a gentleman, and it occasionally drew the scorn of university men who resented writing speeches for persons less educated than themselves, but it was respectable enough: players, if prosperous, were in effect members of the bourgeoisie, and there is nothing to suggest that Stratford considered William Shakespeare less than a solid citizen. When, in 1596, the Shakespeares were granted a coat of arms, the grant was made to Shakespeare's father, but probably William Shakespeare (who the next year bought the second-largest house in town) had arranged the matter on his own behalf. In subsequent transactions he is occasionally styled a gentleman.

Although in 1593 and 1594 Shakespeare published two narrative poems dedicated to the Earl of Southampton, *Venus and Adonis* and *The Rape of Lucrece,* and may well have written most or all of his sonnets in the middle nineties, Shakespeare's literary activity seems to have been almost entirely devoted to the theater. (It may be significant that the two narrative poems were written in years

when the plague closed the theaters for several months.)
In 1594 he was a charter member of a theatrical company
called the Chamberlain's Men (which in 1603 changed
its name to the King's Men); until he retired to Stratford
(about 1611, apparently), he was with this remarkably
stable company. From 1599 the company acted primarily
at the Globe Theatre, in which Shakespeare held a one-
tenth interest. Other Elizabethan dramatists are known to
have acted, but no other is known also to have been en-
titled to a share in the profits of the playhouse.

Shakespeare's first eight published plays did not have
his name on them, but this is not remarkable; the most
popular play of the sixteenth century, Thomas Kyd's *The
Spanish Tragedy,* went through many editions without
naming Kyd, and Kyd's authorship is known only because
a book on the profession of acting happens to quote (and
attribute to Kyd) some lines on the interest of Roman
emperors in the drama. What is remarkable is that after
1598 Shakespeare's name commonly appears on printed
plays—some of which are not his. Another indication of
his popularity comes from Francis Meres, author of *Pal-
ladis Tamia: Wit's Treasury* (1598): in this anthology of
snippets accompanied by an essay on literature, many
playwrights are mentioned, but Shakespeare's name occurs
more often than any other, and Shakespeare is the only
playwright whose plays are listed.

From his acting, playwriting, and share in a theater,
Shakespeare seems to have made considerable money. He
put it to work, making substantial investments in Stratford
real estate. When he made his will (less than a month
before he died), he sought to leave his property intact to
his descendants. Of small bequests to relatives and to
friends (including three actors, Richard Burbage, John
Heminges, and Henry Condell), that to his wife of the
second-best bed has provoked the most comment; perhaps it was the bed the couple had slept in, the best being
reserved for visitors. In any case, had Shakespeare not
excepted it, the bed would have gone (with the rest of his
household possessions) to his daughter and her husband.
On 25 April 1616 he was buried within the chancel of

the church at Stratford. An unattractive monument to his
memory, placed on a wall near the grave, says he died
on 23 April. Over the grave itself are the lines, perhaps
by Shakespeare, that (more than his literary fame) have
kept his bones undisturbed in the crowded burial ground
where old bones were often dislodged to make way for
new:

> Good friend, for Jesus' sake forbear
> To dig the dust enclosèd here.
> Bless be the man that spares these stones
> And cursed be he that moves my bones.

Thirty-seven plays, as well as some nondramatic poems,
are held to constitute the Shakespeare canon. The dates of
composition of most of the works are highly uncertain,
but there is often evidence of a *terminus a quo* (starting
point) and/or a *terminus ad quem* (terminal point) that
provides a framework for intelligent guessing. For example, *Richard II* cannot be earlier than 1595, the publication date of some material to which it is indebted; *The
Merchant of Venice* cannot be later than 1598, the year
Francis Meres mentioned it. Sometimes arguments for a
date hang on an alleged topical allusion, such as the lines
about the unseasonable weather in *A Midsummer Night's
Dream,* II.i.81–117, but such an allusion (if indeed it is an
allusion) can be variously interpreted, and in any case
there is always the possibility that a topical allusion was
inserted during a revision, years after the composition of
a play. Dates are often attributed on the basis of style,
and although conjectures about style usually rest on other
conjectures, sooner or later one must rely on one's literary
sense. There is no real proof, for example, that *Othello* is
not as early as *Romeo and Juliet,* but one feels *Othello*
is later, and because the first record of its performance
is 1604, one is glad enough to set its composition at that
date and not push it back into Shakespeare's early years.
The following chronology, then, is as much indebted to
informed guesswork and sensitivity as it is to fact. The
dates, necessarily imprecise, indicate something like a
scholarly consensus.

PLAYS

1588–93	*The Comedy of Errors*
1588–94	*Love's Labor's Lost*
1590–91	*2 Henry VI*
1590–91	*3 Henry VI*
1591–92	*1 Henry VI*
1592–93	*Richard III*
1592–94	*Titus Andronicus*
1593–94	*The Taming of the Shrew*
1593–95	*The Two Gentlemen of Verona*
1594–96	*Romeo and Juliet*
1595	*Richard II*
1594–96	*A Midsummer Night's Dream*
1596–97	*King John*
1596–97	*The Merchant of Venice*
1597	*1 Henry IV*
1597–98	*2 Henry IV*
1598–99	*Henry V*
1598–1600	*Much Ado About Nothing*
1599	*Julius Caesar*
1599–1600	*As You Like It*
1599–1600	*Twelfth Night*
1600–01	*Hamlet*
1597–1601	*The Merry Wives of Windsor*
1601–02	*Troilus and Cressida*
1602–04	*All's Well That Ends Well*
1603–04	*Othello*
1604	*Measure for Measure*
1605–06	*King Lear*
1605–06	*Macbeth*
1606–07	*Antony and Cleopatra*
1605–08	*Timon of Athens*
1607–09	*Coriolanus*
1608–09	*Pericles*
1609–10	*Cymbeline*
1610–11	*The Winter's Tale*
1611	*The Tempest*
1612–13	*Henry VIII*

POEMS

Shakespeare's Theater

In Shakespeare's infancy, Elizabethan actors performed wherever they could—in great halls, at court, in the courtyards of inns. The innyards must have made rather unsatisfactory theaters: on some days they were unavailable because carters bringing goods to London used them as depots; when available, they had to be rented from the innkeeper; perhaps most important, London inns were subject to the Common Council of London, which was not well disposed toward theatricals. In 1574 the Common Council required that plays and playing places in London be licensed. It asserted that

> sundry great disorders and inconveniences have been found to ensue to this city by the inordinate haunting of great multitudes of people, specially youth, to plays, interludes, and shows, namely occasion of frays and quarrels, evil practices of incontinency in great inns having chambers and secret places adjoining to their open stages and galleries,

and ordered that innkeepers who wished licenses to hold performances put up a bond and make contributions to the poor.

The requirement that plays and innyard theaters be licensed, along with the other drawbacks of playing at inns, probably drove James Burbage (a carpenter-turned-actor) to rent in 1576 a plot of land northeast of the city walls and to build here—on property outside the jurisdiction of the city—England's first permanent construction designed for plays. He called it simply the Theatre. About all that is known of its construction is that it was wood.

It soon had imitators, the most famous being the Globe (1599), built across the Thames (again outside the city's jurisdiction), out of timbers of the Theatre, which had been dismantled when Burbage's lease ran out.

There are three important sources of information about the structure of Elizabethan playhouses—drawings, a contract, and stage directions in plays. Of drawings, only the so-called De Witt drawing (c. 1596) of the Swan—really a friend's copy of De Witt's drawing—is of much significance. It shows a building of three tiers, with a stage jutting from a wall into the yard or center of the building. The tiers are roofed, and part of the stage is covered by a roof that projects from the rear and is supported at its front on two posts, but the groundlings, who paid a penny to stand in front of the stage, were exposed to the sky. (Performances in such a playhouse were held only in the daytime; artificial illumination was not used.) At the rear of the stage are two doors; above the stage is a gallery. The second major source of information, the contract for the Fortune, specifies that although the Globe is to be the model, the Fortune is to be square, eighty feet outside and fifty-five inside. The stage is to be forty-three feet broad, and is to extend into the middle of the yard (i.e., it is twenty-seven and a half feet deep). For patrons willing to pay more than the general admission charged of the groundlings, there were to be three galleries provided with seats. From the third chief source, stage directions, one learns that entrance to the stage was by doors, presumably spaced widely apart at the rear ("Enter one citizen at one door, and another at the other"), and that in addition to the platform stage there was occasionally some sort of curtained booth or alcove allowing for "discovery" scenes, and some sort of playing space "aloft" or "above" to represent (for example) the top of a city's walls or a room above the street. Doubtless each theater had its own peculiarities, but perhaps we can talk about a "typical" Elizabethan theater if we realize that no theater need exactly have fit the description, just as no father is the typical father with 3.7 children. This hypothetical theater is wooden, round or polygonal (in *Henry V* Shake-

speare calls it a "wooden *O*"), capable of holding some
eight hundred spectators standing in the yard around the
projecting elevated stage and some fifteen hundred additional spectators seated in the three roofed galleries. The
stage, protected by a "shadow" or "heavens" or roof, is
entered by two doors; behind the doors is the "tiring
house" (attiring house, i.e., dressing room), and above the
doors is some sort of gallery that may sometimes hold
spectators but that can be used (for example) as the
bedroom from which Romeo—according to a stage direction in one text—"goeth down." Some evidence suggests
that a throne can be lowered onto the platform stage,
perhaps from the "shadow"; certainly characters can descend from the stage through a trap or traps into the
cellar or "hell." Sometimes this space beneath the platform accommodates a sound-effects man or musician (in
Antony and Cleopatra "music of the hautboys is under the
stage") or an actor (in *Hamlet* the "Ghost cries under the
stage"). Most characters simply walk on and off, but because there is no curtain in front of the platform, corpses
will have to be carried off (Hamlet must lug Polonius' guts
into the neighbor room), or will have to fall at the rear,
where the curtain on the alcove or booth can be drawn
to conceal them.

Such may have been the so-called "public theater." Another kind of theater, called the "private theater" because
its much greater admission charge limited its audience to
the wealthy or the prodigal, must be briefly mentioned.
The private theater was basically a large room, entirely
roofed and therefore artificially illuminated, with a stage
at one end. In 1576 one such theater was established in
Blackfriars, a Dominican priory in London that had been
suppressed in 1538 and confiscated by the Crown and
thus was not under the city's jurisdiction. All the actors
in the Blackfriars theater were boys about eight to thirteen
years old (in the public theaters similar boys played female
parts; a boy Lady Macbeth played to a man Macbeth).
This private theater had a precarious existence, and ceased
operations in 1584. In 1596 James Burbage, who had
already made theatrical history by building the Theatre,

began to construct a second Blackfriars theater. He died in 1597, and for several years this second Blackfriars theater was used by a troupe of boys, but in 1608 two of Burbage's sons and five other actors (including Shakespeare) became joint operators of the theater, using it in the winter when the open-air Globe was unsuitable. Perhaps such a smaller theater, roofed, artificially illuminated, and with a tradition of a courtly audience, exerted an influence on Shakespeare's late plays.

Performances in the private theaters may well have had intermissions during which music was played, but in the public theaters the action was probably uninterrupted, flowing from scene to scene almost without a break. Actors would enter, speak, exit, and others would immediately enter and establish (if necessary) the new locale by a few properties and by words and gestures. Here are some samples of Shakespeare's scene painting:

> This is Illyria, lady.

> Well, this is the Forest of Arden.

> This castle hath a pleasant seat; the air
> Nimbly and sweetly recommends itself
> Unto our gentle senses.

On the other hand, it is a mistake to conceive of the Elizabethan stage as bare. Although Shakespeare's Chorus in *Henry V* calls the stage an "unworthy scaffold" and urges the spectators to "eke out our performance with your mind," there was considerable spectacle. The last act of *Macbeth*, for example, has five stage directions calling for "drum and colors," and another sort of appeal to the eye is indicated by the stage direction "Enter Macduff, with Macbeth's head." Some scenery and properties may have been substantial; doubtless a throne was used, and in one play of the period we encounter this direction: "Hector takes up a great piece of rock and casts at Ajax, who tears up a young tree by the roots and assails Hector." The matter is of some importance, and will be glanced at again in the next section.

The Texts of Shakespeare

Though eighteen of his plays were published during his lifetime, Shakespeare seems never to have supervised their publication. There is nothing unusual here; when a playwright sold a play to a theatrical company he surrendered his ownership of it. Normally a company would not publish the play, because to publish it meant to allow competitors to acquire the piece. Some plays, however, did get published: apparently treacherous actors sometimes pieced together a play for a publisher, sometimes a company in need of money sold a play, and sometimes a company allowed a play to be published that no longer drew audiences. That Shakespeare did not concern himself with publication, then, is scarcely remarkable; of his contemporaries only Ben Jonson carefully supervised the publication of his own plays. In 1623, seven years after Shakespeare's death, John Heminges and Henry Condell (two senior members of Shakespeare's company, who had performed with him for about twenty years) collected his plays—published and unpublished—into a large volume, commonly called the First Folio. (A folio is a volume consisting of sheets that have been folded once, each sheet thus making two leaves, or four pages. The eighteen plays published during Shakespeare's lifetime had been issued one play per volume in small books called quartos. Each sheet in a quarto has been folded twice, making four leaves, or eight pages.) The First Folio contains thirty-six plays; a thirty-seventh, *Pericles,* though not in the Folio, is regarded as canonical. Heminges and Condell suggest in an address "To the great variety of readers" that the republished plays are presented in better form than in the quartos: "Before you were abused with diverse stolen and surreptitious copies, maimed and deformed by the frauds and stealths of injurious impostors that exposed them; even those, are now offered to your view cured and perfect of their limbs, and all the rest absolute in their numbers, as he [i.e., Shakespeare] conceived them."

Whoever was assigned to prepare the texts for publication in the First Folio seems to have taken his job seriously and yet not to have performed it with uniform care. The sources of the texts seem to have been, in general, good unpublished copies or the best published copies. The first play in the collection, *The Tempest,* is divided into acts and scenes, has unusually full stage directions and descriptions of spectacle, and concludes with a list of the characters, but the editor was not able (or willing) to present all of the succeeding texts so fully dressed. Later texts occasionally show signs of carelessness: in one scene of *Much Ado About Nothing* the names of actors, instead of characters, appear as speech prefixes, as they had in the quarto, which the Folio reprints; proofreading throughout the Folio is spotty and apparently was done without reference to the printer's copy; the pagination of *Hamlet* jumps from 156 to 257.

A modern editor of Shakespeare must first select his copy; no problem if the play exists only in the Folio, but a considerable problem if the relationship between a quarto and the Folio—or an early quarto and a later one —is unclear. When an editor has chosen what seems to him to be the most authoritative text or texts for his copy, he has not done with making decisions. First of all, he must reckon with Elizabethan spelling. If he is not producing a facsimile, he probably modernizes it, but ought he to preserve the old form of words that apparently were pronounced quite unlike their modern forms—"lanthorn" "alablaster"? If he preserves these forms, is he really preserving Shakespeare's forms or perhaps those of a compositor in the printing house? What is one to do when one finds "lanthorn" and "lantern" in adjacent lines? (The editors of this series in general, but not invariably, assume that words should be spelled in their modern form.) Elizabethan punctuation, too, presents problems. For example in the First Folio, the only text for the play, Macbeth rejects his wife's idea that he can wash the blood from his hand:

> no: this my Hand will rather
> The multitudinous Seas incarnadine,
> Making the Greene one, Red.

Obviously an editor will remove the superfluous capitals, and he will probably alter the spelling to "incarnadine," but will he leave the comma before "red," letting Macbeth speak of the sea as "the green one," or will he (like most modern editors) remove the comma and thus have Macbeth say that his hand will make the ocean *uniformly* red?

An editor will sometimes have to change more than spelling or punctuation. Macbeth says to his wife:

> I dare do all that may become a man,
> Who dares no more, is none.

For two centuries editors have agreed that the second line is unsatisfactory, and have emended "no" to "do": "Who dares do more is none." But when in the same play Ross says that fearful persons

> floate vpon a wilde and violent Sea
> Each way, and moue,

need "move" be emended to "none," as it often is, on the hunch that the compositor misread the manuscript? The editors of the Signet Classic Shakespeare have restrained themselves from making abundant emendations. In their minds they hear Dr. Johnson on the dangers of emending: "I have adopted the Roman sentiment, that it is more honorable to save a citizen than to kill an enemy." Some departures (in addition to spelling, punctuation, and lineation) from the copy text have of course been made, but the original readings are listed in a note following the play, so that the reader can evaluate them for himself.

The editors of the Signet Classic Shakespeare, following tradition, have added line numbers and in many cases act and scene divisions as well as indications of locale at the beginning of scenes. The Folio divided most of the plays into acts and some into scenes. Early eighteenth-century editors increased the divisions. These divisions, which provide a convenient way of referring to passages in the plays, have been retained, but when not in the text chosen as the basis for the Signet Classic text they are enclosed in square brackets [ ] to indicate that they are editorial additions. Similarly, although no play of Shakespeare's published during his lifetime was equipped with indications of locale at the heads of scene divisions, locales have here been added in square brackets for the convenience of the reader, who lacks the information afforded to spectators by costumes, properties, and gestures. The spectator can tell at a glance he is in the throne room, but without an editorial indication the reader may be puzzled for a while. It should be mentioned, incidentally, that there are a few authentic stage directions—perhaps Shakespeare's, perhaps a prompter's—that suggest locales; for example, "Enter Brutus in his orchard," and "They go up into the Senate house." It is hoped that the bracketed additions provide the reader with the sort of help provided in these two authentic directions, but it is equally hoped that the reader will remember that the stage was not loaded with scenery.

No editor during the course of his work can fail to recollect some words Heminges and Condell prefixed to the Folio:

> It had been a thing, we confess, worthy to have been wished, that the author himself had lived to have set forth and overseen his own writings. But since it hath been ordained otherwise, and he by death departed from that right, we pray you do not envy his friends the office of their care and pain to have collected and published them.

Nor can an editor, after he has done his best, forget Heminges and Condell's final words: "And so we leave you to other of his friends, whom if you need can be your guides. If you need them not, you can lead yourselves, and others. And such readers we wish him."

SYLVAN BARNET
Tufts University

Introduction

Measure for Measure was first published in 1623 in the Folio of Shakespeare's works. It was probably written in 1604, for it is on record that a play called *Mesure for Mesure*, by "Shaxberd," was performed before King James I on 26 December of that year, when it was presumably a new play. It was thus composed just before the writing of the great tragedies in which Shakespeare's powers were at their height. It does not seem to have been performed again till 1662, and in fact, till recently, it was not popular on the stage in spite of its theatrical craftsmanship.

It was not popular with the older critics, either. Coleridge, to whom we owe some of our most penetrating Shakespeare criticism, found it "a hateful work," indeed "the only painful play" that Shakespeare ever wrote. Its comedy disgusted him and its tragedy seemed merely horrible. His sense of justice was also revolted by the pardon of Angelo, the corrupt deputy who is virtually guilty of both rape and murder. The heroine, Isabella, was to Coleridge an unamiable character who primly preferred her own chastity to her brother's life. That brother himself, Claudio, was a weak, vacillating youth who expected his sister to save him from the consequences of his own immorality. The play slithered through to an unearned happy ending which was entirely unconvincing. In general, the opinion of the nineteenth century was that *Measure for Measure* was essentially a dark comedy, full of bitter satire and cynicism, reflecting some obscure

phase of tragedy or disillusionment in the personal life
of Shakespeare himself.

In our own day a far different view of the play has
been favored. The twin myths of Shakespeare's personal
sorrows and of a general gloom during the early years
of the sixteenth century are no longer seriously held. It is
urged that the play should be read not as a picture of
normal human affairs with naturalistic character and
action, but as a dramatic parable, embodying some of
the noblest precepts of the Christian religion. The new
interpretation may now and then claim a consistency of
impression not quite warranted by the play itself, but it
seems more coherent than the old view which implicitly
accused Shakespeare of confusing art with life. While this
is the majority view of *Measure for Measure* today, there
are some modern critics who feel that the play is uneven,
though great. They think that Shakespeare's artistic experience has raised questions that cannot properly be
answered, sometimes even asked, in a tragicomedy; the
medium is inhibiting. As for the play's religious significance, they feel that the action and characterization are
more intimately inspired by Shakespeare's immediate
sources in drama and folklore than by Christianity. The
Italian storybook which probably gave him his plot contains several tales on the theme of a woman's forgiving
an enemy who has done her an irreparable wrong, and
the folklore of Shakespeare's day had popularized the
legend of the good monarch who, like the Duke in the
play, moves among his people in disguise to find out the
truth for himself and to protect the good and punish the
bad.

To help us toward a plausible interpretation of the play,
we may briefly look at its sources, and what Shakespeare
made of them. The chief one is almost certainly George
Whetstone's *Promos and Cassandra* (1578), a tedious,
though earnest, play in two parts of five acts each. Whetstone made a prose version of the story for his collection
of stories called the *Heptameron of Civil Discourses*
(1582). In addition to these works, Shakespeare very
probably knew the Italian source of Whetstone, the

Hecatommithi (1565) of Giraldi Cinthio, and Cinthio's dramatized version of the story, *Epitia* (1583). In Whetstone's play, Cassandra pleads with Promos for the life of her brother, Andrugio, who has been condemned to death for fornication. Promos agrees to pardon Andrugio if Cassandra will lie with him. She refuses, but ultimately consents when her brother appeals to her sisterly affection. After she has kept her side of the bargain, Promos goes back on his word, and commands the jailer to behead Andrugio and present the head to Cassandra. The compassionate jailer happens to know the truth and conceals Andrugio, presenting Cassandra with the head of a recently executed felon. Cassandra wants to commit suicide, but decides to appeal to the King first and to seek vengeance on Promos. The King finds that the complaint is true and orders that Promos should marry her and then be put to death. But as soon as the marriage is solemnized, Cassandra finds herself "tied in the greatest bonds of affection to her husband." She now becomes "an earnest suitor for his life" with the King, but in vain. In the meanwhile, her brother, who has been living under a disguise, comes to know of her predicament and reveals himself to the King. Promos is pardoned, and everything ends happily.

When Shakespeare took up this tale for dramatic treatment, he made certain far-reaching changes. In the first place, Cassandra's compelled acceptance of the loathsome and virtually illusory choice thrust on her by Promos hurts the moral feelings of the reader beyond healing, and her last-minute marriage, by royal fiat, to the violator of her honor merely adds insult to injury. Even in Shakespeare's day, Puritan moralists, to specify a single group, held that there were wrongs which no marriage could redress. The sudden change of Cassandra's affections from hatred to love as soon as she is married to Promos is also rather incredible. Very properly, therefore, Shakespeare made his heroine refuse to yield to Angelo. But since the story required that Angelo's condition should somehow be met, he created the character of Mariana and substituted her for Isabella by means of an old folktale device which was presumably acceptable to the original audience. He had already used "the bed trick," as it is usually called, in what is very likely an earlier play, *All's Well That Ends Well*. The "bed trick" does not commend itself to modern taste, and does not also quite agree with the realistic context of the play, but we must remember that Mariana is deeply in love with Angelo, and the consummation of her love leads to her marriage with him at the end. Our sympathies are so fully engaged in her behalf that we want her to be happy, and wink at this otherwise dubious mode of securing her happiness.

Shakespeare also altered the significance of the brother's offense. In Whetstone's play, Andrugio is guilty of fornication, committed, as in Shakespeare's play, with the voluntary consent of the girl. Cassandra attributes her brother's offense partly to the irresistible force of love and partly to his youth. In *Measure for Measure*, however, Claudio explains the reason for his arrest differently:

> From too much liberty, my Lucio, liberty.
> As surfeit is the father of much fast,
> So every scope by the immoderate use
> Turns to restraint. Our natures do pursue,
> Like rats that ravin down their proper bane,
> A thirsty evil, and when we drink, we die. (I.ii.128–33)

In our very nature there is something that drives us into acts of too much liberty, which we loathe even while we indulge in them.

> For that which I do, I allow not: for what I would, that do I not; but what I hate, that do I. . . . For I know that in me (that is, in my flesh) dwelleth no good thing: for to will is present with me; but how to perform that which is good I find not. For the good that I would, I do not: but the evil which I would not, that I do. . . . I find then a law, that, when I would do good, evil is present with me. For I delight in the law of God after the inward man. But I see another law in my members, warring against the law of my mind and

bringing me into captivity to the law of sin which is in
my members.

(Romans 7:15, 18, 19, 21–23)

Claudio is angry and disgusted with himself. But he
does not know what to do with this problem. His friend
Lucio, described in the original list of actors as a "fantastic," does not see that there is a problem. Lucio's view
of the matter is reflected in the imagery of his speech when
he describes Claudio's offense:

> Your brother and his lover have embraced;
> As those that feed grow full, as blossoming time
> That from the seedness the bare fallow brings
> To teeming foison, even so her plenteous womb
> Expresseth his full tilth and husbandry.

(I.iv.40–44)

Juliet's "fertility" was realized by Claudio's "tilth." *Not*
to do as Claudio did is to be guilty of a lack of "husbandry." There is enough truth in this view of human sex
to make it superficially attractive, but we are put on our
guard by being shown its consequences. Lucio has seduced Mistress Kate Keepdown and has abandoned her
and the child. (Incidentally, the child has been looked
after by a bawd, a fact which should make us distrust
theories of Shakespeare's cynicism in *Measure for Measure*.) He has degenerated into a coarse sensualist, bent
on his own pleasures and reckless of all the essential ob-
ligations of a decent life in society. Even his interest in
Claudio's pardon is not quite disinterested. "I pray she
may"—that is, Isabella may persuade Angelo—he tells
Claudio, "as well for the encouragement of the like,
which else would stand under grievous imposition, as for
the enjoying of thy life, who I would be sorry should be
thus foolishly lost at a game of tick-tack." (I.ii.191–95.)
Shakespeare enlarged the role of the overlord in the
story to make him a disguised spectator of and later an
active participant in the action of the play. Duke Vincentio has been rather slack in his princely duties, loving his subjects not wisely but too well, but otherwise

he is a scholar, a statesman, and a soldier. We are told further that his supreme concern has always been to know himself. When he contributes, in his indirect way, to the debate initiated by Claudio, he implies that self-restraint is both essential and possible. When he goes to the prison, disguised as a friar, to console "the afflicted spirits" there, he requests the provost to inform him of the nature of the crimes committed by the condemned prisoners so that he may "minister to them accordingly." With Claudio the ministration takes the form of setting him free from "the deceiving promises of life" and of creating in him a calm resolution to face the approaching end. Sir Thomas More, the Tudor statesman and saint about whom Shakespeare perhaps helped to write a play, declares in his little treatise, *The Four Last Things,* which he wrote to teach "the art of dying well," that nothing can more effectively withdraw the human soul from the wretched affections of the body than a sincere remembrance of death. "The thirsty evil" which Claudio bemoans is the consequence of an excessive attachment to life, itself the result of our forgetfulness of our "glassy essence."

Shakespeare made Isabella a novice of Saint Clare. Why he did so is not quite obvious, for his young women do not need any "motivation" to justify their preference for chastity. Chastity is an absolute value with them. Isabella's novitiate should perhaps be regarded as her answer to the problem of the "prompture of the blood," of which she seems to have some personal knowledge if one may judge from the accents of her admission to Angelo that women, no less than men, are frail:

> Ay, as the glasses where they view themselves,
> Which are as easy broke as they make forms.
> Women! Help heaven! Men their creation mar
> In profiting by them. Nay, call us ten times frail;
> For we are soft as our complexions are,
> And credulous to false prints.
>
> (II.iv.125–30)

Her denunciation of her brother when he timidly suggests that she should yield to Angelo no doubt grates on our ears—Sir Arthur Quiller-Couch was moved to declare that there was something rancid in her chastity—but her harshness reflects her bitterness at being asked to abet the "prompture of the blood." It is significant that the only conventual rule that we hear of in the play relates to receiving male visitors, and that Isabella should desire a stricter restraint upon the votarists of Saint Clare though that order has the reputation of being the strictest women's order of the Roman Catholic Church. At the end of the play, the Duke makes her a proposal which, he says, "much imports her good," surely not a material good, for she is not presented as a girl with whom such frivolous considerations would weigh. Presumably she accepts the Duke's proposal; in Shakespeare's day, it was perfectly in order for a novice to go back to secular life. Though the play itself is ambiguous on the point, it is attractive to believe that Isabella made the discovery that the "prompture of the blood" could be resolved in the married state also.

Halfway through the play, Isabella meets Mariana. Mariana plays a small but significant part in the design of the drama. In spite of Angelo's "unjust unkindness" which should "in all reason" have quenched her love for him, she continues to cherish him. But she will not substitute herself for Isabella until "the friar" whose advice has often stilled her "brawling discontent" assures her that it is no sin. In the last act she pleads that her husband's evil is a passing cloud which will leave him purer than before. Her love is dedicated entirely to the welfare of the beloved's soul, and we may describe it, without undue exaggeration, as a humble human instance of the divine love which found out the remedy when all the souls that were, were forfeit. Mariana's love has transcended the problem of the "prompture of the blood." We know that Isabella is deeply moved by the story of Mariana's love, and it is her appeal that Angelo's very evil may be the cause of his regeneration which in the end wins Isabella over to plead for him. Perhaps Isabella learned the secret of a soul-centered love from Mariana.

Between Isabella and Angelo there is a curious superficial resemblance. Angelo has lived in retirement, and evidently prefers it to the public office which he is summoned to. He has tried to "blunt his natural edge" with "profits of the mind, study and fast." A due sincerity governs his deeds till he looks on Isabella. But the "prompture of the blood" finally overcomes him. Isabella's very virtue corrupts him, while the strumpet with all her double vigor, art and nature, could never once stir him. He has identified virtue wholly with a mode of external conduct. His seemingly virtuous conduct does not represent a transformed will, but is a mere factitious creation, a state whereon he has studied, not a habit of the soul. He himself points out that the problem of "we would" and "we would not" arises when we forget our "grace," a word which may well have a specific Christian sense in view of Isabella's charge that he is not "new made." It is characteristic of him that he should mistake Mariana's love for levity. His ear, coarsened by the strident jazz of a code that is throttling the instincts, cannot catch the quiet melody of an ethic that observes the very rhythm of the blood. So "the natural guiltiness" lurks within, subverting virtue itself to cause his fall. "Sin, taking occasion by the commandment, deceived me, and by it slew me" (Romans 7:11). The sentence of death that the Duke passes on him frees Angelo from an intolerable, meaningless existence, and he welcomes it. He is a new-made man after he is pardoned. To detest him and to disagree with his pardon is natural, for the process of his contrition is rather hurried, but we must try to understand his predicament.

Angelo's ignorance of the inwardness of virtue is also the cause of the excessive legalism of his rule. At bottom, the criticism of the rule of law as Angelo interprets it is that it is ultimately futile. Its severity is aimless, and its achievements are transitory. "There is so great a fever on goodness that the dissolution of it must cure it," says the disguised Duke to Escalus. The time has come when nothing but a total dissolution of the fever that afflicts goodness can restore it to its pristine health. The laws are no doubt "the needful bits and curbs of headstrong weeds," but they can at best regulate conduct; they cannot change the "old man" in us. And as long as that change does not take place, sensuality will prevail in Vienna, openly or covertly.

The wise old Escalus, the most genial character in the play, tries to deal with the problem in his gentle, humanitarian way, but even he is shocked when he discovers that Mistress Overdone is still forfeit in the same kind after double and treble admonition. Pompey refuses to change at all. The Duke himself, as it happens, intervenes to save Claudio's life precisely at the moment when Claudio sues to be rid of it; that is, when Claudio is cured of his malady. In dealing with Barnardine again, the Duke reveals his essentially spiritual approach to the problem of law and justice. Barnardine is a murderer and has a stubborn soul that apprehends no further than this life, and he has squared his life accordingly. When the Duke pardons all his earthly faults, he entrusts him to a friar for advice.

With Angelo, however, he decides on "measure for measure." "Judge not, that ye be not judged. For with what judgment ye judge, ye shall be judged: and with what measure ye mete, it shall be measured to you again" (Matthew 7:1-2). He also reminds Isabella that her brother's ghost cries out for vengeance. In condemning Angelo, the Duke thus seems to observe the law of the Old Testament—an eye for an eye and a tooth for a tooth. But actually he is testing Isabella's adherence to the New Law, which commands that one's enemy shall be loved as a friend, and that good shall be returned for evil. How superbly she answers the test! She does not plead for Angelo's pardon, for she has seen that Mariana's plea for mercy has been disallowed. With a boldness that takes away one's breath, she asserts that Angelo is not guilty at all. There are three charges against him. His "salt imagination" wronged her honor; he violated sacred chastity; and he broke his promise that he would pardon Claudio if the foul ransom were paid. The first charge, the Duke himself has recommended should be

pardoned because that "salt imagination" provided the
opportunity of doing a service to Mariana. The second
charge is not true because Mariana was Angelo's wife
on a precontract. As for the "promise breach," it cannot
be denied that Isabella did not in fact lie with Angelo
or that her brother was guilty, after all, of the crime for
which he was sentenced. The type of betrothal which
Claudio and Juliet had entered upon did not in law give
them any marital rights, whereas Mariana's contract with
Angelo did, at least in law. Finally, it is true that Angelo
intended to violate her, but the intention never became
an act and law cannot take cognizance of thoughts.
"Thoughts are no subjects, / Intents but merely thoughts."
Counsel for the defense submits therefore that the accused is not guilty on any count, does not need a pardon,
and much less can be punished with "measure for measure." The prosperous art which she shows in playing with
reason and discourse could hardly be stretched further.

> Ye have heard that it hath been said, Thou shalt love
> thy neighbor, and hate thine enemy. But I say unto you,
> Love your enemies, bless them that curse you, do good
> to them that hurt you, and pray for them which de-
> spitefully use you and persecute you. That ye may be
> the children of your Father which is in heaven: for he
> maketh his sun to rise on the evil and on the good, and
> sendeth rain on the just and on the unjust. . . . Be ye
> therefore perfect, even as your Father which is in
> heaven is perfect.
>
> (Matthew 5:43–45, 48)

Such then are some of the themes and characters of
the play before us. Shakespeare's contemporaries would
have probably called it a tragicomedy, a new genre in
those days. Tragicomedy is not a loose putting together
of tragedy with comedy, but an independent form of
dramatic composition with an aesthetic of its own. As
the Italian playwright Giambattista Guarini, who had
himself written a tragicomedy, set forth in his *Compendium
of Tragicomic Poetry* (published in 1601): "He who
makes a tragicomedy does not intend to compose sep-

arately either a tragedy or a comedy, but from the two a third thing that will be perfect of its kind, and may take from the others the parts that with most verisimilitude can stand together." From tragedy, said Guarini, tragicomedy takes the movement but not the disturbance of the feelings, the pleasure and not the sadness, the danger but not the death. From comedy, it takes laughter that is not excessive, modest amusement, feigned difficulty, happy reversal, and above all, the comic order. Speaking of the style proper to tragicomedy, Guarini said that the magnificent was its norm, combined not with the grave as in a tragedy, but with the polished. There is something in this description of tragicomedy that reminds us of *Measure for Measure*. For instance, our awareness of the immanence of the Duke, with his declared objective of testing whether power will change purpose effectively, prevents the first part of the play from the tragic course. The "intrigue" of the fourth act does not exist for its own sake, but serves to establish the control of the Duke over the action and to lead to a happy conclusion. The episode of Barnardine makes clear that the resolution to face death which "the friar" has preached to Claudio is far from the insensibility and desperateness of a Barnardine, who will not "wake." The style of the play ranges from the passionate conjurations of Isabella, the tortured self-examinations of Angelo, the exploratory dialectic of Angelo and Isabella, the meditative analysis of the Duke and the surging thrill of terror in Claudio as he stands at the brink of the grave to the irreverent bawdry of Lucio and the petty cunning of Pompey's coiled speech with Escalus. Coleridge was obliged to acknowledge that *Measure for Measure* was Shakespearean throughout. It is indeed one of Shakespeare's most impressive achievements whether we consider the seriousness of the issues it deals with, its characterization, or its construction.

S. Nagarajan
University of Hyderabad

Measure for Measure

The Scene: Vienna

The names of all the actors:

Vincentio, the Duke
Angelo, the Deputy
Escalus, an ancient Lord
Claudio, a young gentleman
Lucio, a fantastic
Two Other Like Gentlemen
Provost
Thomas ⎱
          ⎰ two friars
Peter ⎰
[A Justice]
[Varrius]
Elbow, a simple constable
Froth, a foolish gentleman
Clown [Pompey, servant to Mistress Overdone]
Abhorson, an executioner
Barnardine, a dissolute prisoner
Isabella, sister to Claudio
Mariana, betrothed to Angelo
Juliet, beloved of Claudio
Francisca, a nun
Mistress Overdone, a bawd
[Lords, Officers, Citizens, Boy, and Attendants]

Measure for Measure

ACT I

Scene I. [*The Duke's palace.*]

Enter Duke, Escalus, Lords. [and Attendants].

Duke. Escalus.

Escalus. My lord.

Duke. Of government the properties°1 to unfold,
  Would seem in me t' affect speech and discourse,
  Since I am put to know° that your own science°   5
  Exceeds, in that, the lists° of all advice
  My strength can give you. Then no more remains
  But that, to your sufficiency as your worth is able,°
  And let them work. The nature of our people,
  Our city's institutions, and the terms   10
  For common justice, y'are as pregnant in°
  As art and practice hath enrichèd any
  That we remember. There is our commission,
  From which we would not have you warp.° Call
    hither,

---

1 The degree sign° indicates a footnote, which is keyed to the text by
line number. Text references are printed in *italic* type; the annotation
follows in roman type.
I.1.3 *properties* characteristics 5 *put to know* given to understand
5 *science* knowledge 6 *lists* limits 8 *to your sufficiency. . . able* (perhaps a line is missing after this line) 11 *pregnant in* full of knowledge
14 *warp* deviate

35

13   I say, bid come before us Angelo.
                                        [*Exit an Attendant.*]
            What figure° of us, think you, he will bear?°
            For you must know, we have with special soul°
            Elected him our absence to supply;
            Lent him our terror, dressed him with our love,
20   And given his deputation all the organs°
            Of our own pow'r. What think you of it?

Escalus. If any in Vienna be of worth
            To undergo° such ample grace and honor,
            It is Lord Angelo.

                         Enter Angelo.

Duke.   Look where he comes.

23 *Angelo.* Always obedient to your Grace's will,
            I come to know your pleasure.

Duke.   Angelo,
            There is a kind of character° in thy life,
            That to th' observer doth thy history
            Fully unfold. Thyself and thy belongings°
30   Are not thine own so proper° as to waste
            Thyself upon thy virtues, they on thee.
            Heaven doth with us as we with torches do,°
            Not light them for themselves; for if our virtues
            Did not go forth of us, 'twere all alike
            As if we had them not. Spirits are not finely
35   touched
            But to fine issues,° nor Nature never lends
            The smallest scruple° of her excellence
            But like a thrifty goddess she determines

16 *figure* image 16 *bear* represent 17 *soul* thought 20 *organs*
means of action 23 *undergo* enjoy 27 *character* secret handwriting 29 *belongings* endowments 30 *proper* exclusively 32 *Heaven*
. . . *do* (see Luke 11:33: "No man, when he hath lighted a candle,
putteth it in a secret place, neither under a bushel, but on a candle-
stick that they which come in may see the light." Also Matthew 7:16:
"Ye shall know them by their fruits") 35–36 *Spirits . . . issues* i.e.,
great qualities are bestowed only so that they may lead to great
achievements 37 *scruple* 1/24 oz.

Herself the glory of a creditor,
Both thanks and use.° But I do bend° my speech   40
To one that can my part in him advertise.°
Hold therefore, Angelo:
In our remove° be thou at full ourself;
Mortality and mercy in Vienna
Live in thy tongue and heart. Old Escalus,   45
Though first in question,° is thy secondary.°
Take thy commission.

Angelo.   Now, good my lord,
Let there be some more test made of my mettle°
Before so noble and so great a figure
Be stamped upon it.

Duke.   No more evasion.   50
We have with a leavened° and preparèd choice
Proceeded to you; therefore take your honors.
Our haste from hence is of so quick condition
That it prefers itself,° and leaves unquestioned°
Matters of needful value. We shall write to you,   55
As time and our concernings shall importune,
How it goes with us, and do look to know
What doth befall you here. So fare you well.
To th' hopeful execution do I leave you
Of your commissions.

Angelo.   Yet give leave, my lord,   60
That we may bring° you something on the way.

Duke. My haste may not admit it;
Nor need you, on mine honor, have to do
With any scruple; your scope is as mine own,
So to enforce or qualify the laws   65
As to your soul seems good. Give me your hand.
I'll privily away; I love the people,
But do not like to stage me to their eyes.
Though it do well, I do not relish well

40 *use* interest   40 *bend* address   41 *advertise* display prominently
43 *remove* absence   46 *question* consideration   46 *secondary* sub-
ordinate   48 *mettle* (pun on "metal," i.e., material)   51 *leavened*
i.e., long-pondered   54 *prefers itself* takes precedence   54 *unques-
tioned* unexamined   61 *bring* escort

70   Their loud applause and aves° vehement.
        Nor do I think the man of safe discretion
        That does affect it. Once more, fare you well.

Angelo. The heavens give safety to your purposes.

Escalus. Lead forth and bring you back in happiness.

75 *Duke.* I thank you; fare you well.   *Exit.*

Escalus. I shall desire you, sir, to give me leave
        To have free speech with you; and it concerns me
        To look into the bottom of my place.°
        A pow'r I have, but of what strength and nature,
80   I am not yet instructed.

Angelo. 'Tis so with me. Let us withdraw together,
        And we may soon our satisfaction have
        Touching that point.

Escalus.   I'll wait upon your honor.
                                        Exeunt.

                    Scene II. [*A street.*]

            Enter Lucio and two other Gentlemen.

        Lucio. If the Duke, with the other dukes, come not
            to composition° with the King of Hungary,° why
            then all the dukes fall upon the King.

        First Gentleman. Heaven grant us its peace, but not
5   the King of Hungary's!

        Second Gentleman. Amen.

        Lucio. Thou conclud'st like the sanctimonious pirate,
            that went to sea with the Ten Commandments, but
            scraped one out of the table.

70 *aves* salutations   78 *To look . . . place* i.e., to examine carefully
the range of my authority   I.ii.2 *composition* agreement   2 *Hungary* (perhaps a pun on "hungry")

Second Gentleman. "Thou shalt not steal"? **10**

Lucio. Ay, that he razed.

First Gentleman. Why, 'twas a commandment to command the captain and all the rest from their functions: they put forth to steal. There's not a soldier of us all that, in the thanksgiving before meat, do **15** relish the petition well that prays for peace.

Second Gentleman. I never heard any soldier dislike it.

Lucio. I believe thee, for I think thou never wast where grace was said. **20**

Second Gentleman. No? A dozen times at least.

First Gentleman. What, in meter?

Lucio. In any proportion,° or in any language.

First Gentleman. I think, or in any religion.

Lucio. Ay, why not? Grace is grace, despite of all **25** controversy: as, for example, thou thyself art a wicked villain, despite of all grace.

First Gentleman. Well, there went but a pair of shears between us.°

Lucio. I grant; as there may between the lists° and **30** the velvet. Thou art the list.

First Gentleman. And thou the velvet. Thou art good velvet; thou'rt a three-piled° piece, I warrant thee. I had as lief be a list of an English kersey,° as be piled, as thou art piled, for a French velvet.° Do **35** I speak feelingly° now?

Lucio. I think thou dost; and, indeed, with most pain-

23 *proportion* length　28–29 *there . . . us* i.e., we are cut from the same cloth　30 *lists* selvage or border of a cloth (usually of a different material from the body)　33 *three-piled* (1) pile of a treble thickness (2) "piled" (bald) as a result of venereal disease　34 *kersey* coarse cloth (therefore "plain and honest")　35 *French velvet* (1) excellent velvet (2) French prostitute (syphilis was also known as "the French disease")　35–36 *Do . . . feelingly* i.e., do I touch you there?

ful feeling° of thy speech. I will, out of thine own
confession, learn to begin thy health; but, whilst I
40   live, forget to drink after thee.°

First Gentleman. I think I have done myself wrong,
have I not?

Second Gentleman. Yes, that thou hast, whether thou
art tainted or free.

Enter Bawd [Mistress Overdone].

45 *Lucio.* Behold, behold, where Madam Mitigation
comes! I have purchased as many diseases under
her roof as come to—

Second Gentleman. To what, I pray?

Lucio. Judge.

50 *Second Gentleman.* To three thousand dolors° a year.

First Gentleman. Ay, and more.

Lucio. A French crown° more.

First Gentleman. Thou art always figuring diseases in
me, but thou art full of error. I am sound.

55 *Lucio.* Nay, not as one would say, healthy, but so
sound as things that are hollow. Thy bones are
hollow; impiety° has made a feast of thee.

First Gentleman. How now! Which of your hips has
the most profound sciatica?

60 *Mistress Overdone.* Well, well; there's one yonder arrested and carried to prison was worth five thousand of you all.

Second Gentleman. Who's that, I pray thee?

Mistress Overdone. Marry,° sir, that's Claudio,
65   Signior Claudio.

38 *feeling* personal experience 39–40 *learn . . . thee* drink to your
health but not after you from the same cup (to avoid the infection)
50 *dolors* (pun on "dollars") 52 *French crown* (1) *écu* (2) head
that has gone bald from venereal disease 57 *impiety* immorality
64 *Marry* (a light oath, from "by the Virgin Mary")

First Gentleman. Claudio to prison? 'Tis not so.

Mistress Overdone. Nay, but I know 'tis so. I saw
him arrested; saw him carried away, and which
is more, within these three days his head to be
chopped off.   70

Lucio. But, after all this fooling, I would not have it
so. Art thou sure of this?

Mistress Overdone. I am too sure of it; and it is for
getting Madam Julietta with child.

Lucio. Believe me, this may be. He promised to meet   75
me two hours since, and he was ever precise in
promise-keeping.

Second Gentleman. Besides, you know, it draws
something near to the speech we had to such a
purpose.   80

First Gentleman. But, most of all, agreeing with the
proclamation.

Lucio. Away! Let's go learn the truth of it.
                              Exit [Lucio with Gentlemen].

Mistress Overdone. Thus, what with the war, what
with the sweat,° what with the gallows, and what   85
with poverty, I am custom-shrunk.

                    Enter Clown [Pompey].

How now? What's the news with you?

Pompey. Yonder man is carried to prison.

Mistress Overdone. Well; what has he done?

Pompey. A woman.   90

Mistress Overdone. But what's his offense?

Pompey. Groping for trouts in a peculiar° river.

Mistress Overdone. What? Is there a maid with child
by him?

85 *sweat* sweating sickness, plague   92 *peculiar* private

95 *Pompey.* No, but there's a woman with maid by him.
      You have not heard of the proclamation, have you?

    Mistress Overdone. What proclamation, man?

    Pompey. All houses in the suburbs° of Vienna must
      be plucked down.

100 *Mistress Overdone.* And what shall become of those
      in the city?

    Pompey. They shall stand for seed: they had gone
      down too, but that a wise burgher put in for them.

    Mistress Overdone. But shall all our houses of resort
105   in the suburbs be pulled down?

    Pompey. To the ground, mistress.

    Mistress Overdone. Why, here's a change indeed in
      the commonwealth! What shall become of me?

    Pompey. Come, fear not you; good counselors lack
110   no clients. Though you change your place, you
      need not change your trade; I'll be your tapster°
      still. Courage, there will be pity taken on you; you
      that have worn your eyes almost out in the service,
      you will be considered.

115 *Mistress Overdone.* What's to do here, Thomas
      Tapster? Let's withdraw.

    Pompey. Here comes Signior Claudio, led by the
      provost to prison; and there's Madam Juliet.
                                              Exeunt.

            Enter Provost, Claudio, Juliet, Officers, Lucio,
                      and two Gentlemen.

    Claudio. Fellow, why dost thou show me thus to th'
      world?
120   Bear me to prison, where I am committed.

    Provost. I do it not in evil disposition,

    98 *suburbs* (in Shakespeare's London, the area of the brothels)
    111 *tapster* bartender, waiter (here, pimp)

But from Lord Angelo, by special charge.

Claudio. Thus can the demigod Authority
Make us pay down for our offense by weight.
The words of heaven: on whom it will, it will;   125
On whom it will not, so. Yet still 'tis just.°

Lucio. Why, how now, Claudio! Whence comes this
restraint?

Claudio. From too much liberty, my Lucio, liberty.
As surfeit is the father of much fast,
So every scope by the immoderate use   130
Turns to restraint. Our natures do pursue,
Like rats that ravin down their proper bane,°
A thirsty evil, and when we drink, we die.

Lucio. If I could speak so wisely under an arrest, I
would send for certain of my creditors. And yet, to   135
say the truth, I had as lief have the foppery° of
freedom as the mortality of imprisonment. What's
thy offense, Claudio?

Claudio. What but to speak of would offend again.

Lucio. What, is't murder?   140

Claudio. No.

Lucio. Lechery?

Claudio. Call it so.

Provost. Away, sir, you must go.

Claudio. One word, good friend. Lucio, a word with
you.   145

Lucio. A hundred, if they'll do you any good.
Is lechery so looked after?

Claudio. Thus stands it with me: upon a true contract

125–26 *The words . . . just* (see Romans 9:15,18: "For he saith to
Moses, I will have mercy on whom I will have mercy, and I will
have compassion on whom I will have compassion. . . . Therefore
hath he mercy on whom he will have mercy, and whom he will he
hardeneth")   132 *ravin . . . bane* greedily devour what is poisonous
to them   136 *foppery* foolishness

I got possession of Julietta's bed.
150 You know the lady, she is fast my wife,
Save that we do the denunciation° lack
Of outward order. This we came not to,
Only for propagation° of a dower
Remaining in the coffer of her friends,°
155 From whom we thought it meet to hide our love
Till time had made them for us. But it chances
The stealth of our most mutual entertainment
With character too gross is writ on Juliet.

Lucio. With child, perhaps?

Claudio.   Unhappily, even so.
160 And the new deputy now for the Duke—
Whether it be the fault and glimpse of newness,°
Or whether that the body public be
A horse whereon the governor doth ride,
Who, newly in the seat, that it may know
165 He can command, lets it straight feel the spur;
Whether the tyranny be in his place,
Or in his eminence that fills it up,
I stagger in°—but this new governor
Awakes me all the enrollèd° penalties
170 Which have, like unscoured armor, hung by th' wall
So long, that nineteen zodiacs° have gone round,
And none of them been worn; and, for a name,
Now puts the drowsy and neglected act
Freshly on me. 'Tis surely for a name.

175 *Lucio.* I warrant it is, and thy head stands so tickle°
on thy shoulders, that a milkmaid, if she be in love,
may sigh it off. Send after the Duke, and appeal
to him.

Claudio. I have done so, but he's not to be found.
180 I prithee, Lucio, do me this kind service:
This day my sister should the cloister enter,

151 *denunciation* formal announcement   153 *propagation* increase
154 *friends* relatives   161 *fault and glimpse of newness* i.e., weakness arising from the sudden vision of new authority   168 *stagger in* am not sure   169 *enrollèd* inscribed in the rolls of the laws
171 *zodiacs* i.e., years   175 *tickle* insecure

And there receive her approbation.°
Acquaint her with the danger of my state;
Implore her, in my voice, that she make friends
To the strict deputy; bid herself assay° him.　　185
I have great hope in that; for in her youth
There is a prone° and speechless dialect,
Such as move men; beside, she hath prosperous art
When she will play with reason and discourse,
And well she can persuade.　　190

Lucio. I pray she may; as well for the encouragement
of the like, which else would stand under grievous
imposition, as for the enjoying of thy life, who I
would be sorry should be thus foolishly lost at a
game of tick-tack.° I'll to her.　　195

Claudio. I thank you, good friend Lucio.

Lucio. Within two hours.

Claudio.　　　　　　　Come, officer, away!

　　　　　　　　　　　　　　　　Exeunt.

Scene III. [*A monastery.*]

Enter Duke and Friar Thomas.

Duke. No, holy father; throw away that thought;
Believe not that the dribbling dart° of love
Can pierce a complete° bosom. Why I desire thee
To give me secret harbor, hath a purpose
More grave and wrinkled° than the aims and ends　　5
Of burning youth.

---

182 *approbation* novitiate　185 *assay* test, i.e., attempt to persuade
187 *prone* winning　195 *tick-tack* (literally, a game using a board
into which pegs were fitted)　I.iii.2 *dribbling dart* arrow feebly shot
3 *complete* protected, independent　5 *wrinkled* mature, aged

Friar Thomas.   May your Grace speak of it?

Duke. My holy sir, none better knows than you
       How I have ever loved the life removed,
       And held in idle price to haunt assemblies
10   Where youth and cost, witless bravery° keeps.
       I have delivered to Lord Angelo,
       A man of stricture° and firm abstinence,
       My absolute power and place here in Vienna,
       And he supposes me traveled to Poland;
15   For so I have strewed it in the common ear,°
       And so it is received. Now, pious sir,
       You will demand of me why I do this.

Friar Thomas. Gladly, my lord.

Duke. We have strict statutes and most biting laws,
20   The needful bits and curbs to headstrong weeds,
       Which for this fourteen° years we have let slip,
       Even like an o'ergrown lion in a cave,
       That goes not out to prey. Now, as fond fathers,
       Having bound up the threat'ning twigs of birch,
25   Only to stick it in their children's sight
       For terror, not to use; in time the rod
       Becomes more mocked than feared; so our decrees,
       Dead to infliction,° to themselves are dead,
       And Liberty° plucks Justice by the nose;
30   The baby beats the nurse, and quite athwart
       Goes all decorum.

Friar Thomas.   It rested in your Grace
       To unloose this tied-up Justice when you pleased,
       And it in you more dreadful would have seemed
       Than in Lord Angelo.

Duke.   I do fear, too dreadful:
35   Sith° 'twas my fault to give the people scope,
       'Twould be my tyranny to strike and gall them

10 *witless bravery* senseless show   12 *stricture* strictness   15 *common ear* the ear of the people   21 *fourteen* (in I.ii.171 the time has been "nineteen" years. Doubtless the printer's copy in both lines had either xiv or xix and in one line was misread)   28 *Dead to infliction* utterly unenforced   29 *Liberty* license   35 *Sith* since

For what I bid them do; for we bid this be done
When evil deeds have their permissive pass,
And not the punishment. Therefore, indeed, my
    father,
I have on Angelo imposed the office,   40
Who may, in th' ambush° of my name, strike home,
And yet my nature never in the fight
To do it slander. And to behold his sway,
I will, as 'twere a brother of your order,
Visit both prince and people. Therefore, I prithee,   45
Supply me with the habit° and instruct me
How I may formally in person bear
Like a true friar. Moe° reasons for this action
At our more leisure shall I render you;
Only, this one: Lord Angelo is precise,°   50
Stands at a guard with envy;° scarce confesses
That his blood flows, or that his appetite
Is more to bread than stone. Hence shall we see,
If power change purpose, what our seemers be.

                                      Exit [*with Friar*].

Scene IV. [*A nunnery.*]

Enter Isabella and Francisca, a nun.

Isabella. And have you nuns no farther privileges?

Francisca. Are not these large enough?

Isabella. Yes, truly. I speak not as desiring more,
    But rather wishing a more strict restraint
    Upon the sisterhood, the votarists of Saint Clare.°   5

Lucio. (*Within*) Ho! Peace be in this place!

41 *in th' ambush* under cover   46 *habit* garment   48 *Moe* more
50 *precise* fastidiously strict   51 *Stands . . . envy* defies all malicious
criticism I.iv.5 *Saint Clare* (a notably strict order)

Isabella.   Who's that which calls?

Francisca. It is a man's voice. Gentle Isabella,
    Turn you the key, and know his business of him.
    You may, I may not: you are yet unsworn.
    When you have vowed, you must not speak with
10   men
    But in the presence of the prioress:
    Then, if you speak, you must not show your face,
    Or, if you show your face, you must not speak.
    He calls again; I pray you, answer him.   [*Exit.*]

15 *Isabella.* Peace and prosperity! Who is't that calls?

[*Enter Lucio.*]

Lucio. Hail, virgin—if you be, as those cheek-roses
    Proclaim you are no less! Can you so stead° me
    As bring me to the sight of Isabella,
    A novice of this place and the fair sister
20   To her unhappy brother, Claudio?

Isabella. Why "her unhappy brother"? Let me ask,
    The rather for I now must make you know
    I am that Isabella and his sister.

Lucio. Gentle and fair, your brother kindly greets you.
25   Not to be weary with you, he's in prison.

Isabella. Woe me! For what?

Lucio. For that which, if myself might be his judge,
    He should receive his punishment in thanks:
    He hath got his friend with child.

Isabella. Sir! Make me not your story.°

30 *Lucio.*   'Tis true.
    I would not, though 'tis my familiar sin
    With maids to seem the lapwing,° and to jest,
    Tongue far from heart, play with all virgins so.
    I hold you as a thing enskied and sainted,
35   By your renouncement, an immortal spirit;

17 *stead* help   30 *story* subject for mirth   32 *lapwing* pewit (a bird
which runs away from its nest to mislead intruders)

And to be talked with in sincerity,
As with a saint.

Isabella. You do blaspheme the good in mocking me.

Lucio. Do not believe it. Fewness and truth,° 'tis thus:
Your brother and his lover have embraced;   40
As those that feed grow full, as blossoming time
That from the seedness° the bare fallow brings
To teeming foison,° even so her plenteous womb
Expresseth his full tilth and husbandry.

Isabella. Someone with child by him? My cousin
Juliet?   45

Lucio. Is she your cousin?

Isabella. Adoptedly, as schoolmaids change their
names
By vain, though apt, affection.

Lucio.   She it is.

Isabella. O, let him marry her.

Lucio.   This is the point:
The Duke is very strangely gone from hence;   50
Bore many gentlemen, myself being one,
In hand and hope of action,° but we do learn
By those that know the very nerves of state,
His givings-out were of an infinite distance
From his true-meant design. Upon his place,   55
And with full line of his authority,
Governs Lord Angelo, a man whose blood
Is very snow-broth; one who never feels
The wanton stings and motions of the sense,
But doth rebate and blunt his natural edge   60
With profits of the mind, study and fast.
He—to give fear to use and liberty,°
Which have for long run by the hideous law,
As mice by lions—hath picked out an act,

39 *Fewness and truth* briefly and truly   42 *seedness* sowing   43
foison harvest   51–52 *Bore . . . action* deluded . . . with the hope
of military action   62 *use and liberty* habitual license

...der whose heavy sense° your brother's life
Falls into forfeit; he arrests him on it,
And follows close the rigor of the statute,
To make him an example. All hope is gone,
Unless you have the grace by your fair prayer
70   To soften Angelo. And that's my pith of business
'Twixt you and your poor brother.

Isabella. Doth he so? Seek his life?

Lucio.   Has censured° him
Already, and, as I hear, the provost hath
A warrant for's execution.

75   *Isabella.* Alas, what poor ability's in me
To do him good?

Lucio.   Assay the pow'r you have.

Isabella. My power? Alas, I doubt—

Lucio.   Our doubts are traitors,
And makes° us lose the good we oft might win,
By fearing to attempt. Go to Lord Angelo,
80   And let him learn to know, when maidens sue,
Men give like gods; but when they weep and kneel,
All their petitions are as freely theirs
As they themselves would owe° them.

Isabella. I'll see what I can do.

Lucio.   But speedily.

85   *Isabella.* I will about it straight,
No longer staying but to give the Mother
Notice of my affair. I humbly thank you;
Commend me to my brother; soon at night
I'll send him certain word of my success.°

Lucio. I take my leave of you.

90   *Isabella.*   Good sir, adieu.
                                    Exeunt.

65 *sense* interpretation   72 *censured* pronounced judgment on   78
makes (a plural subject sometimes takes a verb ending in -*s*)
83 *owe* own   89 *success* outcome

ACT II

Scene I. [*A room.*]

Enter Angelo, Escalus, and Servants, Justice.

Angelo. We must not make a scarecrow of the law,
  Setting it up to fear the birds of prey,
  And let it keep one shape, till custom make it
  Their perch and not their terror.

Escalus.   Ay, but yet
  Let us be keen, and rather cut° a little,   5
  Than fall,° and bruise to death. Alas, this gentleman
  Whom I would save had a most noble father.
  Let but your honor know,
  Whom I believe to be most strait° in virtue,
  That, in the working of your own affections,°   10
  Had time cohered with place or place with wishing,
  Or that the resolute acting of your blood
  Could have attained th' effect of your own purpose,
  Whether you had not sometime in your life
  Erred in this point which now you censure him,   15
  And pulled the law upon you.

Angelo. 'Tis one thing to be tempted, Escalus,
  Another thing to fall. I not deny,

II.i.5 *cut* prune 6 *fall* let the ax fall 9 *strait* strict 10 *affections*
passions

51

The jury, passing on the prisoner's life,
20   May in the sworn twelve have a thief or two
     Guiltier than him they try. What's open made to
       Justice,
     That Justice seizes. What knows the laws
     That thieves do pass on thieves? 'Tis very preg-
       nant,°
     The jewel that we find, we stoop and take't
25   Because we see it; but what we do not see
     We tread upon, and never think of it.
     You may not so extenuate his offense
     For I have had such faults; but rather tell me,
     When I, that censure him, do so offend,
30   Let mine own judgment pattern out my death,
     And nothing come in partial. Sir, he must die.

Escalus. Be it as your wisdom will.

Angelo.   Where is the provost?

Enter Provost.

Provost. Here, if it like your honor.

Angelo.   See that Claudio
     Be executed by nine tomorrow morning.
35   Bring him his confessor, let him be prepared,
     For that's the utmost of his pilgrimage.
                                          [*Exit Provost.*]

Escalus. Well, Heaven forgive him, and forgive us all.
     Some rise by sin, and some by virtue fall:
     Some run from breaks of ice,° and answer none;
40   And some condemnèd for a fault° alone.

Enter Elbow, Froth, Clown [Pompey], Officers.

Elbow. Come, bring them away. If these be good peo-
     ple in a commonweal that do nothing but use their
     abuses in common houses, I know no law. Bring
     them away.

23 *pregnant* clear 39 *Some . . . ice* some escape after gross violations
of chastity (? the passage is much disputed) 40 *fault* (1) small crack
in the ice (2) act of sex

Angelo. How now, sir! What's your name? And what's 45
the matter?

Elbow. If it please your honor, I am the poor Duke's
constable, and my name is Elbow. I do lean upon
justice, sir, and do bring in here before your good
honor two notorious benefactors. 50

Angelo. Benefactors? Well, what benefactors are they?
Are they not malefactors?

Elbow. If it please your honor, I know not well what
they are, but precise villains they are, that I am
sure of, and void of all profanation in the world 55
that good Christians ought to have.

Escalus. This comes off well; here's a wise officer.

Angelo. Go to: what quality° are they of? Elbow is
your name? Why dost thou not speak, Elbow?

Pompey. He cannot, sir; he's out at elbow.° 60

Angelo. What are you, sir?

Elbow. He, sir! A tapster, sir, parcel-bawd,° one that
serves a bad woman whose house, sir, was, as they
say, plucked down in the suburbs, and now she
professes a hothouse,° which, I think, is a very ill 65
house too.

Escalus. How know you that?

Elbow. My wife, sir, whom I detest° before Heaven
and your honor—

Escalus. How! Thy wife? 70

Elbow. Ay, sir—whom, I thank Heaven, is an honest°
woman—

Escalus. Dost thou detest her therefore?

Elbow. I say, sir, I will detest myself also, as well as

58 *quality* profession 60 *out at elbow* (1) somewhat seedy (2) speechless (out at the sound of his name) 62 *parcel-bawd* partly a bawd
65 *hothouse* bathhouse 68 *detest* i.e., protest 71 *honest* chaste

she, that this house, if it be not a bawd's house, it
is pity of her life, for it is a naughty° house.

Escalus. How dost thou know that, constable?

Elbow. Marry, sir, by my wife, who, if she had been a
woman cardinally° given, might have been accused
80 in fornication, adultery, and all uncleanliness there.

Escalus. By the woman's means?

Elbow. Ay, sir, by Mistress Overdone's means; but as
she spit in his face, so she defied him.

Pompey. Sir, if it please your honor, this is not so.

85 *Elbow.* Prove it before these varlets here, thou honorable man; prove it.

Escalus. Do you hear how he misplaces?

Pompey. Sir, she came in great with child; and longing,
saving your honor's reverence, for stewed prunes.°
90 Sir, we had but two in the house, which at that very
distant time stood, as it were, in a fruit dish, a dish
of some threepence; your honors have seen such
dishes; they are not china dishes, but very good
dishes—

95 *Escalus.* Go to, go to; no matter for the dish, sir.

Pompey. No, indeed, sir, not of a pin; you are therein
in the right; but to the point. As I say, this Mistress
Elbow, being, as I say, with child, and being great-
bellied, and longing, as I said, for prunes; and hav-
100 ing but two in the dish, as I said, Master Froth here,
this very man, having eaten the rest, as I said, and,
as I say, paying for them very honestly; for, as you
know, Master Froth, I could not give you threepence again.

105 *Froth.* No, indeed.

Pompey. Very well, you being then, if you be remem-

76 *naughty* immoral   79 *cardinally* i.e., carnally   89 *stewed prunes*
(supposed to be a favorite dish among prostitutes)

b'red, cracking the stones of the foresaid prunes—

Froth. Ay, so I did indeed.

Pompey. Why, very well; I telling you then, if you be rememb'red, that such a one and such a one were 110 past cure of the thing you wot° of, unless they kept very good diet, as I told you—

Froth. All this is true.

Pompey. Why, very well, then—

Escalus. Come, you are a tedious fool; to the purpose. 115 What was done to Elbow's wife, that he hath cause to complain of? Come me to what was done to her.

Pompey. Sir, your honor cannot come to that yet.°

Escalus. No, sir, nor I mean it not.

Pompey. Sir, but you shall come to it, by your honor's 120 leave. And, I beseech you, look into Master Froth here, sir, a man of fourscore pound a year, whose father died at Hallowmas.° Was't not at Hallowmas, Master Froth?

Froth. All-hallond Eve.°   125

Pompey. Why, very well; I hope here be truths. He, sir, sitting, as I say, in a lower chair, sir, 'twas in the Bunch of Grapes, where, indeed, you have a delight to sit, have you not?

Froth. I have so, because it is an open room, and 130 good for winter.

Pompey. Why, very well, then; I hope here be truths.

Angelo. This will last out a night in Russia,
When nights are longest there. I'll take my leave,
And leave you to the hearing of the cause, 135
Hoping you'll find good cause to whip them all.

111 *wot* know   117–18 *Come me . . . that yet* (the verbs carry a sexual innuendo)   123 *Hallowmas* All Saints' Day, November 1st   125 *All-hallond Eve* October 31st

Escalus. I think no less. Good morrow to your lord-
      ship.   *Exit* [*Angelo*].
    Now, sir, come on: what was done to Elbow's wife,
    once more?

140 *Pompey.* Once, sir? There was nothing done to her
    once.

Elbow. I beseech you, sir, ask him what this man did
    to my wife.

Pompey. I beseech your honor, ask me.

145 *Escalus.* Well, sir; what did this gentleman to her?

Pompey. I beseech you, sir, look in this gentleman's
    face. Good Master Froth, look upon his honor;
    'tis for a good purpose. Doth your honor mark his
    face?

150 *Escalus.* Ay, sir, very well.

Pompey. Nay, I beseech you, mark it well.

Escalus. Well, I do so.

Pompey. Doth your honor see any harm in his face?

Escalus. Why, no.

155 *Pompey.* I'll be supposed° upon a book, his face is the
    worst thing about him. Good, then; if his face be
    the worst thing about him, how could Master Froth
    do the constable's wife any harm? I would know
    that of your honor.

160 *Escalus.* He's in the right. Constable, what say you
    to it?

Elbow. First, and° it like you, the house is a re-
    spected° house; next, this is a respected fellow;
    and his mistress is a respected woman.

165 *Pompey.* By this hand, sir, his wife is a more respected
    person than any of us all.

155 *supposed* i.e., deposed   162 *and* if   162–63 *respected* i.e., sus-
pected

Elbow. Varlet, thou liest; thou liest, wicked varlet! The
time is yet to come that she was ever respected with
man, woman, or child.

Pompey. Sir, she was respected with him before he   170
married with her.

Escalus. Which is the wiser here, Justice or Iniquity?°
Is this true?

Elbow. O thou caitiff! O thou varlet! O thou wicked
Hannibal!° I respected with her before I was mar-   175
ried to her! If ever I was respected with her, or she
with me, let not your worship think me the poor
Duke's officer. Prove this, thou wicked Hannibal,
or I'll have mine action of batt'ry on thee.

Escalus. If he took you a box o' th' ear, you might   180
have your action of slander too.

Elbow. Marry, I thank your good worship for it. What
is't your worship's pleasure I shall do with this
wicked caitiff?

Escalus. Truly, officer, because he hath some offenses   185
in him that thou wouldst discover if thou couldst,
let him continue in his courses till thou know'st
what they are.

Elbow. Marry, I thank your worship for it. Thou seest,
thou wicked varlet, now, what's come upon thee.   190
Thou art to continue now, thou varlet; thou art to
continue.

Escalus. Where were you born, friend?

Froth. Here in Vienna, sir.

Escalus. Are you of fourscore pounds a year?   195

Froth. Yes, and't please you, sir.

Escalus. So. [*To Pompey*] What trade are you of, sir?

Pompey. A tapster, a poor widow's tapster.

172 *Justice or Iniquity* (personified characters in morality plays)
175 *Hannibal* i.e., cannibal, fleshmonger (?)

Escalus. Your mistress' name?

200 *Pompey.* Mistress Overdone.

Escalus. Hath she had any more than one husband?

Pompey. Nine, sir; Overdone by the last.

Escalus. Nine! Come hither to me, Master Froth.
Master Froth, I would not have you acquainted
205   with tapsters: they will draw you,° Master Froth,
and you will hang them. Get you gone, and let me
hear no more of you.

Froth. I thank your worship. For mine own part, I
never come into any room in a taphouse, but I am
210   drawn in.

Escalus. Well, no more of it, Master Froth; farewell.
[*Exit Froth.*]
Come you hither to me, Master Tapster. What's
your name, Master Tapster?

Pompey. Pompey.

215 *Escalus.* What else?

Pompey. Bum, sir.

Escalus. Troth, and your bum is the greatest thing
about you; so that, in the beastliest sense, you are
Pompey the Great. Pompey, you are partly a bawd,
220   Pompey, howsoever you color° it in being a tapster,
are you not? Come, tell me true; it shall be the
better for you.

Pompey. Truly, sir, I am a poor fellow that would live.

Escalus. How would you live, Pompey? By being a
225   bawd? What do you think of the trade, Pompey?
Is it a lawful trade?

Pompey. If the law would allow it, sir.

205 *draw you* (1) draw drinks for you (2) empty you, disembowel
you   220 *color* camouflage

Escalus. But the law will not allow, it, Pompey; nor it shall not be allowed in Vienna.

Pompey. Does your worship mean to geld and splay all the youth of the city?   230

Escalus. No, Pompey.

Pompey. Truly, sir, in my poor opinion, they will to't, then. If your worship will take order for the drabs and the knaves, you need not to fear the bawds.   235

Escalus. There is pretty orders beginning, I can tell you; it is but heading° and hanging.

Pompey. If you head and hang all that offend that way but for ten year together, you'll be glad to give out a commission for more heads; if this law hold 240 in Vienna ten year, I'll rent the fairest house in it after threepence a bay;° if you live to see this come to pass, say Pompey told you so.

Escalus. Thank you, good Pompey; and, in requital of your prophecy, hark you: I advise you, let me 245 not find you before me again upon any complaint whatsoever; no, not for dwelling where you do. If I do, Pompey, I shall beat you to your tent, and prove a shrewd Caesar to you; in plain dealing, Pompey, I shall have you whipped. So, for this 250 time, Pompey, fare you well.

Pompey. I thank your worship for your good counsel; [*aside*] but I shall follow it as the flesh and fortune shall better determine.
Whip me? No, no; let carman whip his jade.°   255
The valiant heart's not whipped out of his trade.
                                        Exit.

Escalus. Come hither to me, Master Elbow; come hither, Master constable. How long have you been in this place of constable?

---

237 *heading* beheading   242 *bay* space under a single gable   255
carman whip his jade (the cartman whipped the whore after carting
her through the streets; a "jade" is literally a nag)

260 *Elbow.* Seven year and a half, sir.

Escalus. I thought, by the readiness in the office, you
  had continued in it some time. You say, seven years
  together?

Elbow. And a half, sir.

265 *Escalus.* Alas, it hath been great pains to you. They
  do you wrong to put you so oft upon't.° Are there
  not men in your ward sufficient to serve it?

Elbow. Faith, sir, few of any wit in such matters. As
  they are chosen, they are glad to choose me for
270 them; I do it for some piece of money, and go
  through with all.

Escalus. Look you bring me in the names of some
  six or seven, the most sufficient of your parish.

Elbow. To your worship's house, sir?

275 *Escalus.* To my house. Fare you well. [*Exit Elbow.*]
  What's o'clock, think you?

Justice. Eleven, sir.

Escalus. I pray you home to dinner with me.

Justice. I humbly thank you.

280 *Escalus.* It grieves me for the death of Claudio,
  But there's no remedy.

Justice. Lord Angelo is severe.

Escalus.   It is but needful:
  Mercy is not itself, that oft looks so;
  Pardon is still° the nurse of second woe.
285 But yet—poor Claudio! There is no remedy.
  Come, sir.   *Exeunt.*

266 *put you so oft upon't* i.e., impose on you the task of being
constable   284 *still* always

Scene II. [*A room.*]

Enter Provost, [*and a*] *Servant.*

Servant. He's hearing of a cause; he will come straight:
  I'll tell him of you.

Provost.   Pray you, do. [*Exit Servant.*] I'll know
  His pleasure; maybe he will relent. Alas,
  He hath but as offended in a dream.
  All sects,° all ages smack of this vice; and he   *5*
  To die for't!

Enter Angelo.

Angelo.   Now, what's the matter, provost?

Provost. Is it your will Claudio shall die tomorrow?

Angelo. Did not I tell thee yea? Hadst thou not order?
  Why dost thou ask again?

Provost.   Lest I might be too rash.
  Under your good correction, I have seen,   *10*
  When, after execution, judgment hath
  Repented o'er his doom.

Angelo.   Go to; let that be mine.°
  Do you your office, or give up your place,
  And you shall well be spared.

Provost.   I crave your honor's
      pardon.
  What shall be done, sir, with the groaning Juliet?   *15*
  She's very near her hour.

Angelo.   Dispose of her
  To some more fitter place, and that with speed.

I.ii.5 *sects* classes   12 *mine* i.e., my responsibility

[Re-enter Servant.]

Servant. Here is the sister of the man condemned
    Desires access to you.

Angelo.   Hath he a sister?

20 *Provost.* Ay, my good lord, a very virtuous maid
    And to be shortly of a sisterhood,
    If not already.

Angelo.   Well, let her be admitted.

                            [Exit Servant.]

    See you the fornicatress be removed;
    Let her have needful, but not lavish, means;
    There shall be order for't.

Enter Lucio and Isabella.

25 *Provost.*   'Save your honor.

Angelo. Stay a little while. [*To Isabella*] Y'are wel-
    come: what's your will?

Isabella. I am a woeful suitor to your honor,
    Please but your honor hear me.

Angelo.   Well; what's your suit?

Isabella. There is a vice that most I do abhor,
30   And most desire should meet the blow of justice,
    For which I would not plead, but that I must,
    For which I must not plead, but that I am
    At war 'twixt will and will not.

Angelo.   Well: the matter?

Isabella. I have a brother is condemned to die.
35   I do beseech you, let it be his fault,°
    And not my brother.

Provost.   [*Aside*] Heaven give thee moving graces.

Angelo. Condemn the fault, and not the actor of it?
    Why, every fault's condemned ere it be done.

35 *let it be his fault* i.e., condemn his fault, not him

Mine were the very cipher of a function,
To fine the faults whose fine° stands in record,   40
And let go by the actor.

Isabella.   O just but severe law!
I had a brother, then. Heaven keep your honor.

Lucio. [*Aside to Isabella*] Give't not o'er so. To him
  again, entreat him,
Kneel down before him, hang upon his gown;
You are too cold; if you should need a pin,   45
You could not with more tame a tongue desire it.
To him, I say!

Isabella. Must he needs die?

Angelo.   Maiden, no remedy.

Isabella. Yes; I do think that you might pardon him,
And neither heaven nor man grieve at the mercy.   50

Angelo. I will not do't.

Isabella.   But can you, if you would?

Angelo. Look what° I will not, that I cannot do.

Isabella. But might you do't, and do the world no
  wrong,
If so your heart were touched with that remorse°
As mine is to him?

Angelo.   He's sentenced; 'tis too late.   55

Lucio. [*Aside to Isabella*] You are too cold.

Isabella. Too late? Why, no: I, that do speak a word,
May call it again. Well, believe this:
No ceremony° that to great ones 'longs,°
Not the king's crown, nor the deputed sword,   60
The marshal's truncheon, nor the judge's robe,
Become them with one half so good a grace
As mercy does.
If he had been as you, and you as he,

40 *fine . . . fine* penalize . . . penalty 52 *Look what* whatever 54 *re-morse* compassion 59 *ceremony* insignia of greatness 59 *'longs* belongs

65   You would have slipped like him; but he, like you,
         Would not have been so stern.

Angelo.   Pray you, be gone.

Isabella. I would to heaven I had your potency,
         And you were Isabel; should it then be thus?
         No; I would tell what 'twere to be a judge,
         And what a prisoner.

Lucio. [*Aside to Isabella*] Ay, touch him; there's the
70   vein.

Angelo. Your brother is a forfeit of the law,
         And you but waste your words.

Isabella.   Alas, alas!
         Why, all the souls that were were forfeit once;
         And He that might the vantage best have took
75   Found out the remedy. How would you be,
         If He, which is the top of judgment, should
         But judge you as you are? O, think on that,
         And mercy then will breathe within your lips,
         Like man new made.

Angelo.   Be you content, fair maid;
80   It is the law, not I, condemn your brother.
         Were he my kinsman, brother, or my son,
         It should be thus with him; he must die tomorrow

Isabella. Tomorrow! O, that's sudden! Spare him,
         spare him!
         He's not prepared for death. Even for our kitchens
85   We kill the fowl of season:° shall we serve heaven
         With less respect than we do minister
         To our gross selves? Good, good my lord, bethink
         you:
         Who is it that hath died for this offense?
         There's many have committed it.

Lucio. [*Aside to Isabella*]   Ay, well said.

Angelo. The law hath not been dead, though it hath
90   slept.

85 *of season* in season

Those many had not dared to do that evil,
If the first that did th' edict infringe
Had answered for his deed. Now 'tis awake,
Takes note of what is done, and, like a prophet,
Looks in a glass, that shows what future evils,
Either new, or by remissness new conceived,°   95
And so in progress to be hatched and born,
Are now to have no successive degrees,
But here they live, to end.

Isabella.   Yet show some pity.

Angelo. I show it most of all when I show justice,   100
For then I pity those I do not know,
Which a dismissed° offense would after gall;
And do him right that, answering one foul wrong,
Lives not to act another. Be satisfied;
Your brother dies tomorrow; be content.   105

Isabella. So you must be the first that gives this sen-
    tence,
And he, that suffers. O, it is excellent �
● To have a giant's strength; but it is tyrannous
To use it like a giant.

Lucio. [*Aside to Isabella*] That's well said.

Isabella. Could great men thunder   110
As Jove himself does, Jove would ne'er be quiet,
For every pelting,° petty officer
Would use his heaven for thunder.
Nothing but thunder. Merciful heaven,
Thou rather with thy sharp and sulfurous bolt   115
Splits the unwedgeable and gnarlèd oak
Than the soft myrtle. But man, proud man,
Dressed in a little brief authority,
Most ignorant of what he's most assured,

95–96 *future. . . conceived* i.e., evils that will take place in future,
but that are either now planned or may be planned later ("remissness": careless omission of duty)   102 *dismissed* forgiven   112 *pelt-*
ing paltry

120   His glassy essence,° like an angry ape,
      Plays such fantastic tricks before high heaven
      As makes the angels weep; who, with our spleens,°
      Would all themselves laugh mortal.

  Lucio. [*Aside to Isabella*] O, to him, to him, wench!
      He will relent;
      He's coming; I perceive't.

125 *Provost.*   [*Aside*] Pray heaven she win him.

  Isabella. We cannot weigh our brother with ourself:
      Great men may jest with saints; 'tis wit in them;
      But in the less, foul profanation.

  Lucio. Thou'rt i' th' right, girl; more o' that.

130 *Isabella.* That in the captain's but a choleric word,
      Which in the soldier is flat blasphemy.

  Lucio. [*Aside to Isabella*] Art avised° o' that? More
      on't.

  Angelo. Why do you put these sayings upon me?

  Isabella. Because authority, though it err like others,
135   Hath yet a kind of medicine in itself,
      That skins the vice° o' th' top; go to your bosom,
      Knock there, and ask your heart what it doth know
      That's like my brother's fault; if it confess
      A natural guiltiness such as is his,
140   Let it not sound a thought upon your tongue
      Against my brother's life.

  Angelo.   [*Aside*] She speaks, and 'tis
      Such sense, that my sense breeds with it. [*Aloud*]
      Fare you well.

  Isabella. Gentle my lord, turn back.

  Angelo. I will bethink me; come again tomorrow.

120 *glassy essence* the rational soul which reveals to man, as in a
mirror, what constitutes him a human being (?) fragile nature (?)
122 *spleens* (the spleen was believed the seat of mirth and anger)
132 *avised* informed   136 *skins the vice* i.e., covers the sore of vice
with a skin, but does not heal it (or perhaps "skims off the visible
layer of vice")

Isabella. Hark how I'll bribe you; good my lord, turn
    back.   149

Angelo. How? Bribe me?

Isabella. Ay, with such gifts that heaven shall share
    with you.

Lucio. [*Aside to Isabella*] You had marred all else.

Isabella. Not with fond sicles° of the tested gold,
    Or stones whose rate are either rich or poor   150
    As fancy values them; but with true prayers
    That shall be up at heaven, and enter there
    Ere sunrise, prayers from preservèd souls,
    From fasting maids whose minds are dedicate
    To nothing temporal.

Angelo.   Well; come to me tomorrow.   155

Lucio. [*Aside to Isabella*] Go to; 'tis well; away.

Isabella. Heaven keep your honor safe.

Angelo.   [*Aside*] Amen:
    For I am that way going to temptation,
    Where prayers cross.°

Isabella.   At what hour tomorrow
    Shall I attend your lordship?

Angelo.   At any time 'fore noon.   160

Isabella. 'Save your honor.

    [*Exeunt Isabella, Lucio, and Provost.*]

Angelo.   From thee, even from thy virtue!
    What's this? What's this? Is this her fault or mine?
    The tempter or the tempted, who sins most?
    Ha, not she. Nor doth she tempt; but it is I
    That, lying by the violet in the sun,   165
    Do as the carrion does, not as the flow'r,
    Corrupt with virtuous season.° Can it be

149 *fond sicles* foolish shekels 159 *cross* are at cross purposes 167
Corrupt with virtuous season go bad in the season that blossoms the
flower

That modesty may more betray our sense
Than woman's lightness? Having waste ground
    enough,
170   Shall we desire to raze the sanctuary,
And pitch our evils° there? O fie, fie, fie!
What dost thou, or what art thou, Angelo?
Dost thou desire her foully for those things
That make her good? O, let her brother live:
175   Thieves for their robbery have authority
When judges steal themselves. What, do I love her,
That I desire to hear her speak again,
And feast upon her eyes? What is't I dream on?
O cunning enemy, that, to catch a saint,
180   With saints dost bait thy hook! Most dangerous
Is that temptation that doth goad us on
To sin in loving virtue. Never could the strumpet,
With all her double vigor, art and nature,
Once stir my temper; but this virtuous maid
185   Subdues me quite. Ever till now,
When men were fond,° I smiled, and wond'red
    how.   Exit.

Scene III. [The prison.]

Enter Duke [disguised as a friar] and Provost.

Duke. Hail to you, provost—so I think you are.

Provost. I am the provost. What's your will, good
    friar?

Duke. Bound by my charity and my blest order,
    I come to visit the afflicted spirits
5   Here in the prison. Do me the common right
    To let me see them, and to make me know

171 evils evil structures (e.g., perhaps whorehouses or privies)
186 fond infatuated

    The nature of their crimes, that I may minister
    To them accordingly.

Provost. I would do more than that, if more were
    needful.

Enter Juliet.

    Look, here comes one: a gentlewoman of mine,   *10*
    Who, falling in the flaws° of her own youth,
    Hath blistered her report:° she is with child;
    And he that got it, sentenced; a young man
    More fit to do another such offense
    Than die for this.   *15*

Duke. When must he die?

Provost.   As I do think, tomorrow.
    [*To Juliet*] I have provided for you; stay awhile,
    And you shall be conducted.

Duke. Repent you, fair one, of the sin you carry?

Juliet. I do, and bear the shame most patiently.   *20*

Duke. I'll teach you how you shall arraign° your con-
    science,
    And try your penitence, if it be sound
    Or hollowly put on.

Juliet.   I'll gladly learn.

Duke. Love you the man that wronged you?

Juliet. Yes, as I love the woman that wronged him.   *25*

Duke. So, then, it seems your most offenseful act
    Was mutually committed?

Juliet.   Mutually.

Duke. Then was your sin of heavier kind than his.

Juliet. I do confess it, and repent it, father.

Duke. 'Tis meet so, daughter. But lest you do repent   *30*

II.iii.11 *flaws* sudden gusts of wind   12 *report* reputation   21 *ar-
raign* interrogate

As that the sin hath brought you to this shame—
Which sorrow is always toward ourselves, not heaven,
Showing we would not spare heaven as we love it,
But as we stand in fear—

Juliet. I do repent me, as it is an evil,
And take the shame with joy.

Duke. There rest.
Your partner, as I hear, must die tomorrow,
And I am going with instruction to him.
Grace go with you, *Benedicite!*° *Exit.*

Juliet. Must die tomorrow! O injurious love,
That respites° me a life, whose very comfort
Is still a dying horror.

Provost. 'Tis pity of him. *Exeunt.*

Scene IV. [*A room.*]

Enter Angelo.

Angelo. When I would pray and think, I think and pray
To several° subjects: heaven hath my empty words,
Whilst my invention,° hearing not my tongue,
Anchors on Isabel: heaven in my mouth,
As if I did but only chew his name,
And in my heart the strong and swelling evil
Of my conception.° The state,° whereon I studied,
Is like a good thing, being often read,
Grown seared° and tedious; yea, my gravity,
Wherein, let no man hear me, I take pride,

39 *Benedicite* bless you 41 *respites* saves II.iv.2 *several* separate 3 *invention* imagination 7 *conception* thought 7 *state* attitude (?) statecraft (?) 9 *seared* worn out

Could I with boot° change for an idle plume
Which the air beats for vain. O place, O form,
How often dost thou with thy case,° thy habit,°
Wrench awe from fools, and tie the wiser souls
To thy false seeming! Blood, thou art blood.   15
Let's write "good angel" on the devil's horn,°
'Tis not the devil's crest. How now, who's there?

Enter Servant.

Servant. One Isabel, a sister, desires access to you.

Angelo. Teach her the way. [*Exit Servant.*] O heavens,
Why does my blood thus muster to my heart,   20
Making both it unable for itself,
And dispossessing all my other parts
Of necessary fitness?
So play the foolish throngs with one that swounds,°
Come all to help him, and so stop the air   25
By which he should revive; and even so
The general,° subject to a well-wished king,
Quit their own part, and in obsequious fondness
Crowd to his presence, where their untaught love
Must needs appear offense.

Enter Isabella.

                    How now, fair maid?   30

Isabella. I am come to know your pleasure.

Angelo. That you might know it, would much better
    please me
    Than to demand what 'tis. Your brother cannot
    live.

Isabella. Even so. Heaven keep your honor.

Angelo. Yet may he live awhile, and it may be,   35
    As long as you or I; yet he must die.

Isabella. Under your sentence?

11 *with boot* with profit   13 *case* (either "chance" or "outside")
13 *habit* (either "behavior" or "garment")   16 *horn* phallus (?)
24 *swounds* swoons   27 *general* multitude

Angelo. Yea.

Isabella. When? I beseech you that in his reprieve,
40   Longer or shorter, he may be so fitted
    That his soul sicken not.

Angelo. Ha! Fie, these filthy vices! It were as good
    To pardon him that hath from nature stol'n
    A man already made, as to remit
45   Their saucy sweetness° that do coin heaven's image
    In stamps that are forbid: 'tis all as easy
    Falsely to take away a life true made,
    As to put metal in restrainèd° means
    To make a false one.

50 *Isabella.* 'Tis set down so in heaven, but not in earth.

Angelo. Say you so? Then I shall pose° you quickly.
    Which had you rather: that the most just law
    Now took your brother's life; or, to redeem him,
    Give up your body to such sweet uncleanness
    As she that he hath stained?

55 *Isabella.*   Sir, believe this:
    I had rather give my body than my soul.

Angelo. I talk not of your soul; our compelled sins
    Stand more for number than for accompt.°

Isabella.   How say you?

Angelo. Nay, I'll not warrant that; for I can speak
60   Against the thing I say. Answer to this:
    I, now the voice of the recorded law,
    Pronounce a sentence on your brother's life;
    Might there not be a charity in sin
    To save this brother's life?

Isabella.   Please you to do't,
65   I'll take it as a peril to my soul,
    It is no sin at all, but charity.

44–45 *to remit . . . sweetness* to pardon their lascivious pleasures
48 *restrainèd* forbidden   51 *pose* baffle (with a difficult question)
58 *Stand . . . accompt* are enumerated but not counted against us

Angelo. Pleased you to do't at peril of your soul,
    Were equal poise° of sin and charity.

Isabella. That I do beg his life, if it be sin,
    Heaven let me bear it. You granting of my suit,   70
    If that be sin, I'll make it my morn prayer
    To have it added to the faults of mine,
    And nothing of your answer.

Angelo.   Nay, but hear me.
    Your sense pursues not mine; either you are ig-
        norant,
    Or seem so, crafty; and that's not good.   75

Isabella. Let me be ignorant, and in nothing good,
    But graciously to know I am no better.

Angelo. Thus wisdom wishes to appear most bright
    When it doth tax° itself, as these black masks
    Proclaim an enshield° beauty ten times louder   80
    Than beauty could, displayed. But mark me;
    To be receivèd plain, I'll speak more gross:
    Your brother is to die.

Isabella. So.

Angelo. And his offense is so, as it appears,   85
    Accountant° to the law upon that pain.°

Isabella. True.

Angelo. Admit no other way to save his life—
    As I subscribe° not that, nor any other,
    But in the loss of question°—that you, his sister,   90
    Finding yourself desired of such a person
    Whose credit with the judge, or own great place,
    Could fetch your brother from the manacles
    Of the all-binding law; and that there were
    No earthly mean to save him, but that either   95
    You must lay down the treasures of your body
    To this supposed, or else to let him suffer:

68 *poise* balance   79 *tax* censure   80 *enshield* concealed   86 *Accountant* accountable   86 *pain* punishment   89 *subscribe* assent to   90 *But . . . question* except to keep alive the argument

What would you do?

Isabella. As much for my poor brother as myself:
100   That is, were I under the terms of death,
        Th' impression of keen whips I'd wear as rubies,
        And strip myself to death as to a bed
        That longing have been sick for, ere I'd yield
        My body up to shame.

Angelo.   Then must your brother die.

105 *Isabella.* And 'twere the cheaper way.
        Better it were a brother died at once
        Than that a sister, by redeeming him,
        Should die forever.

Angelo. Were not you, then, as cruel as the sentence
110   That you have slandered so?

Isabella. Ignomy in ransom and free pardon
        Are of two houses; lawful mercy
        Is nothing kin to foul redemption.

Angelo. You seemed of late to make the law a tyrant,
115   And rather proved the sliding of your brother
        A merriment than a vice.

Isabella. O, pardon me, my lord. It oft falls out,
        To have what we would have, we speak not what
            we mean.
        I something do excuse the thing I hate
120   For his advantage that I dearly love.

Angelo. We are all frail.

Isabella.   Else let my brother die,
        If not a fedary, but only he
        Owe and succeed thy weakness.°

Angelo. Nay, women are frail too.

    Isabella. Ay, as the glasses where they view them-
125   selves,

122–23 *If . . . weakness* (the meaning seems to be: "Let my brother
die if he is the only inheritor of human frailty instead of being a mere
vassal to it")

Which are as easy broke as they make forms.°
Women! Help heaven! Men their creation mar
In profiting by them. Nay, call us ten times frail;
For we are soft as our complexions are,
And credulous° to false prints.

Angelo.   I think it well,   130
And from this testimony of your own sex—
Since, I suppose, we are made to be no stronger
Than faults may shake our frames—let me be bold:
I do arrest your words.° Be that you are,
That is, a woman; if you be more, you're none;   135
If you be one, as you are well expressed°
By all external warrants, show it now,
By putting on the destined livery.°

Isabella. I have no tongue but one; gentle my lord,
Let me entreat you speak the former language.   140

Angelo. Plainly conceive, I love you.

Isabella. My brother did love Juliet,
And you tell me that he shall die for't.

Angelo. He shall not, Isabel, if you give me love.

Isabella. I know your virtue hath a license in't,   145
Which seems a little fouler than it is,
To pluck on° others.

Angelo.   Believe me, on mine honor,
My words express my purpose.

Isabella. Ha! Little honor to be much believed,
And most pernicious purpose. Seeming, seeming!   150
I will proclaim thee, Angelo; look for't:
Sign me a present pardon for my brother,
Or with an outstretched throat I'll tell the world
    aloud
What man thou art.

---

126 *forms* images, appearances   130 *credulous* receptive   134 *I do arrest your words* I take you at your word   136 *expressed* shown to be   138 *the destined livery* the dress that it is the destiny of a woman to wear   147 *pluck on* draw on

Angelo.   Who will believe thee, Isabel?
155   My unsoiled name, th' austereness of my life,
       My vouch° against you, and my place i' th' state,
       Will so your accusation overweigh,
       That you shall stifle in your own report,
       And smell of calumny. I have begun,
160   And now I give my sensual race the rein.
       Fit thy consent to my sharp appetite,
       Lay by all nicety and prolixious° blushes,
       That banish what they sue for; redeem thy brother
       By yielding up thy body to my will,°
165   Or else he must not only die the death,
       But thy unkindness shall his death draw out
       To ling'ring sufferance.° Answer me tomorrow,
       Or, by the affection° that now guides me most,
       I'll prove a tyrant to him. As for you,
170   Say what you can, my false o'erweighs your true.
                                                 Exit.

Isabella. To whom should I complain? Did I tell this,
       Who would believe me? O perilous mouths,
       That bear in them one and the selfsame tongue,
       Either of condemnation or approof;°
175   Bidding the law make curtsy to their will,
       Hooking both right and wrong to th' appetite,
       To follow as it draws. I'll to my brother.
       Though he hath fall'n by prompture of the blood,
       Yet hath he in him such a mind of honor,
180   That, had he twenty heads to tender down
       On twenty bloody blocks, he'd yield them up,
       Before his sister should her body stoop
       To such abhorred pollution.
          Then, Isabel, live chaste, and, brother, die:
185   More than our brother is our chastity.
       I'll tell him yet of Angelo's request,
       And fit his mind to death, for his soul's rest.   *Exit.*

---

156 *vouch* testimony   162 *prolixious* tediously drawn-out   164 *will*
carnal appetite   167 *sufferance* torture   168 *affection* passion   174
approof approval

ACT III

Scene I. [*The prison.*]

Enter Duke [as friar], Claudio, and Provost.

Duke. So then, you hope of pardon from Lord Angelo?

Claudio. The miserable have no other medicine
But only hope:
I have hope to live, and am prepared to die.

Duke. Be absolute° for death; either death or life   5
Shall thereby be the sweeter. Reason thus with life:
If I do lose thee, I do lose a thing
That none but fools would keep; a breath thou art,
Servile to all the skyey influences,°
That dost this habitation, where thou keep'st,°   10
Hourly afflict; merely, thou art death's fool,°
For him thou labor'st by thy flight to shun,
And yet run'st toward him still. Thou art not noble,
For all th' accommodations° that thou bear'st
Are nursed by baseness. Thou'rt by no means valiant,   15
For thou dost fear the soft and tender fork°
Of a poor worm. Thy best of rest is sleep,

III.i.5 *absolute* unconditionally prepared   9 *skyey influences* influence of the stars   10 *keep'st* dwellest   11 *fool* (the professional jester in a nobleman's household whose job was to keep his master amused)   14 *accommodations* necessities   16 *fork* forked tongue (of a snake)

77

And that thou oft provok'st;° yet grossly fear'st
Thy death, which is no more. Thou art not thyself;
20 For thou exists on many a thousand grains
That issue out of dust. Happy thou art not,
For what thou hast not, still thou striv'st to get,
And what thou hast, forget'st. Thou art not certain,°
For thy complexion shifts to strange effects,
25 After the moon.° If thou art rich, thou'rt poor.
For, like an ass whose back with ingots bows,
Thou bear'st thy heavy riches but a journey,
And death unloads thee. Friend hast thou none,
For thine own bowels,° which do call thee sire,
30 The mere effusion of thy proper loins,°
Do curse the gout, serpigo,° and the rheum,°
For ending thee no sooner. Thou hast nor youth
        nor age,
But, as it were, an after-dinner's sleep,
Dreaming on both; for all thy blessèd youth
35 Becomes as agèd, and doth beg the alms
Of palsied eld,° and when thou art old and rich,
Thou has neither heat, affection,° limb, nor beauty,
To make thy riches pleasant. What's yet in this
That bears° the name of life? Yet in this life
40 Lie hid moe thousand deaths; yet death we fear,
That makes these odds all even.

Claudio.   I humbly thank you.
To sue to live, I find I seek to die,
And seeking death, find life: let it come on.

Enter Isabella.

Isabella. What, ho! Peace here; grace and good company!

Provost. Who's there? Come in, the wish deserves a
45 welcome.

18 *provok'st* invokest   23 *certain* invariable   24–25 *For . . . moon*
your temperament (desire?) moves to numerous things, changeable
as (or "influenced by") the moon   29 *bowels* offspring   30 *The
mere . . . loins* the very issue of your own loins   31 *serpigo* a skin
disease   31 *rheum* catarrh   36 *eld* old age   37 *affection* feeling
39 *bears* deserves

Duke. Dear sir, ere long I'll visit you again.

Claudio. Most holy sir, I thank you.

Isabella. My business is a word or two with Claudio.

Provost. And very welcome. Look, signior, here's your sister.

Duke. Provost, a word with you.   30

Provost. As many as you please.

Duke. Bring me to hear them speak, where I may be concealed.   [*Duke and Provost withdraw.*]

Claudio. Now, sister, what's the comfort?

Isabella. Why,   35
As all comforts are, most good, most good indeed.
Lord Angelo, having affairs to heaven,
Intends you for his swift ambassador,
Where you shall be an everlasting leiger:°
Therefore your best appointment° make with speed;   60
Tomorrow you set on.

Claudio.   Is there no remedy?

Isabella. None, but such remedy as, to save a head,
To cleave a heart in twain.

Claudio.   But is there any?

Isabella. Yes, brother, you may live;
There is a devilish mercy in the judge,   65
If you'll implore it, that will free your life,
But fetter you till death.

Claudio.   Perpetual durance?°

Isabella. Ay, just; perpetual durance, a restraint,
Though all the world's vastidity° you had,
To a determined scope.°

59 *leiger* resident ambassador 60 *appointment* preparation 67 *durance* imprisonment 69 *vastidity* vast spaces 70 *determined scope* fixed limit (i.e., the reprieve may win him the world, but will cost him his soul)

70 *Claudio.*   But in what nature?
   Isabella. In such a one as, you consenting to't,
        Would bark your honor from that trunk you bear,
        And leave you naked.

   Claudio.   Let me know the point.

   Isabella. O, I do fear thee, Claudio, and I quake,
75   Lest thou a feverous life shouldst entertain,
        And six or seven winters more respect
        Than a perpetual honor. Dar'st thou die?
        The sense° of death is most in apprehension,°
        And the poor beetle that we tread upon
80   In corporal sufferance finds a pang as great
        As when a giant dies.

   Claudio.   Why give you me this shame?
        Think you I can a resolution fetch
        From flow'ry tenderness? If I must die,
        I will encounter darkness as a bride,
85   And hug it in mine arms.

   Isabella. There spake my brother, there my father's
              grave
        Did utter forth a voice. Yes, thou must die,
        Thou art too noble to conserve a life
        In base appliances.° This outward-sainted deputy,
90   Whose settled visage and deliberate word
        Nips youth i' th' head, and follies doth enmew°
        As falcon doth the fowl, is yet a devil;
        His filth within being cast,° he would appear
        A pond as deep as hell.

   Claudio.   The prenzie° Angelo!

95 *Isabella.* O, 'tis the cunning livery of hell,
        The damned'st body to invest and cover
        In prenzie guards.° Dost thou think, Claudio,
        If I would yield him my virginity,

---

78 *sense* feeling 78 *apprehension* imagination 89 *appliances* devices
91 *enmew* drive into the water (as a hawk drives a fowl) 93 *cast*
vomited up 94 *prenzie* (meaning uncertain; often emended to "princely," or "precise") 97 *guards* trimmings

Thou mightst be freed?

Claudio.   O heavens, it cannot be.

Isabella. Yes, he would give't thee, from this rank
   offense,   100
   So to offend him still. This night's the time
   That I should do what I abhor to name,
   Or else thou diest tomorrow.

Claudio.   Thou shalt not do't.

Isabella. O, were it but my life,
   I'd throw it down for your deliverance   105
   As frankly as a pin.

Claudio.   Thanks, dear Isabel.

Isabella. Be ready, Claudio, for your death tomorrow.

Claudio. Yes. Has he affections° in him,
   That thus can make him bite the law by th' nose,
   When he would force° it? Sure, it is no sin,   110
   Or of the deadly seven° it is the least.

Isabella. Which is the least?

Claudio. If it were damnable, he being so wise,
   Why would he for the momentary trick
   Be perdurably fined?° O Isabel!   115

Isabella. What says my brother?

Claudio.   Death is a fearful thing.

Isabella. And shamèd life a hateful.

Claudio. Ay, but to die, and go we know not where,
   To lie in cold obstruction° and to rot,
   This sensible° warm motion° to become   120
   A kneaded clod; and the delighted° spirit
   To bathe in fiery floods, or to reside

108 *affections* sensual appetites   110 *force* enforce   111 *deadly*
seven (pride, envy, wrath, sloth, avarice, gluttony, lechery)   114–15
Why . . . fined i.e., why for the momentary trifle (of sexual intercourse) would he be eternally damned   119 *obstruction* motionless-
ness   120 *sensible* feeling   120 *motion* organism   121 *delighted*
capable of delight

In thrilling region of thick-ribbèd ice;
To be imprisoned in the viewless winds,
125 And blown with restless violence round about
The pendent° world; or to be worse than worst
Of those that lawless and incertain thought
Imagine howling—'tis too horrible!
The weariest and most loathèd worldly life
130 That age, ache, penury, and imprisonment
Can lay on nature is a paradise
To what we fear of death.

Isabella. Alas, alas.

Claudio.   Sweet sister, let me live:
What sin you do to save a brother's life,
135 Nature dispenses with° the deed so far
That it becomes a virtue.

Isabella.   O you beast,
O faithless coward, O dishonest wretch!
Wilt thou be made a man out of my vice?
Is't not a kind of incest, to take life
From thine own sister's shame? What should I
140   think?
Heaven shield my mother played my father fair,
For such a warpèd slip of wilderness°
Ne'er issued from his blood. Take my defiance,
Die, perish! Might but my bending down
145 Reprieve thee from thy fate, it should proceed.
I'll pray a thousand prayers for thy death,
No word to save thee.

Claudio. Nay, hear me, Isabel.

Isabella.   O, fie, fie, fie!
Thy sin's not accidental, but a trade.
150 Mercy to thee would prove itself a bawd,
'Tis best that thou diest quickly.

Claudio.   O, hear me, Isabella!

---

126 *pendent* hanging in space   135 *dispenses with* grants a dispensation for   142 *wilderness* wild nature without nurture

[*The Duke comes forward.*]

Duke. Vouchsafe a word, young sister, but one word.

Isabella. What is your will?

Duke. Might you dispense with your leisure, I would
   by and by have some speech with you: the satis-   *155*
   faction I would require is likewise your own benefit.

Isabella. I have no superfluous leisure; my stay must
   be stolen out of other affairs, but I will attend you
   awhile.

Duke. [*Aside to Claudio*] Son, I have overheard what   *160*
   hath passed between you and your sister. Angelo
   had never the purpose to corrupt her; only he hath
   made an assay° of her virtue to practice his judgment with the disposition of natures. She, having
   the truth of honor in her, hath made him that   *165*
   gracious denial which he is most glad to receive. I
   am confessor to Angelo, and I know this to be true;
   therefore prepare yourself to death. Do not satisfy
   your resolution with hopes that are fallible. Tomorrow you must die; go to your knees, and make   *170*
   ready.

Claudio. Let me ask my sister pardon. I am so out
   of love with life, that I will sue to be rid of it.

Duke. Hold you there; farewell. [*Exit Claudio.*] Provost, a word with you.   *175*

[*Enter Provost.*]

Provost. What's your will, father?

Duke. That now you are come, you will be gone.
   Leave me awhile with the maid. My mind promises
   with my habit° no loss shall touch her by my company.   *180*

Provost. In good time.°   *Exit.*

Duke. The hand that hath made you fair hath made

163 *assay* test   179 *habit* religious dress   181 *In good time* very
well

you good. The goodness that is cheap in beauty
makes beauty brief in goodness; but grace, being
185   the soul of your complexion,° shall keep the body
of it ever fair. The assault that Angelo hath made
to you, fortune hath conveyed to my understanding, and, but that frailty hath examples for his falling, I should wonder at Angelo. How will you do
190   to content this substitute, and to save your brother?

Isabella. I am now going to resolve° him. I had rather
my brother die by the law than my son should be
unlawfully born. But O, how much is the good
Duke deceived in Angelo! If ever he return and I
195   can speak to him, I will open my lips in vain, or
discover his government.°

Duke. That shall not be much amiss. Yet, as the matter now stands, he will avoid your accusation: he
made trial of you only. Therefore fasten your ear
200   on my advisings; to the love I have in doing good
a remedy presents itself. I do make myself believe
that you may most uprighteously do a poor
wronged lady a merited benefit; redeem your
brother from the angry law; do no stain to your
205   own gracious person; and much please the absent
Duke, if peradventure he shall ever return to have
hearing of this business.

Isabella. Let me hear you speak farther. I have spirit
to do anything that appears not foul in the truth
210   of my spirit.

Duke. Virtue is bold, and goodness never fearful.
Have you not heard speak of Mariana, the sister
of Frederick, the great soldier who miscarried at
sea?

215 *Isabella.* I have heard of the lady, and good words
went with her name.

---

185 *complexion* character   191 *resolve* answer   196 *discover his government* expose his rule

Duke. She should this Angelo have married; was affianced to her by oath, and the nuptial appointed:
between which time of the contract and limit of the
solemnity,° her brother Frederick was wracked at   220
sea, having in that perished vessel the dowry of his
sister. But mark how heavily this befell to the poor
gentlewoman: there she lost a noble and renowned
brother, in his love toward her ever most kind and
natural; with him, the portion and sinew of her for-   225
tune, her marriage dowry; with both, her com-
binate° husband, this well-seeming Angelo.

Isabella. Can this be so? Did Angelo so leave her?

Duke. Left her in her tears, and dried not one of them
with his comfort; swallowed his vows whole, pre-   230
tending in her discoveries of dishonor: in few, bestowed her on her own lamentation, which she yet
wears for his sake; and he, a marble to her tears,
is washed with them, but relents not.

Isabella. What a merit were it in death to take this   235
poor maid from the world! What corruption in this
life, that it will let this man live! But how out of
this can she avail?°

Duke. It is a rupture that you may easily heal, and
the cure of it not only saves your brother, but   240
keeps you from dishonor in doing it.

Isabella. Show me how, good father.

Duke. This forenamed maid hath yet in her the continuance of her first affection; his unjust unkindness, that in all reason should have quenched her   245
love, hath, like an impediment in the current, made
it more violent and unruly. Go you to Angelo;
answer his requiring with a plausible obedience;
agree with his demands to the point; only refer
yourself to this advantage: first, that your stay with   250
him may not be long; that the time may have all

219–20 *limit of the solemnity* date set for the marriage ceremony
226–27 *combinate* betrothed   238 *avail* benefit

shadow and silence in it; and the place answer to
convenience. This being granted in course—and
now follows all—we shall advise this wronged maid
255 to stead up° your appointment, go in your place.
If the encounter° acknowledge itself hereafter, it
may compel him to her recompense: and here, by
this, is your brother saved, your honor untainted,
the poor Mariana advantaged, and the corrupt dep-
260 uty scaled.° The maid will I frame° and make fit
for his attempt. If you think well to carry this, as
you may, the doubleness of the benefit defends the
deceit from reproof. What think you of it?

Isabella. The image of it gives me content already,
263 and I trust it will grow to a most prosperous per-
fection.

Duke. It lies much in your holding up. Haste you
speedily to Angelo: if for this night he entreat you
to his bed, give him promise of satisfaction. I will
270 presently to Saint Luke's; there at the moated
grange° resides this dejected Mariana. At that
place call upon me, and dispatch with Angelo, that
it may be quickly.

Isabella. I thank you for this comfort. Fare you well,
273 good father.   *Exit.*

[Scene II. *Before the prison.*]

Enter, [*to the Duke,*] Elbow, Clown
[*Pompey, and*] Officers.

Elbow. Nay, if there be no remedy for it, but that
you will needs buy and sell men and women like

255 *stead up* keep   256 *encounter* i.e., sexual union   260 *scaled*
weighed   260 *frame* prepare   271 *grange* farm

beasts, we shall have all the world drink brown and
white bastard.°

Duke. O heavens! What stuff is here?   5

Pompey. 'Twas never merry world since, of two
usuries,° the merriest was put down, and the worser
allowed by order of law a furred gown to keep him
warm; and furred with fox and lamb skins too, to
signify that craft, being richer than innocency,   10
stands for the facing.°

Elbow. Come your way, sir. 'Bless you, good father
friar.

Duke. And you, good brother father. What offense
hath this man made you, sir?   15

Elbow. Marry, sir, he hath offended the law; and, sir,
we take him to be a thief too, sir; for we have
found upon him, sir, a strange picklock, which we
have sent to the deputy.

Duke. Fie, sirrah, a bawd, a wicked bawd!   20
The evil that thou causest to be done,
That is thy means to live. Do thou but think
What 'tis to cram a maw° or clothe a back
From such a filthy vice; say to thyself,
From their abominable and beastly touches
I drink, I eat, array myself, and live.   25
Canst thou believe thy living is a life,
So stinkingly depending? Go mend, go mend.

Pompey. Indeed, it does stink in some sort, sir; but
yet, sir, I would prove—
                                                     30
Duke. Nay, if the devil have given thee proofs for sin,
Thou wilt prove his. Take him to prison, officer.
Correction and instruction must both work
Ere this rude beast will profit.

Elbow. He must before the deputy, sir; he has given   35
him warning. The deputy cannot abide a whore-

III.ii.4 *bastard* sweet Spanish wine   5–6 *two usuries* lending money at
interest (a way of breeding barren metal) and fornication   11 *stands
for the facing* represents the trimming   23 *maw* belly

4

master; if he be a whoremonger, and comes before
him, he were as good go a mile on his errand.°

Duke. That we were all, as some would seem to be,
40   From our faults, as faults from seeming, free!

Enter Lucio.

Elbow. His neck will come to your waist—a cord,° sir.

Pompey. I spy comfort; I cry bail. Here's a gentleman
and a friend of mine.

Lucio. How now, noble Pompey! What, at the wheels
45   of Caesar? Art thou led in triumph? What, is there
none of Pygmalion's images,° newly made woman,
to be had now, for putting the hand in the pocket
and extracting it clutched? What reply, ha? What
say'st thou to this tune, matter and method? Is't not
50   drowned i' th' last rain, ha? What say'st thou, Trot?
Is the world as it was, man? Which is the way? Is
it sad, and few words? Or how? The trick of it?

Duke. Still thus, and thus; still worse.

Lucio. How doth my dear morsel, thy mistress? Pro-
55   cures she still, ha?

Pompey. Troth, sir, she hath eaten up all her beef,°
and she is herself in the tub.°

Lucio. Why, 'tis good. It is the right of it; it must be
so: ever your fresh whore and your powdered bawd,
60   an unshunned consequence; it must be so. Art going
to prison, Pompey?

Pompey. Yes, faith, sir.

Lucio. Why, 'tis not amiss, Pompey. Farewell; go, say

---

38 *he were . . . errand* i.e., he has a hard (or fruitless?) journey
ahead   41 *cord* i.e., the cord around the Friar's waist   46 *Pygmalion's
images* i.e., prostitutes (Pompey is compared to Pygmalion, sculptor of
a female statue that came to life)   56 *beef* prostitutes (who serve as
flesh-food)   57 *in the tub* taking the cure for venereal disease (a tub
was also used for corning beef, hence the reference to powdering—
pickling—in Lucio's next speech)

I sent thee thither. For debt, Pompey? Or how?

Elbow. For being a bawd, for being a bawd.   65

Lucio. Well, then, imprison him. If imprisonment be
the due of a bawd, why, 'tis his right. Bawd is he
doubtless, and of antiquity too, bawd-born. Farewell, good Pompey. Commend me to the prison,
Pompey, you will turn good husband° now, Pom-   70
pey, you will keep the house.

Pompey. I hope, sir, your good worship will be my
bail.

Lucio. No, indeed, will I not, Pompey, it is not the
wear.° I will pray, Pompey, to increase your bond-   75
age. If you take it not patiently, why, your mettle°
is the more. Adieu, trusty Pompey. 'Bless you, friar.

Duke. And you.

Lucio. Does Bridget paint still, Pompey, ha?

Elbow. Come your ways, sir, come.   80

Pompey. You will not bail me then, sir?

Lucio. Then, Pompey, nor now. What news abroad,
friar, what news?

Elbow. Come your ways, sir, come.

Lucio. Go to kennel, Pompey, go. [*Exeunt Elbow,*   85
Pompey, and Officers.] What news, friar, of the
Duke?

Duke. I know none. Can you tell me of any?

Lucio. Some say he is with the Emperor of Russia;
other some, he is in Rome: but where is he, think   90
you?

Duke. I know not where; but wheresoever, I wish him
well.

Lucio. It was a mad fantastical trick of him to steal

70 *husband* housekeeper, manager   75 *wear* fashion   76 *mettle*
spirit (pun on metal of chains)

95 from the state, and usurp the beggary he was neve
born to. Lord Angelo dukes it well in his absence
he puts transgression to't.

Duke. He does well in't.

Lucio. A little more lenity to lechery would do n
100 harm in him; something too crabbed that way, friar

Duke. It is too general a vice, and severity mus
cure it.

Lucio. Yes, in good sooth, the vice is of a grea
kindred, it is well allied; but it is impossible t
105 extirp it quite, friar, till eating and drinking b
put down. They say this Angelo was not made b
man and woman after this downright way of cre
ation. Is it true, think you?

Duke. How should he be made, then?

110 *Lucio.* Some report a sea maid° spawned him; some
that he was begot between two stockfishes.° But i
is certain that when he makes water his urine i
congealed ice; that I know to be true. And he is
motion generative;° that's infallible.

115 *Duke.* You are pleasant, sir, and speak apace.

Lucio. Why, what a ruthless thing is this in him, fo
the rebellion of a codpiece to take away the life o
a man! Would the Duke that is absent have don
this? Ere he would have hanged a man for the get
120 ting a hundred bastards, he would have paid fo
the nursing a thousand. He had some feeling of th
sport; he knew the service, and that instructed him
to mercy.

Duke. I never heard the absent Duke much detecte
125 for° women; he was not inclined that way.

Lucio. O, sir, you are deceived.

110 *sea maid* (to explain his piscatory coldness)   111 *stockfishe*
dried cod   114 *motion generative* masculine puppet   124–25 *de*
tected for accused of

Duke. 'Tis not possible.

Lucio. Who, not the Duke? Yes, your beggar of fifty,
and his use was to put a ducat in her clack-dish;°
the Duke had crotchets° in him. He would be drunk *130*
too; that let me inform you.

Duke. You do him wrong, surely.

Lucio. Sir, I was an inward° of his. A shy fellow was
the Duke, and I believe I know the cause of his
withdrawing. *135*

Duke. What, I prithee, might be the cause?

Lucio. No, pardon; 'tis a secret must be locked within
the teeth and the lips; but this I can let you understand, the greater file° of the subject held the Duke
to be wise. *140*

Duke. Wise! Why, no question but he was.

Lucio. A very superficial, ignorant, unweighing fellow.

Duke. Either this is envy in you, folly, or mistaking.
The very stream of his life and the business he hath
helmed must, upon a warranted need,° give him a *145*
better proclamation. Let him be but testimonied in
his own bringings-forth,° and he shall appear to the
envious a scholar, a statesman, and a soldier. Therefore you speak unskillfully; or if your knowledge
be more, it is much dark'ned in your malice. *150*

Lucio. Sir, I know him, and I love him.

Duke. Love talks with better knowledge, and knowledge with dearer love.

Lucio. Come, sir, I know what I know.

Duke. I can hardly believe that, since you know not *155*
what you speak. But, if ever the Duke return, as
our prayers are he may, let me desire you to make

129 *clack-dish* beggar's bowl (metaphorical here)   130 *crotchets*
whims   133 *inward* intimate companion   139 *greater file* majority
145 *upon a warranted need* if proof be demanded   147 *bringings-
forth* actions

your answer before him. If it be honest you have
spoke, you have courage to maintain it. I am bound
160 to call upon you, and I pray you, your name?

Lucio. Sir, my name is Lucio, well known to the Duke.

Duke. He shall know you better, sir, if I may live to
report you.

Lucio. I fear you not.

165 *Duke.* O, you hope the Duke will return no more, or
you imagine me too unhurtful an opposite. But,
indeed, I can do you little harm; you'll forswear
this again.

Lucio. I'll be hanged first; thou art deceived in me,
170 friar. But no more of this. Canst thou tell if Claudio
die tomorrow or no?

Duke. Why should he die, sir?

Lucio. Why? For filling a bottle with a tundish.° I
would the Duke we talk of were returned again;
175 this ungenitured° agent will unpeople the province
with continency; sparrows must not build in his
house-eaves, because they are lecherous. The Duke
yet would have dark deeds darkly answered; he
would never bring them to light. Would he were
180 returned! Marry, this Claudio is condemned for untrussing.° Farewell, good friar; I prithee, pray for
me. The Duke, I say to thee again, would eat mutton on Fridays.° He's not past it, yet, and I say
to thee, he would mouth with a beggar, though she
185 smelled brown bread and garlic. Say that I said so.
Farewell.   *Exit.*

Duke. No might nor greatness in mortality
    Can censure 'scape; back-wounding calumny
    The whitest virtue strikes. What king so strong

173 *tundish* funnel   175 *ungenitured* sexless   180–81 *untrussing*
undressing   182–83 *eat mutton on Fridays* (the Duke allegedly
ate mutton on a Friday, which was a fast day, and also practiced
venery; "mutton" also means "harlot," and Friday is the day of the
planet Venus)

Can tie the gall up in the slanderous tongue?   *190*
But who comes here?

Enter Escalus, Provost, and [Officers with]
Bawd [Mistress Overdone].

Escalus. Go, away with her to prison!

Mistress Overdone. Good my lord, be good to me.
Your honor is accounted a merciful man, good my
lord.   *195*

Escalus. Double and treble admonition, and still forfeit in the same kind! This would make mercy
swear, and play the tyrant.

Provost. A bawd of eleven years' continuance, may
it please your honor.   *200*

Mistress Overdone. My lord, this is one Lucio's information against me. Mistress Kate Keepdown was
with child by him in the Duke's time; he promised
her marriage; his child is a year and a quarter old,
come Philip and Jacob;° I have kept it myself, and   *205*
see how he goes about to abuse me.

Escalus. That fellow is a fellow of much license; let
him be called before us. Away with her to prison.
Go to, no more words. [*Exeunt Officers with Mistress Overdone.*] Provost, my brother Angelo will   *210*
not be altered; Claudio must die tomorrow. Let him
be furnished with divines, and have all charitable
preparation. If my brother wrought by my pity,
it should not be so with him.

Provost. So please you, this friar hath been with him, *215*
and advised him for th' entertainment of death.

Escalus. Good even, good father.

Duke. Bliss and goodness on you!

Escalus. Of whence are you?

205 *Philip and Jacob* May 1st

commentary on times

220 *Duke.* Not of this country, though my chance is now
        To use it for my time; I am a brother
        Of gracious order, late come from the See
        In special business from his Holiness.

Escalus. What news abroad i' th' world?

225 *Duke.* None, but that there is so great a fever on good-
        ness, that the dissolution of it must cure it,° novelty
        is only in request,° and it is as dangerous to be
        aged° in any kind of course as it is virtuous to be
        constant in any undertaking. There is scarce truth
230   enough alive to make societies secure, but security°
        enough to make fellowships° accursed. Much upon
        this riddle runs the wisdom of the world. This news
        is old enough, yet it is every day's news. I pray
        you, sir, of what disposition was the Duke?

235 *Escalus.* One that, above all other strifes, contended
        especially to know himself.

Duke. What pleasure was he given to?

Escalus. Rather rejoicing to see another merry, than
        merry at anything which professed to make him
240   rejoice: a gentleman of all temperance. But leave
        we him to his events, with a prayer they may prove
        prosperous, and let me desire to know how you
        find Claudio prepared. I am made to understand
        that you have lent him visitation.

245 *Duke.* He professes to have received no sinister meas-
        ure from his judge, but most willingly humbles him-
        self to the determination of justice; yet had he
        framed to himself, by the instruction of his frailty,
        many deceiving promises of life; which I, by my
250   good leisure, have discredited to him, and now is
        he resolved to die.

Escalus. You have paid the heavens your function,

225–26 *fever . . . cure it* i.e., the dissolution of the fever alone can
now restore goodness to its pristine health   226–27 *novelty is only
in request* change is urgently needed   228 *aged* old and worn out
230 *security* heedlessness   231 *fellowships* human societies

and the prisoner the very debt of your calling. I
have labored for the poor gentleman to the extremest shore of my modesty,° but my brother   255
justice have I found so severe, that he hath forced
me to tell him he is indeed Justice.

Duke. If his own life answer the straitness of his pro-
ceeding, it shall become him well; wherein if he
chance to fail, he hath sentenced himself.   260

Escalus. I am going to visit the prisoner. Fare you
well.

Duke. Peace be with you!
                    [*Exeunt Escalus and Provost.*]
 He who the sword of heaven will bear
 Should be as holy as severe;   265
 Pattern in himself to know
 Grace to stand, and virtue go;°
 More nor less to others paying
 Than by self-offenses weighing.
 Shame to him whose cruel striking   270
 Kills for faults of his own liking.
 Twice treble shame on Angelo,
 To weed my° vice and let his grow.
 O, what may man within him hide,
 Though angel on the outward side!   275
 How may likeness made in crimes,
 Making practice° on the times,
 To draw with idle spiders' strings
 Most ponderous and substantial things?
 Craft against vice I must apply: 280
 With Angelo tonight shall lie
 His old betrothèd but despisèd;
 So disguise shall, by th' disguisèd,
 Pay with falsehood false exacting,
 And perform an old contracting.   285

Exit

254–55 *extremest shore of my modesty* i.e., as far as is proper
266–67 *Pattern . . . go* i.e., he should have a model in himself of
grace which will stand if virtue elsewhere ebbs   273 *my* (used
impersonally)   277 *Making practice* practicing deception

ACT IV

Scene I. [*The moated grange.*]

Enter Mariana and Boy singing.

SONG

Take, O, take those lips away,
   That so sweetly were forsworn;
And those eyes, the break of day,
   Lights that do mislead the morn;
5   But my kisses bring again, bring again;
   Seals of love, but sealed in vain, sealed in vain.

Enter Duke [disguised as before].

Mariana. Break off thy song, and haste thee quick
    away.
  Here comes a man of comfort, whose advice
  Hath often stilled my brawling discontent.

                        [Exit Boy.]

10 I cry you mercy, sir; and well could wish
  You had not found me here so musical.
  Let me excuse me, and believe me so,
  My mirth it much displeased, but pleased my woe.

Duke. 'Tis good; though music oft hath such a charm

To make bad good, and good provoke to harm.   15
I pray you, tell me, hath anybody inquired for me
here today? Much upon this time have I promised
here to meet.

Mariana. You have not been inquired after; I have
sat here all day.   20

                    Enter Isabella.

Duke. I do constantly believe you. The time is come
even now. I shall crave your forbearance a little;
may be I will call upon you anon, for some advantage to yourself.

Mariana. I am always bound to you.   *Exit.* 25

Duke. Very well met, and well come.
What is the news from this good deputy?

Isabella. He hath a garden circummured° with brick,
Whose western side is with a vineyard backed;
And to that vineyard is a planchèd° gate,   30
That makes his opening with this bigger key.
This other doth command a little door
Which from the vineyard to the garden leads.
There have I made my promise
Upon the heavy middle of the night   35
To call upon him.

Duke. But shall you on your knowledge find this way?

Isabella. I have ta'en a due and wary note upon't.
With whispering and most guilty diligence,
In action all of precept,° he did show me   40
The way twice o'er.

Duke.   Are there no other tokens
Between you 'greed concerning her observance?°

Isabella. No, none, but only a repair i' th' dark,
And that I have possessed° him my most stay

IV.i.28 *circummured* walled around   30 *planchèd* planked   40 *In
. . . precept* teaching by gestures   42 *her observance* what she must
do   44 *possessed* informed

45   Can be but brief; for I have made him know
I have a servant comes with me along,
That stays upon° me, whose persuasion° is
I come about my brother.

Duke.   'Tis well borne up.
I have not yet made known to Mariana
50 A word of this. What, ho, within! Come forth.

Enter Mariana.

I pray you, be acquainted with this maid;
She comes to do you good.

Isabella.   I do desire the like.

Duke. Do you persuade yourself that I respect you?

Mariana. Good friar, I know you do, and have found
it.

55 *Duke.* Take, then, this your companion by the hand,
Who hath a story ready for your ear.
I shall attend your leisure, but make haste;
The vaporous night approaches.

Mariana. Will't please you walk aside?
                            Exit [with Isabella].

60 *Duke.* O place and greatness, millions of false eyes
Are stuck upon thee; volumes of report
Run with these false and most contrarious quests°
Upon thy doings; thousand escapes° of wit
Make thee the father of their idle dreams,
And rack thee in their fancies.

Enter Mariana and Isabella.

65   Welcome, how agreed?

Isabella. She'll take the enterprise upon her, father,
If you advise it.

Duke.   It is not my consent

47 *stays upon* waits for   47 *persuasion* conviction   62 *quests* cry
of the hound on the scent   63 *escapes* sallies

But my entreaty too.

Isabella.   Little have you to say
When you depart from him, but, soft and low,
"Remember now my brother."

Mariana.   Fear me not.   *70*

Duke. Nor, gentle daughter, fear you not at all.
He is your husband on a precontract;°
To bring you thus together, 'tis no sin,
Sith that the justice of your title to him
Doth flourish the deceit. Come, let us go: *75*
Our corn's to reap, for yet our tithe's° to sow.

                        Exeunt.

Scene II. [*The prison.*]

Enter Provost and Clown [Pompey].

Provost. Come hither, sirrah. Can you cut off a man's head?

Pompey. If the man be a bachelor, sir, I can; but if he be a married man, he's his wife's head,° and I can never cut off a woman's head.   *5*

Provost. Come, sir, leave me your snatches,° and yield me a direct answer. Tomorrow morning are to die Claudio and Barnardine. Here is in our prison a common executioner, who in his office lacks a helper. If you will take it on you to assist him, it   *10* shall redeem you from your gyves;° if not, you shall have your full time of imprisonment, and your

72 *precontract* legally binding betrothal agreement 75 *tithe* tithe corn IV.ii.4 *he's his wife's head* (see Ephesians 5:23: "For the husband is the head of the wife") 6 *snatches* quibbles 11 *gyves* shackles

deliverance with an unpitied whipping, for you have been a notorious bawd.

15 *Pompey.* Sir, I have been an unlawful bawd time out of mind, but yet I will be content to be a lawful hangman. I would be glad to receive some instruction from my fellow partner.

Provost. What, ho, Abhorson!° Where's Abhorson, 20 there?

Enter Abhorson.

Abhorson. Do you call, sir?

Provost. Sirrah, here's a fellow will help you tomorrow in your execution. If you think it meet, compound° with him by the year, and let him abide 25 here with you; if not, use him for the present, and dismiss him. He cannot plead his estimation° with you; he hath been a bawd.

Abhorson. A bawd, sir? Fie upon him! He will discredit our mystery.°

30 *Provost.* Go to, sir; you weigh equally; a feather will turn the scale.   *Exit.*

Pompey. Pray, sir, by your good favor—for surely, sir, a good favor° you have, but that you have a hanging look—do you call, sir, your occupation 35 a mystery?

Abhorson. Ay, sir; a mystery.

Pompey. Painting, sir, I have heard say, is a mystery; and your whores, sir, being members of my occupation, using painting, do prove my occupation a 40 mystery; but what mystery there should be in hanging, if I should be hanged, I cannot imagine.

Abhorson. Sir, it is a mystery.

19 *Abhorson* (pun on "ab, whore, son," son from a whore)   23–24 *compound* settle   26 *estimation* reputation   29 *mystery* craft   33 *favor* countenance

Pompey. Proof?

Abhorson. Every true man's apparel fits your thief: if
it be too little for your thief, your true man thinks it　　45
big enough; if it be too big for your thief, your thief
thinks it little enough: so every true man's apparel
fits your thief.°

Enter Provost.

Provost. Are you agreed?

Pompey. Sir, I will serve him; for I do find your hang-　　50
man is a more penitent trade than your bawd; he
doth oft'ner ask forgiveness.°

Provost. You, sirrah, provide your block and your ax
tomorrow four o'clock.

Abhorson. Come on, bawd. I will instruct thee in my　　55
trade; follow.

Pompey. I do desire to learn, sir; and I hope, if you
have occasion to use me for your own turn,°
you shall find me yare;° for, truly, sir, for your
kindness I owe you a good turn.　　60

Provost. Call hither Barnardine and Claudio.

Exit [Pompey with Abhorson].

Th' one has my pity; not a jot the other,
Being a murderer, though he were my brother.

Enter Claudio.

Look, here's the warrant, Claudio, for thy death.
'Tis now dead midnight, and by eight tomorrow　　65
Thou must be made immortal. Where's Barnardine?

Claudio. As fast locked up in sleep as guiltless labor
When it lies starkly° in the traveler's bones;
He will not wake.

44–48 *every . . . thief* (interpretation uncertain)　52 *ask forgiveness*
(the executioner always asked the condemned man to forgive him)
58 *turn* execution (pun)　59 *yare* ready　68 *starkly* stiffly

Provost.   Who can do good on him?
Well, go, prepare yourself. [*Knocking within.*] But,
70   hark, what noise?—
Heaven give your spirits comfort. [*Exit Claudio.*]
By and by.
I hope it is some pardon or reprieve
For the most gentle Claudio. Welcome, father.

Enter Duke [disguised as before].

Duke. The best and wholesom'st spirits of the night
Envelop you, good provost! Who called here of
75   late?

Provost. None since the curfew rung.

Duke. Not Isabel?

Provost.   No.

Duke.   They will, then, ere't be long.

Provost. What comfort is for Claudio?

Duke. There's some in hope.

80 *Provost.* It is a bitter deputy.

Duke. Not so, not so; his life is paralleled
Even with the stroke and line of his great justice.
He doth with holy abstinence subdue
That in himself which he spurs on his pow'r
85   To qualify° in others; were he mealed° with that
Which he corrects, then were he tyrannous;
But this being so, he's just.   [*Knocking within.*]
                              Now are they come.
                                        [*Exit Provost.*]
This is a gentle provost—seldom when
The steelèd jailer is the friend of men.
                              [*Knocking within.*]
How now, what noise? That spirit's possessed with
90   haste

85 *qualify* moderate   85 *mealed* stained

That wounds th' unsisting° postern° with these
 strokes.

[*Enter Provost.*]

Provost. There he must stay until the officer
 Arise to let him in; he is called up.

Duke. Have you no countermand for Claudio yet,
 But he must die tomorrow?

Provost.   None, sir, none.   95

Duke. As near the dawning, provost, as it is,
 You shall hear more ere morning.

Provost.   Happily
 You something know; yet I believe there comes
 No countermand; no such example have we.
 Besides, upon the very siege° of justice   100
 Lord Angelo hath to the public ear
 Professed the contrary.

Enter a Messenger.

                    This is his lord's man.

Duke. And here comes Claudio's pardon.

Messenger. My lord hath sent you this note, and by
 me this further charge, that you swerve not from   105
 the smallest article of it, neither in time, matter,
 or other circumstance. Good morrow; for, as I
 take it, it is almost day.

Provost. I shall obey him.

                              [*Exit Messenger.*]

Duke. [*Aside*] This is his pardon, purchased by such
 sin   110
 For which the pardoner himself is in.
 Hence hath offense his quick celerity,

91 *unsisting* (perhaps "unassisting," perhaps a printer's slip for
"resisting")   91 *postern* small door   100 *siege* seat

When it is borne in high authority.
When vice makes mercy, mercy's so extended,
115 That for the fault's love is th' offender friended.
Now, sir, what news?

Provost. I told you. Lord Angelo, belike° thinking
me remiss in mine office, awakens me with this un-
wonted putting-on;° methinks strangely, for he hath
120 not used it before.

Duke. Pray you, let's hear.

Provost. [*Reads*] *the letter.* "Whatsoever you may hear
to the contrary, let Claudio be executed by four
of the clock; and in the afternoon Barnardine. For
125 my better satisfaction, let me have Claudio's head
sent me by five. Let this be duly performed with a
thought that more depends on it than we must yet
deliver. Thus fail not to do your office, as you will
answer it at your peril."
130 What say you to this, sir?

Duke. What is that Barnardine who is to be executed
in th' afternoon?

Provost. A Bohemian born, but here nursed up and
bred; one that is a prisoner nine years old.

135 *Duke.* How came it that the absent Duke had not
either delivered him to his liberty or executed him?
I have heard it was ever his manner to do so.

Provost. His friends still wrought reprieves for him;
and, indeed, his fact,° till now in the government
140 of Lord Angelo, came not to an undoubtful proof.

Duke. It is now apparent?

Provost. Most manifest, and not denied by himself.

Duke. Hath he borne himself penitently in prison?
How seems he to be touched?

145 *Provost.* A man that apprehends death no more dreadfully but as a drunken sleep; careless, reckless, and

117 *belike* perhaps 119 *putting-on* urging 139 *fact* evil deed

fearless of what's past, present, or to come; insensible of mortality, and desperately mortal.°

Duke. He wants° advice.

Provost. He will hear none. He hath evermore had the 150
liberty of the prison; give him leave to escape hence,
he would not: drunk many times a day, if not many
days entirely drunk. We have very oft awaked him,
as if to carry him to execution, and showed him a
seeming warrant for it; it hath not moved him at all. 155

Duke. More of him anon. There is written in your
brow, provost, honesty and constancy: if I read it
not truly, my ancient skill beguiles me; but, in the
boldness of my cunning,° I will lay myself in hazard.° Claudio, whom here you have warrant to exe- 160
cute, is no greater forfeit to the law than Angelo who
hath sentenced him. To make you understand this
in a manifested effect,° I crave but four days' res-
pite, for the which you are to do me both a
present° and a dangerous courtesy. 165

Provost. Pray, sir, in what?

Duke. In the delaying death.

Provost. Alack, how may I do it, having the hour limited,° and an express command, under penalty, to
deliver his head in the view of Angelo? I may make 170
my case as Claudio's, to cross this in the smallest.

Duke. By the vow of mine Order I warrant you, if my
instructions may be your guide. Let this Barnardine
be this morning executed, and his head borne to
Angelo. 175

Provost. Angelo hath seen them both, and will discover the favor.°

Duke. O, death's a great disguiser; and you may add

148 *desperately mortal* about to die without hope of the future
149 *wants* needs 159 *cunning* knowledge 159–60 *lay myself in
hazard* take a risk 163 *in a manifested effect* by open proof
165 *present* immediate 168–69 *limited* determined 176–77 *discover the favor* recognize the face

to it. Shave the head, and tie the beard; and say it
180   was the desire of the penitent to be so bared° before his death; you know the course is common.
If anything fall to you upon this, more than thanks
and good fortune, by the saint whom I profess, I
will plead against it with my life.

185   *Provost.* Pardon me, good father; it is against my oath.

Duke. Were you sworn to the Duke, or to the deputy?

Provost. To him, and to his substitutes.

Duke. You will think you have made no offense, if the
Duke avouch the justice of your dealing?

190   *Provost.* But what likelihood is in that?

Duke. Not a resemblance, but a certainty. Yet since
I see you fearful,° that neither my coat, integrity,
nor persuasion can with ease attempt° you, I will
go further than I meant, to pluck all fears out of
195   you. Look you, sir, here is the hand and seal of the
Duke. You know the character,° I doubt not, and
the signet is not strange to you.

Provost. I know them both.

Duke. The contents of this is the return of the Duke.
200   You shall anon overread it at your pleasure, where
you shall find, within these two days he will be
here. This is a thing that Angelo knows not; for he
this very day receives letters of strange tenor, perchance of the Duke's death, perchance entering into
205   some monastery, but by chance nothing of what is
writ. Look, th' unfolding star° calls up the shepherd. Put not yourself into amazement how these
things should be: all difficulties are but easy when
they are known. Call your executioner, and off with
210   Barnardine's head; I will give him a present shrift,°

180 *bared* shaved   192 *fearful* full of fear   193 *attempt* move
196 *character* handwriting   206 *unfolding star* morning star (signal-
ing the shepherd to lead the sheep from the fold)   210 *shrift*
absolution

and advise him for a better place. Yet you are
amazed; but this shall absolutely resolve° you.
Come away; it is almost clear dawn.

Exit [with Provost].

Scene III. [*The prison.*]

Enter Clown [Pompey].

Pompey. I am as well acquainted here as I was in our
house of profession: one would think it were Mistress Overdone's own house, for here be many of
her old customers. First, here's young Master Rash;
he's in for a commodity° of brown paper and old   5
ginger, ninescore and seventeen pounds, of which
he made five marks,° ready money; marry, then
ginger was not much in request, for the old women
were all dead. Then is there here one Master Caper,
at the suit of Master Three-pile the mercer, for   10
some four suits of peach-colored satin, which now
peaches° him a beggar. Then have we here young
Dizzy, and young Master Deep-vow, and Master
Copper-spur,° and Master Starve-lackey, the rapier
and dagger man, and young Drop-heir that killed   15
lusty Pudding, and Master Forthright the tilter,°
and brave Master Shoe-tie° the great traveler, and
wild Half-can° that stabbed Pots, and, I think,
forty more; all great doers in our trade, and are
now "for the Lord's sake."°   20

212 *resolve* convince   IV.iii.5 *commodity* (worthless goods whose
purchase at a heavy price was forced on a debtor in dire need by
a usurious creditor, who thus circumvented the contemporary laws
against usury)   7 *marks* (a mark was about two-thirds of a pound)
12 *peaches* betrays   14 *Copper-spur* i.e., Master Pretentious (cop-
per was a bogus substitute for gold)   16 *tilter* fighter   17 *Shoe-tie*
rosette (worn by gallants)   18 *Half-can* (a larger vessel than a
pot)   20 *"for the Lord's sake"* (the cry of prisoners begging alms
from passers-by)

Enter Abhorson.

Abhorson. Sirrah, bring Barnardine hither.

Pompey. Master Barnardine! You must rise and be
hanged, Master Barnardine!

Abhorson. What, ho, Barnardine!

25 *Barnardine.* (*Within*) A pox o' your throats! Who
makes that noise there? What are you?

Pompey. Your friends, sir; the hangman. You must
be so good, sir, to <u>rise and be put to death</u>.

Barnardine. [*Within*] Away, you rogue, away! I am
30 sleepy.

Abhorson. Tell him he must awake, and that quickly
too.

Pompey. Pray, Master Barnardine, <u>awake till you are</u>
<u>executed, and sleep afterwards</u>.

35 *Abhorson.* Go into him, and fetch him out.

Pompey. He is coming, sir, he is coming; I hear his
straw rustle.

Enter Barnardine.

Abhorson. Is the ax upon the block, sirrah?

Pompey. Very ready, sir.

40 *Barnardine.* How now, Abhorson? What's the news
with you?

Abhorson. Truly, sir, I would desire you to clap into
your prayers; for, look you, the warrant's come.

Barnardine. You rogue, I have been drinking all night;
45 I am not fitted for't.

Pompey. O, the better, sir: for he that drinks all
night, and is hanged betimes° in the morning, may
sleep the sounder all the next day.

47 *betimes* early

Enter Duke [disguised as before].

Abhorson. Look you, sir; here comes your ghostly°
   father. Do we jest now, think you?   50

Duke. Sir, induced by my charity, and hearing how
   hastily you are to depart, I am come to advise you,
   comfort you, and pray with you.

Barnardine. Friar, not I: I have been drinking hard
   all night, and I will have more time to prepare me,   55
   or they shall beat out my brains with billets.° I will
   not consent to die this day, that's certain.

Duke. O, sir, you must; and therefore I beseech you
   Look forward on the journey you shall go.

Barnardine. I swear I will not die today for any man's   60
   persuasion.

Duke. But hear you—

Barnardine. Not a word. If you have anything to say
   to me, come to my ward, for thence will not I today.
                                                 Exit.

Enter Provost.

Duke. Unfit to live or die. O gravel heart!   65
   After him, fellows; bring him to the block.
                     [*Exeunt Abhorson and Pompey.*]

Provost. Now, sir, how do you find the prisoner?

Duke. A creature unprepared, unmeet for death;
   And to transport him in the mind he is
   Were damnable.

Provost.   Here in the prison, father,   70
   There died this morning of a cruel fever
   One Ragozine, a most notorious pirate,
   A man of Claudio's years, his beard and head
   Just of his color. What if we do omit
   This reprobate till he were well inclined,   75
   And satisfy the deputy with the visage

49 *ghostly* spiritual   56 *billets* cudgels

Of Ragozine, more like to Claudio?

Duke. O, 'tis an accident that heaven provides.
Dispatch it presently;° the hour draws on
80   Prefixed° by Angelo. See this be done,
And sent according to command, whiles I
Persuade this rude wretch willingly to die.

Provost. This shall be done, good father, presently;
But Barnardine must die this afternoon,
85   And how shall we continue Claudio,
To save me from the danger that might come
If he were known alive?

Duke.   Let this be done:
Put them in secret holds,° both Barnardine and
    Claudio.
Ere twice the sun hath made his journal° greeting
90   To yonder generation, you shall find
Your safety manifested.

Provost. I am your free dependant.°

Duke. Quick, dispatch, and send the head to Angelo.
                          Exit [*Provost*].
Now will I write letters to Angelo—
95   The provost, he shall bear them—whose contents
Shall witness to him I am near at home,
And that by great injunctions I am bound
To enter publicly. Him I'll desire
To meet me at the consecrated fount,
100   A league below the city; and from thence,
By cold gradation° and well-balanced form,
We shall proceed with Angelo.

Enter Provost.

Provost. Here is the head; I'll carry it myself.

Duke. Convenient is it. Make a swift return,

79 *presently* at once   80 *Prefixed* predetermined   88 *holds* cells
89 *journal* daily   92 *your free dependant* freely at your service
101 *cold gradation* deliberate steps

　　For I would commune with you of such things　*105*
　　That want° no ear but yours.

Provost.　　　　　　　　　I'll make all speed.
　　　　　　　　　　　　　　　　　　Exit.

Isabella. (Within) Peace, ho, be here!

Duke. The tongue of Isabel. She's come to know
　　If yet her brother's pardon be come hither.
　　But I will keep her ignorant of her good,　*110*
　　To make her heavenly comforts of despair
　　When it is least expected.

　　　　　　　Enter Isabella.

Isabella.　　　　　　　Ho, by your leave!

Duke. Good morning to you, fair and gracious daugh-
　　ter.

Isabella. The better, given me by so holy a man.
　　Hath yet the deputy sent my brother's pardon?　*115*

Duke. He hath released him, Isabel, from the world;
　　His head is off, and sent to Angelo.

Isabella. Nay, but it is not so.

Duke. It is no other. Show your wisdom, daughter,
　　In your close° patience.　*120*

Isabella. O, I will to him and pluck out his eyes!

Duke. You shall not be admitted to his sight.

Isabella. Unhappy Claudio, wretched Isabel,
　　Injurious world, most damnèd Angelo!

Duke. This nor hurts him nor profits you a jot;　*125*
　　Forbear it therefore, give your cause to heaven.
　　Mark what I say, which you shall find
　　By every syllable a faithful verity.
　　The Duke comes home tomorrow—nay, dry your
　　　eyes—
　　One of our covent,° and his confessor,　*130*

106 *want* need　**120** *close* deep, secret　**130** *covent* convent

Gives me this instance:° already he hath carried
Notice to Escalus and Angelo,
Who do prepare to meet him at the gates,
There to give up their pow'r. If you can, pace°
    your wisdom
135 In that good path that I would wish it go,
And you shall have your bosom° on this wretch,
Grace of the Duke, revenges to your heart,
And general honor.

Isabella.   I am directed by you.

Duke. This letter, then, to Friar Peter give;
140 'Tis that he sent me of the Duke's return.
Say, by this token, I desire his company
At Mariana's house tonight. Her cause and yours
I'll perfect him withal, and he shall bring you
Before the Duke; and to the head of Angelo
145 Accuse him home and home. For my poor self,
I am combinèd° by a sacred vow,
And shall be absent. Wend you with this letter;
Command these fretting waters from your eyes
With a light heart; trust not my holy Order,
150 If I pervert your course. Who's here?

Enter Lucio.

Lucio. Good even. Friar, where's the provost?

Duke. Not within, sir.

Lucio. O pretty Isabella, I am pale at mine heart to
    see thine eyes so red; thou must be patient. I am
155 fain to dine and sup with water and bran; I dare
    not for my head fill my belly; one fruitful meal
    would set me to't. But they say the Duke will be
    here tomorrow. By my troth, Isabel, I loved thy
    brother. If the old fantastical Duke of dark cor-
160 ners had been at home, he had lived.
                                      [*Exit Isabella.*]

131 *instance* proof 134 *pace* conduct 136 *bosom* desire 146
combinèd bound

Duke. Sir, the Duke is marvelous little beholding to
   your reports; but the best is, he lives not in them.

Lucio. Friar, thou knowest not the Duke so well as I
   do; he's a better woodman° than thou tak'st him
   for.   *165*

Duke. Well, you'll answer this one day. Fare ye well.

Lucio. Nay, tarry, I'll go along with thee: I can tell
   thee pretty tales of the Duke.

Duke. You have told me too many of him already,   *170*
   sir, if they be true; if not true, none were enough.

Lucio. I was once before him for getting a wench
   with child.

Duke. Did you such a thing?

Lucio. Yes, marry, did I; but I was fain to forswear
   it: they would else have married me to the rotten   *175*
   medlar.°

Duke. Sir, your company is fairer than honest. Rest
   you well.

Lucio. By my troth, I'll go with thee to the lane's end.
   If bawdy talk offend you, we'll have very little of   *180*
   it. Nay, friar, I am a kind of burr; I shall stick.

                                                Exeunt.

Scene IV. [*A room.*]

Enter Angelo and Escalus.

Escalus. Every letter he hath writ hath disvouched
   other.

---

164 *woodman* hunter (here, of women)   176 *medlar* applelike fruit
edible only when partly decayed (here, a prostitute)

Claudio regrets his doings

Angelo. In most uneven and distracted manner. His
actions show much like to madness; pray heaven
his wisdom be not tainted. And why meet him at
the gates, and redeliver our authorities there?

Escalus. I guess not.

Angelo. And why should we proclaim it in an hour
before his ent'ring, that if any crave redress of injustice, they should exhibit their petitions in the
street?

Escalus. He shows his reason for that: to have a dispatch of complaints, and to deliver us from devices°
hereafter which shall then have no power to stand
against us.

Angelo. Well, I beseech you, let it be proclaimed.
Betimes i' th' morn I'll call you at your house. Give
notice to such men of sort and suit° as are to meet
him.

Escalus. I shall, sir. Fare you well.   *Exit.*

Angelo. Good night.
          This deed unshapes me quite, makes me unpreg-
               nant,°
          And dull to all proceedings. A deflow'red maid,
          And by an eminent body that enforced
          The law against it! But that her tender shame
          Will not proclaim against her maiden loss,°
          How might she tongue me! Yet reason dares her no;
          For my authority bears of a credent bulk,°
          That no particular scandal once can touch
          But it confounds the breather. He should have
               lived,
          Save that his riotous youth, with dangerous sense,°
          Might in the times to come have ta'en revenge,
          By so receiving a dishonored life

IV.iv.13 *devices* false complaints   18 *men of sort and suit* noble-
men   22 *unpregnant* unreceptive   26 *maiden loss* loss of maidenhood   28 *bears of a credent bulk* is derived from trusted material
31 *sense* feeling

With ransom of such shame. Would yet he had
   lived!
Alack, when once our grace we have forgot,   *33*
Nothing goes right; we would, and we would not.
                                               Exit.

Scene V. [*Outside the town.*]

Enter Duke [in his own habit] and Friar Peter.

Duke. These letters at fit time deliver me.°
   The provost knows our purpose and our plot.
   The matter being afoot, keep your instruction,
   And hold you ever to our special drift,
   Though sometimes you do blench° from this to that,   *5*
   As cause doth minister. Go call at Flavius' house,
   And tell him where I stay; give the like notice
   To Valencius, Rowland, and to Crassus,
   And bid them bring the trumpets to the gate;
   But send me Flavius first.

Friar Peter.   It shall be speeded well.   *10*
                                               [*Exit.*]

Enter Varrius.

Duke. I thank thee, Varrius; thou hast made good
   haste.
   Come, we will walk. There's other of our friends
   Will greet us here anon, my gentle Varrius. *Exeunt.*

IV.v.1 *me* for me   5 *blench* deviate

Scene VI. [*Near the city gate.*]

Enter Isabella and Mariana.

Isabella. To speak so indirectly I am loath:
  I would say the truth; but to accuse him so,
  That is your part. Yet I am advised to do it,
  He says, to veil full purpose.

Mariana.   Be ruled by him.

5 *Isabella.* Besides, he tells me that, if peradventure
  He speak against me on the adverse side,
  I should not think it strange; for 'tis a physic
  That's bitter to sweet end.

Mariana. I would Friar Peter—

Enter Friar Peter.

Isabella.   O peace! The friar is come.

Friar Peter. Come, I have found you out a stand most
10   fit
  Where you may have such vantage° on the Duke,
  He shall not pass you. Twice have the trumpets
      sounded.
  The generous° and gravest citizens
  Have hent° the gates, and very near upon
15 The Duke is ent'ring: therefore, hence, away!
                                   Exeunt.

IV.vi.11 *vantage* advantageous position   13 *generous* highborn   14
hent gathered at

ACT V

Scene I. [*The city gate.*]

*Enter Duke, Varrius, Lords, Angelo, Escalus,
Lucio, [Provost, Officers, and] Citizens, at
several doors.*

Duke. My very worthy cousin,° fairly met.
  Our old and faithful friend, we are glad to see you.

Angelo, Escalus. Happy return be to your royal
  Grace.

Duke. Many and hearty thankings to you both.
  We have made inquiry of you, and we hear   5
  Such goodness of your justice, that our soul
  Cannot but yield you forth to public thanks,
  Forerunning more requital.°

Angelo.   You make my bonds still greater.

Duke. O, your desert speaks loud, and I should wrong
    it
  To lock it in the wards of covert bosom,°   10

V.i.1 *cousin* (a sovereign's address to a nobleman) 8 *Forerunning
more requital* preceding additional reward 10 *To . . . bosom* i.e.,
to keep it locked hidden in my heart

117

When it deserves, with characters of brass,
A forted residence 'gainst the tooth of time
And razure° of oblivion. Give me your hand,
And let the subject see, to make them know
15 That outward courtesies would fain proclaim
Favors that keep° within. Come, Escalus,
You must walk by us on our other hand—
And good supporters are you.

Enter [Friar] Peter and Isabella.

Friar Peter. Now is your time: speak loud, and kneel
before him.

20 *Isabella.* Justice, O royal Duke! Vail your regard°
Upon a wronged—I would fain have said, a maid.
O worthy prince, dishonor not your eye
By throwing it on any other object
Till you have heard me in my true complaint,
25 And given me justice, justice, justice, justice!

Duke. Relate your wrongs. In what? By whom? Be
brief.
Here is Lord Angelo shall give you justice;
Reveal yourself to him.

Isabella.   O worthy Duke,
You bid me seek redemption of the devil.
30 Hear me yourself, for that which I must speak
Must either punish me, not being believed,
Or wring redress from you. Hear me, O hear me,
here!

Angelo. My lord, her wits, I fear me, are not firm.
She hath been a suitor to me for her brother
Cut off by course of justice—

35 *Isabella.*   By course of justice!

Angelo. And she will speak most bitterly and strange.

Isabella. Most strange, but yet most truly, will I speak.

13 *razure* erasure   16 *keep* dwell   20 *Vail your regard* cast your
attention

That Angelo's forsworn, is it not strange?
That Angelo's a murderer, is't not strange?
That Angelo is an adulterous thief,   40
An hypocrite, a virgin-violator;
Is it not strange, and strange?

Duke.   Nay, it is ten times strange.

Isabella. It is not truer he is Angelo
Than this is all as true as it is strange.
Nay, it is ten times true, for truth is truth   45
To th' end of reck'ning.

Duke.   Away with her! Poor soul,
She speaks this in th' infirmity of sense.

Isabella. O prince, I conjure thee, as thou believ'st
There is another comfort than this world,
That thou neglect me not, with that opinion   50
That I am touched with madness. Make not impos-
    sible
That which but seems unlike. 'Tis not impossible
But one, the wicked'st caitiff on the ground,
May seem as shy, as grave, as just, as absolute°
As Angelo; even so may Angelo,   55
In all his dressings, caracts,° titles, forms,
Be an arch-villain. Believe it, royal prince;
If he be less, he's nothing; but he's more,
Had I more name for badness.

Duke.   By mine honesty,
If she be mad, as I believe no other,   60
Her madness hath the oddest frame of sense,
Such a dependency of thing on thing,
As e'er I heard in madness.

Isabella.   O gracious Duke,
Harp not on that; nor do not banish reason
For inequality,° but let your reason serve   65
To make the truth appear where it seems hid,
And hide the false seems° true.

54 *absolute* perfect   56 *caracts* symbols of office   65 *inequality* injustice   67 *seems* which seems

Duke.   Many that are not mad
    Have, sure, more lack of reason. What would you
    say?

Isabella. I am the sister of one Claudio,
70   Condemned upon the act of fornication
    To lose his head, condemned by Angelo.
    I, in probation° of a sisterhood,
    Was sent to by my brother, one Lucio
    As then the messenger—

Lucio.   That's I, and't like° your Grace.
75   I came to her from Claudio, and desired her
    To try her gracious fortune with Lord Angelo
    For her poor brother's pardon.

Isabella.   That's he indeed.

Duke. You were not bid to speak.

Lucio.   No, my good lord,
    Nor wished to hold my peace.

Duke.   I wish you now, then;
80   Pray you, take note of it, and when you have
    A business for yourself, pray heaven you then
    Be perfect.°

Lucio.   I warrant your honor.

Duke. The warrant's° for yourself; take heed to't.

Isabella. This gentleman told somewhat of my tale—

85 *Lucio.* Right.

Duke. It may be right; but you are i' the wrong
    To speak before your time. Proceed.

Isabella.   I went
    To this pernicious caitiff deputy—

Duke. That's somewhat madly spoken.

---

72 *probation* novitiate   74 *and't like* if it please   82 *perfect* thoroughly prepared   83 *warrant* warning

Isabella.   Pardon it;
  The phrase is to the matter.°   90

Duke. Mended again. The matter: proceed.

Isabella. In brief, to set the needless process by,
  How I persuaded, how I prayed, and kneeled,
  How he refelled° me, and how I replied—
  For this was of much length—the vild° conclusion   95
  I now begin with brief and shame to utter.
  He would not, but by gift of my chaste body
  To his concupiscible intemperate lust,
  Release my brother; and after much debatement,
  My sisterly remorse° confutes mine honor,   100
  And I did yield to him; but the next morn betimes,
  His purpose surfeiting,° he sends a warrant
  For my poor brother's head.

Duke.   This is most likely!

Isabella. O, that it were as like as it is true!

Duke. By heaven, fond wretch, thou know'st not what
    thou speak'st,   105
  Or else thou art suborned against his honor
  In hateful practice.° First, his integrity
  Stands without blemish. Next, it imports no reason°
  That with such vehemency he should pursue
  Faults proper° to himself: if he had so offended,   110
  He would have weighed thy brother by himself,
  And not have cut him off. Someone hath set you on;
  Confess the truth, and say by whose advice
  Thou cam'st here to complain.

Isabella.   And is this all?
  Then, O you blessèd ministers above,   115
  Keep me in patience, and with ripened time
  Unfold the evil which is here wrapped up
  In countenance. Heaven shield your Grace from
    woe,

90 *to the matter* appropriate 94 *refelled* repelled 95 *vild* vile 100 *remorse* pity 102 *surfeiting* satiating 107 *practice* plot 108 *imports no reason* does not attend to reason 110 *proper* belonging

      As I, thus wronged, hence unbelievèd go!

120 *Duke.* I know you'd fain be gone. An officer,
      To prison with her! Shall we thus permit
      A blasting and a scandalous breath to fall
      On him so near us? This needs must be a practice.
      Who knew of your intent and coming hither?

125 *Isabella.* One that I would were here, Friar Lodowick.

    Duke. A ghostly father, belike. Who knows that
      Lodowick?

    Lucio. My lord, I know him; 'tis a meddling friar,
      I do not like the man. Had he been lay,° my lord,
      For certain words he spake against your Grace
130   In your retirement, I had swinged° him soundly.

    Duke. Words against me! This's a good friar, belike!
      And to set on this wretched woman here
      Against our substitute! Let this friar be found.

    Lucio. But yesternight, my lord, she and that friar,
135   I saw them at the prison; a saucy friar,
      A very scurvy° fellow.

    Friar Peter. Blessed be your royal Grace!
      I have stood by, my lord, and I have heard
      Your royal ear abused. First, hath this woman
140   Most wrongfully accused your substitute,
      Who is as free from touch or soil with her
      As she from one ungot.

    Duke.   We did believe no less.
      Know you that Friar Lodowick that she speaks of?

    Friar Peter. I know him for a man divine and holy;
145   Not scurvy, nor a temporary meddler,°
      As he's reported by this gentleman;
      And, on my trust, a man that never yet
      Did, as he vouches, misreport your Grace.

    Lucio. My lord, most villainously; believe it.

128 *lay* layman   130 *swinged* thrashed   136 *scurvy* worthless   145
temporary meddler meddler in temporal affairs

Friar Peter. Well, he in time may come to clear him-
 self,   *150*
 But at this instant he is sick, my lord,
 Of a strange fever. Upon his mere request,
 Being come to knowledge that there was complaint
 Intended 'gainst Lord Angelo, came I hither,
 To speak, as from his mouth, what he doth know *155*
 Is true and false; and what he with his oath
 And all probation° will make up full clear,
 Whensoever he's convented.° First, for this woman,
 To justify this worthy nobleman,
 So vulgarly and personally accused,   *160*
 Her shall you hear disprovèd to her eyes,
 Till she herself confess it.

Duke.   Good friar, let's hear it.
     [*Isabella is carried off guarded.*]

      Enter Mariana [*veiled*].

Do you not smile at this, Lord Angelo?
O heaven, the vanity of wretched fools!
Give us some seats. Come, cousin Angelo,   *165*
In this I'll be impartial; be you judge
Of your own cause. Is this the witness, friar?
First, let her show her face, and after speak.

Mariana. Pardon, my lord; I will not show my face
 Until my husband bid me.   *170*

Duke. What, are your married?

Mariana. No, my lord.

Duke. Are you a maid?

Mariana. No, my lord.

Duke. A widow, then?   *175*

Mariana. Neither, my lord.

Duke. Why, you are nothing, then: neither maid,
 widow, nor wife?

157 *probation* proof 158 *convented* sent for

Lucio. My lord, she may be a punk;° for many of
180　them are neither maid, widow, nor wife.

Duke. Silence that fellow. I would he had some cause
To prattle for himself.

Lucio. Well, my lord.

Mariana. My lord, I do confess I ne'er was married,
185　And I confess, besides, I am no maid.
I have known° my husband; yet my husband
Knows not that ever he knew me.

Lucio. He was drunk, then, my lord; it can be no
better.

190　*Duke.* For the benefit of silence, would thou wert so
too!

Lucio. Well, my lord.

Duke. This is no witness for Lord Angelo.

Mariana. Now I come to't, my lord:
195　She that accuses him of fornication,
In selfsame manner doth accuse my husband,
And charges him, my lord, with such a time
When I'll depose I had him in mine arms
With all th' effect of love.

Angelo. Charges she moe than me?

200　*Mariana.*　　　　　　　　　　　Not that I know.

Duke. No? You say your husband?

Mariana. Why, just, my lord, and that is Angelo,
Who thinks he knows that he ne'er knew my body,
But knows he thinks that he knows Isabel's.

205　*Angelo.* This is a strange abuse. Let's see thy face.

Mariana. My husband bids me; now I will unmask.
　　　　　　　　　　　　　　　　[*Unveiling.*]
　　This is that face, thou cruel Angelo,

179 *punk* harlot　186 *known* had intercourse with

Which once thou swor'st was worth the looking on;
This is the hand which, with a vowed contract,
Was fast belocked in thine; this is the body　　210
That took away the match° from Isabel,
And did supply thee at thy garden house
In her imagined person.

Duke.　　　　　　　Know you this woman?

Lucio. Carnally, she says.

Duke.　　　　　　　Sirrah, no more!

Lucio. Enough, my lord.　　　　　　　215

Angelo. My lord, I must confess I know this woman:
And five years since there was some speech of marriage
Betwixt myself and her, which was broke off,
Partly for that her promisèd proportions°
Came short of composition,° but in chief,　　220
For that her reputation was disvalued
In levity;° since which time of five years
I never spake with her, saw her, nor heard from her,
Upon my faith and honor.

Mariana.　　　　　　Noble prince,
As there comes light from heaven and words from breath,　　225
As there is sense in truth and truth in virtue,
I am affianced this man's wife as strongly
As words could make up vows; and, my good lord,
But Tuesday night last gone in's garden house
He knew me as a wife. As this is true,　　230
Let me in safety raise me from my knees,
Or else forever be confixèd° here,
A marble monument.

Angelo.　　　　　I did but smile till now;
Now, good my lord, give me the scope of justice;
My patience here is touched. I do perceive　　235

211 *match* meeting　219 *proportions* dowry　220 *composition* previous agreement　221–22 *disvalued/In levity* discredited for lightness　232 *confixèd* fixed firmly

These poor informal° women are no more
But instruments of some more mightier member
That sets them on. Let me have way, my lord,
To find this practice out.

Duke.   Ay, with my heart,
240 And punish them to your height of pleasure.
Thou foolish friar and thou pernicious woman,
Compact° with her that's gone, think'st thou thy
   oaths,
Though they would swear down each particular
   saint,
Were testimonies against his worth and credit,
245 That's sealed in approbation?° You, Lord Escalus,
Sit with my cousin; lend him your kind pains
To find out this abuse, whence 'tis derived.
There is another friar that set them on;
Let him be sent for.

Friar Peter. Would he were here, my lord, for he, in-
250 deed,
Hath set the women on to this complaint:
Your provost knows the place where he abides,
And he may fetch him.

Duke.   Go, do it instantly. [*Exit Provost.*]
And you, my noble and well-warranted cousin,
255 Whom it concerns to hear this matter forth,
Do with your injuries as seems you best,
In any chastisement. I for a while
Will leave you, but stir not you till you have
Well determined upon these slanderers.

260 *Escalus.* My lord, we'll do it throughly.   *Exit* [*Duke*].
Signior Lucio, did not you say you knew that Friar
Lodowick to be a dishonest person?

Lucio. Cucullus non facit monachum;° honest in
nothing but in his clothes, and one that hath spoke
265 most villainous speeches of the Duke.

236 *informal* (1) rash (2) informing   242 *Compact* in collusion
245 *approbation* attested integrity   263 *Cucullus non facit monachum* the cowl does not make the monk (Latin)

Escalus. We shall entreat you to abide here till he
come, and enforce° them against him; we shall find
this friar a notable° fellow.

Lucio. As any in Vienna, on my word.

Escalus. Call that same Isabel here once again; I 270
would speak with her. [*Exit an Attendant.*] Pray
you, my lord, give me leave to question; you shall
see how I'll handle her.

Lucio. Not better than he, by her own report.

Escalus. Say you?

Lucio. Marry, sir, I think, if you handled her pri- 275
vately, she would sooner confess; perchance, publicly, she'll be ashamed.

　　*Enter Duke [as friar], Provost, Isabella,
　　　　　[and Officers].*

Escalus. I will go darkly° to work with her.

Lucio. That's the way; for women are light at mid- 280
night.

Escalus. Come on, mistress, here's a gentlewoman
denies all that you have said.

Lucio. My lord, here comes the rascal I spoke of—
here with the provost.

Escalus. In very good time. Speak not you to him till 285
we call upon you.

Lucio. Mum.

Escalus. Come, sir, did you set these women on to
slander Lord Angelo? They have confessed you did. 290

Duke. 'Tis false.

Escalus. How! Know you where you are?

Duke. Respect to your great place; and let the devil

267 *enforce* urge 268 *notable* notoroius 279 *darkly* subtly

Be sometime honored for his burning throne.
295   Where is the Duke? 'Tis he should hear me speak.

Escalus. The Duke's in us, and we will hear you speak.
Look you speak justly.

Duke. Boldly, at least. But, O poor souls,
Come you to seek the lamb here of the fox?
300   Good night to your redress. Is the Duke gone?
Then is your cause gone too. The Duke's unjust,
Thus to retort° your manifest° appeal,
And put your trial in the villain's mouth
Which here you come to accuse.

305   *Lucio.* This is the rascal; this is he I spoke of.

Escalus. Why, thou unreverend and unhallowed friar,
Is't not enough thou hast suborned these women
To accuse this worthy man, but in foul mouth,
And in the witness of his proper° ear,
310   To call him villain? And then to glance from him
To th' Duke himself, to tax him with injustice?
Take him hence; to th' rack with him. We'll touse°
    you
Joint by joint, but we will know his purpose.
What, "unjust"!

Duke.   Be not so hot. The Duke
315   Dare no more stretch this finger of mine than he
Dare rack his own: his subject am I not,
Nor here provincial.° My business in this state
Made me a looker-on here in Vienna,
Where I have seen corruption boil and bubble
320   Till it o'errun the stew. Laws for all faults,
But faults so countenanced, that the strong statutes
Stand like the forfeits° in a barber's shop,
As much in mock as mark.°

Escalus. Slander to th' state! Away with him to prison!

302 *retort* refer back   302 *manifest* clear   309 *proper* very   312
touse pull   317 *provincial* belonging to the province or state
322 *forfeits* extracted teeth (barbers acted as dentists)   323 *As
much . . . mark* to be mocked at as much as to be seen

Angelo. What can you vouch against him, Signior 325
    Lucio? Is this the man that you did tell us of?

Lucio. 'Tis he, my lord. Come hither, goodman bald-
    pate; do you know me?

Duke. I remember you, sir, by the sound of your
    voice. I met you at the prison, in the absence of 330
    the Duke.

Lucio. O, did you so? And do you remember what
    you said of the Duke?

Duke. Most notedly, sir.

Lucio. Do you so, sir? And was the Duke a flesh- 335
    monger, a fool, and a coward, as you then reported
    him to be?

Duke. You must, sir, change persons with me, ere you
    make that my report. You, indeed, spoke so of
    him; and much more, much worse. 340

Lucio. O thou damnable fellow! Did not I pluck thee
    by the nose for thy speeches?

Duke. I protest I love the Duke as I love myself.

Angelo. Hark, how the villain would close° now, after
    his treasonable abuses. 345

Escalus. Such a fellow is not to be talked withal.
    Away with him to prison! Where is the provost?
    Away with him to prison, lay bolts enough upon
    him, let him speak no more. Away with those gig-
    lets° too, and with the other confederate compan- 350
    ion.

Duke. [*To the Provost*] Stay, sir; stay awhile.

Angelo. What, resists he? Help him, Lucio.

Lucio. Come, sir; come, sir; come, sir; foh, sir! Why,
    you bald-pated, lying rascal, you must be hooded, 355
    must you? Show your knave's visage, with a pox

344 *close* come to agreement   **349–50** *giglets* wanton women

to you. Show your sheep-biting° face, and be
hanged an hour. Will't not off?
[*Pulls off the friar's hood, and discovers the Duke.*]

Duke. Thou art the first knave that e'er mad'st a
Duke.
360 First, provost, let me bail these gentle three.
[*To Lucio*] Sneak not away, sir; for the friar and
you
Must have a word anon. Lay hold on him.

Lucio. This may prove worse than hanging.

Duke [*To Escalus*] What you have spoke I pardon.
Sit you down.
We'll borrow place of him. [*To Angelo*] Sir, by
365 your leave.
Hast thou or word, or wit, or impudence,
That yet can do thee office?° If thou hast,
Rely upon it till my tale be heard,
And hold no longer out.

Angelo.   O my dread lord,
370 I should be guiltier than my guiltiness,
To think I can be undiscernible,
When I perceive your Grace, like pow'r divine,
Hath looked upon my passes.° Then, good prince,
No longer session° hold upon my shame,
375 But let my trial be mine own confession.
Immediate sentence then, and sequent death,
Is all the grace I beg.

Duke.   Come hither, Mariana.
Say, wast thou e'er contracted to this woman?

Angelo. I was, my lord.

380 *Duke.* Go take her hence, and marry her instantly.
Do you the office, friar, which consummate,
Return him here again. Go with him, provost.

Exit [*Angelo with Mariana, Friar Peter, and Provost*].

357 *sheep-biting* currish 367 *office* service 373 *passes* trespasses 374
session trial

Escalus. My lord, I am more amazed at his dishonor
  Than at the strangeness of it.

Duke.   Come hither, Isabel.
  Your friar is now your prince. As I was then   *385*
  Advertising and holy° to your business,
  Not changing heart with habit, I am still
  Attorneyed at your service.

Isabella.   O, give me pardon,
  That I, your vassal, have employed and pained
  Your unknown sovereignty!

Duke.   You are pardoned, Isabel: *390*
  And now, dear maid, be you as free to us.
  Your brother's death, I know, sits at your heart,
  And you may marvel why I obscured myself,
  Laboring to save his life, and would not rather
  Make rash remonstrance of my hidden pow'r   *395*
  Than let him so be lost. O most kind maid,
  It was the swift celerity of his death,
  Which I did think with slower foot came on,
  That brained my purpose. But, peace be with him.
  That life is better life, past fearing death,   *400*
  Than that which lives to fear. Make it your comfort,
  So happy is your brother.

    Enter Angelo, Mariana, [Friar] Peter, Provost.

Isabella.   I do, my lord.

Duke. For this new-married man, approaching here,
  Whose salt° imagination yet hath wronged
  Your well-defended honor, you must pardon   *405*
  For Mariana's sake. But as he adjudged your
    brother,
  Being criminal, in double violation,
  Of sacred chastity, and of promise-breach,
  Thereon dependent, for your brother's life,
  The very mercy of the law cries out   *410*

386 *Advertising and holy* attentive and devoted   404 *salt* lecherous

Most audible, even from his proper tongue,
"An Angelo for Claudio, death for death!"
Haste still pays haste, and leisure answers leisure;
Like doth quit like, and Measure still for Measure.°
415   Then, Angelo, thy fault's thus manifested;
Which, though thou wouldst deny, denies thee van-
    tage.
We do condemn thee to the very block
Where Claudio stooped to death, and with like
    haste.
Away with him.

Mariana.   O my most gracious lord,
420   I hope you will not mock me with a husband.

Duke. It is your husband mocked you with a husband.
Consenting to the safeguard of your honor,
I thought your marriage fit; else imputation,°
For that he knew you, might reproach your life,
425   And choke your good to come. For his possessions,
Although by confiscation they are ours,
We do instate and widow you withal,
To buy you a better husband.

Mariana.   O my dear lord,
I crave no other, nor no better man.

430   *Duke.* Never crave him; we are definitive.°

Mariana. Gentle my liege—   [*Kneeling.*]

Duke.   You do but lose your labor.
Away with him to death! [*To Lucio*] Now, sir, to
    you.

Mariana. O my good lord! Sweet Isabel, take my part,
Lend me your knees, and all my life to come
435   I'll lend you all my life to do you service.

Duke. Against all sense you do importune her;

414 *Measure still for Measure* (see Matthew 7:1–2: "Judge not,
that ye be not judged. For with what judgment ye judge, ye shall
be judged: and with what measure ye mete, it shall be measured
to you again")   423 *imputation* accusation   430 *definitive* determined

Should she kneel down in mercy of this fact,°
Her brother's ghost his pavèd° bed would break,
And take her hence in horror.

Mariana.　　　　　　　　Isabel,
Sweet Isabel, do yet but kneel by me,　　　　　　　440
Hold up your hands, say nothing, I'll speak all.
They say, best men are molded out of faults;
And, for the most, become much more the better
For being a little bad; so may my husband.
O Isabel, will you not lend a knee?　　　　　　　445

Duke. He dies for Claudio's death.

Isabella. [*Kneeling*]　　　　Most bounteous sir,
Look, if it please you, on this man condemned,
As if my brother lived. I partly think
A due sincerity governèd his deeds,
Till he did look on me. Since it is so,　　　　　　450
Let him not die. My brother had but justice,
In that he did the thing for which he died.
For Angelo,
His act did not o'ertake his bad intent,
And must be buried but as an intent　　　　　　455
That perished by the way. Thoughts are no sub-
    jects,°
Intents but merely thoughts.

Mariana.　　　　　　　Merely, my lord.

Duke. Your suit's unprofitable; stand up, I say.
I have bethought me of another fault.
Provost, how came it Claudio was beheaded
At an unusual hour?　　　　　　　　　　　460

Provost.　　　　　It was commanded so.

Duke. Had you a special warrant for the deed?

Provost. No, my good lord; it was by private message.

Duke. For which I do discharge you of your office;
    Give up your keys.

437 *fact* crime　438 *pavèd* slab-covered　456 *no subjects* i.e., not
subject to law

465 *Provost.*   Pardon me, noble lord.
    I thought it was a fault, but knew it not;°
    Yet did repent me, after more advice;°
    For testimony whereof, one in the prison,
    That should by private order else have died,
    I have reserved alive.

Duke.   What's he?

470 *Provost.*   His name is Barnardine.

Duke. I would thou hadst done so by Claudio.
    Go fetch him hither; let me look upon him.
                   [Exit Provost.]

Escalus. I am sorry, one so learnèd and so wise
    As you, Lord Angelo, have still° appeared,
475   Should slip so grossly, both in the heat of blood,
    And lack of tempered judgment afterward.

Angelo. I am sorry that such sorrow I procure,
    And so deep sticks it in my penitent heart,
    That I crave death more willingly than mercy;
480   'Tis my deserving, and I do entreat it.

Enter Barnardine and Provost,
Claudio [muffled], Juliet.

Duke. Which is that Barnardine?

Provost.   This, my lord.

Duke. There was a friar told me of this man.
    Sirrah, thou art said to have a stubborn soul,
    That apprehends no further than this world,
    And squar°st thy life according. Thou'rt con-
485   demned;
    But, for those earthly faults, I quit° them all,
    And pray thee take this mercy to provide
    For better times to come. Friar, advise him;
    I leave him to your hand. What muffled fellow's
      that?

466 *knew it not* was not sure   467 *advice* thought   474 *still*
ever   485 *squar'st* regulate   486 *quit* pardon

Provost. This is another prisoner that I saved,   490
  Who should have died when Claudio lost his head;
  As like almost to Claudio as himself.
                          [*Unmuffles Claudio.*]

Duke. [*To Isabella*] If he be like your brother, for his
      sake
  Is he pardoned; and, for your lovely sake,
  Give me your hand, and say you will be mine,
  He is my brother too; but fitter time for that.   495
  By this Lord Angelo perceives he's safe;
  Methinks I see a quick'ning° in his eye.
  Well, Angelo, your evil quits you well;
  Look that you love your wife; her worth, worth
      yours.
  I find an apt remission° in myself,   500
  And yet here's one in place I cannot pardon.
  [*To Lucio*] You, sirrah, that knew me for a fool, a
      coward,
  One all of luxury,° an ass, a madman;
  Wherein have I so deserved of you,
  That you extol me thus?   505

Lucio. 'Faith, my lord, I spoke it but according to the
  trick.° If you will hang me for it, you may; but I
  had rather it would please you I might be whipped.

Duke. Whipped first, sir, and hanged after.   510
  Proclaim it, provost, round about the city,
  If any woman wronged by this lewd fellow—
  As I have heard him swear himself there's one
  Whom he begot with child—let her appear,
  And he shall marry her. The nuptial finished,   515
  Let him be whipped and hanged.

Lucio. I beseech your highness, do not marry me to a
  whore. Your highness said even now, I made you a
  duke: good my lord, do not recompense me in
  making me a cuckold.   520

---

498 *quick'ning* animation   501 *remission* wish to forgive   504 *luxury* lust   508 *trick* fashion

Duke. Upon mine honor, thou shalt marry her.
   Thy slanders I forgive; and therewithal
   Remit thy other forfeits. Take him to prison,
   And see our pleasure herein executed.

325 *Lucio.* Marrying a punk, my lord, is pressing to death,
   whipping, and hanging.

Duke. Slandering a prince deserves it.
                        [Exeunt Officers with Lucio.]
   She, Claudio, that you wronged, look you restore.°
   Joy to you, Mariana. Love her, Angelo;
530 I have confessed her, and I know her virtue.
   Thanks, good friend Escalus, for thy much good-
       ness;
   There's more behind° that is more gratulate.°
   Thanks, provost, for thy care and secrecy;
   We shall employ thee in a worthier place.
535 Forgive him, Angelo, that brought you home
   The head of Ragozine for Claudio's;
   Th' offense pardons itself. Dear Isabel,
   I have a motion° much imports your good,
   Whereto if you'll a willing ear incline,
540 What's mine is yours, and what is yours is mine.
   So, bring us to our palace, where we'll show
   What's yet behind, that's meet° you all should
      know.   *[Exeunt.]*

FINIS.

---

528 *restore* i.e., by marriage   532 *behind* to come   532 *gratulate*
gratifying   538 *motion* proposal   542 *meet* fitting

Textual Note

Our only authority for the text of *Measure for Measure* is the First Folio, whose text is on the whole a good one, probably based on a transcript of Shakespeare's manuscripts made by Ralph Crane, the scrivener of the King's Players. It seems a little disturbed in Act IV; the Duke's speech on "place and greatness" in this act would be more appropriate preceding his lines in III.ii, after the exit of Lucio. In the present text the act and scene divisions are translated from Latin and in two places depart from the Folio in order to correspond to the Globe text (the Globe's divisions are used in most books on Shakespeare): Globe I.ii is split in the Folio into a new scene after the exit of Pompey, and Globe III.ii is not marked in the Folio. The present edition corrects obvious typographical errors, modernizes spelling and punctuation, expands and regularizes speech prefixes, adjusts the lineation of a few passages, transfers the indication of locale ("The Scene: Vienna") and the *dramatis personae* ("The names of all the actors.") from the end to the beginning, and slightly alters the position of a few stage directions. Other substantial departures from the Folio are listed below, the present reading in italics and then the Folio reading in roman.

I.iii.27 *Becomes more* More   43 *it* in

I.iv.54 *givings-out* giuing-out

II.i.12 *your* our   39 *breaks* brakes

II.ii.96 *new* now   111 *ne'er* neuer

II.iv.9 *seared* feard   53 *or, to* and to   76 *Let me be* Let be   94 *all-binding* all-building

III.i.31 *serpigo* Sapego   52 *Bring me to hear them* Bring them to heare me   69 *Though* Through   130 *penury* periury   218 *by oath* oath

III.ii.26 *eat, array* eate away   48 *extracting it* extracting   153 *dearer* deare   227 *and it* and as it   278 *strings* stings

IV.i.62 *quests* Quest   64 *dreams* dreame

IV.ii.44–48 *If it be too little . . . fits your thief* [F gives to Pompey]

IV.iii.16 *Forthright* Forthlight   90 *yonder* yond

IV.iv.6 *redeliver* reliuer

V.i.13 *me* we   168 *her face* your face   426 *confiscation* confutation   542 *that's* that

A Note on
the Sources of *Measure for Measure*

The principal sources of *Measure for Measure* are
George Whetstone's play of *Promos and Cassandra* (1578)
and its prose redaction in the same author's *Heptameron
of Civil Discourses* (1582). Whetstone's own source was
Giraldi Cinthio's *Hecatommithi* (1565); and Shakespeare
almost certainly knew this work, which contains the story
of Othello. He may, in addition, have also known Cinthio's posthumously published play of *Epitia* (1583).
Brief summaries of these sources are given here for comparison with Shakespeare's treatment of the story.

CINTHIO'S *Hecatommithi*, DECADE 8, NOVELLA 5

The Emperor Maximian appoints one of his trusted
men, Juriste, to rule over the city of Innsbruck. He
charges him particularly to observe justice scrupulously.
Juriste, who lacks all self-knowledge, accepts the grave
responsibility with alacrity and for a while he is a model
ruler.

A young man called Vico is brought before Juriste for
violating a virgin, and is condemned to death according
to the laws of the city. Vico's sister, Epitia, who is a
student of philosophy and has a sweet way of speaking,

139

pleads for her brother. Her brother is very young; he was moved by the impulse of love; the ravished maiden is unmarried and Vico is willing to marry her. The law was made so severe only to deter would-be offenders, not really to be enforced. Captivated by Epitia's beauty and eloquence, Juriste promises to reconsider the case. When she meets him again, he proposes that she should lie with him if she wants her brother's sentence to be mitigated. Epitia refuses unless Juriste is willing to marry her afterward. Juriste does not promise to do this, though he hints at the possibility. When Epitia goes to the prison to prepare her brother for his fate, Vico pleads passionately with her and appeals to her sisterly affection to save him. So Epitia reluctantly consents to Juriste's proposal. Juriste, however, orders the execution of Vico before lying with her.

In the morning Epitia goes home to find that Juriste has indeed kept his promise to release her brother—dead. She thinks of revenge, but instead appeals to the Emperor. The Emperor sends for Juriste and finds that the complaint is true. He first forces Juriste to marry Epitia, who is quite unwilling, and then he orders that Juriste be put to death. Now that Juriste is her husband, Epitia is in a cruel dilemma. She discourses to the Emperor on the superiority of clemency to justice. The Emperor is impressed with her forgiving nature and pardons Juriste. Epitia and her husband live happily ever after.

CINTHIO's *Epitia*

The story is much the same as that in the *Hecatommithi,* but there are some new characters and the brother is secretly saved by the captain of the prison. The latter announces this fact at the end of the play, to the astonishment of the other characters and also the reader, who is not given a hint of it in the prefatory "argument."

Principal among the new characters are Angela, Juriste's sister, who conveys an offer of marriage from him to Epitia and testifies against him before the Emperor when

Juriste breaks his word; a secretary and a podesta who argue respectively for and against forgiving Vico; a messenger who reports how Vico was put to death on special commission from the podesta, who had Juriste's authority to do so; and the captain of the prison, who brings the supposed head of Vico to Epitia.

Epitia refuses to plead for Juriste until she learns that her brother is alive. Believing that Juriste should be punished for evil intent, the Emperor is at first unwilling to pardon him even after Vico reappears, but he finally grants Epitia's suit in order that she may have "complete contentment."

WHETSTONE's *Promos and Cassandra* AND *Heptameron*

In the play, Promos is appointed to rule over the city of Julio, and declares his resolve to render justice impartially. Reviving a defunct law, he sentences Andrugio to death for incontinence. The law will not accept marriage as sufficient recompense for the wrong. Andrugio's sister, Cassandra, weeps over the hard fate of her young brother, who appeals to her to plead with Promos. She therefore meets Promos and obtains a postponement of the execution. After she has left, Promos reveals in a soliloquy that he has fallen in love with her but is determined to overcome the temptation. However, having been encouraged by his corrupt servant, Phallax, to believe that Cassandra might be overcome, he is unable to subdue his desire for her. When she meets him again to know his final decision, he first defends the law and then, when she pleads for mercy, makes his infamous proposal.

Amazed and horrified, Cassandra refuses. Promos promises to make her his wife and gives her two days in which to think it over. She goes to her brother's cell to inform him of Promos' vile condition and to prepare him for death. Andrugio, taken aback that a judge of Promos' supposed integrity has been corrupted by the same lust for which he would condemn another, appeals to his sister to accept the proposed terms and thereby save his life.

Brother and sister argue, but finally Cassandra is won over.

After satisfying his desire, Promos decides to break his word, since no one knows of his promise and Cassandra cannot reveal her own shame. He orders that Andrugio should be executed secretly and his head sent to Cassandra. While the girl is eagerly looking forward to welcoming her brother, the jailer brings her the severed head. She conceals her grief, pretending to be quite satisfied. She thinks of suicide, but later decides to appeal to the King. The jailer has in fact brought her the head of an executed criminal and released Andrugio, who goes into hiding. Promos is secretly troubled at what he has done.

In the second part of the play, the King comes to Julio. He hears Cassandra's story and promises to see that justice is done. Upon examination, Promos at once confesses, and the King orders that he first be married to Cassandra and then put to death. Promos pleads for mercy, but in vain. In the meantime, Andrugio, hiding in the woods, comes to know what is happening. Cassandra bewails her hard fate. Duty commands that she should love the husband for whose sentence she has been responsible. She appeals to the King to pardon him, but the ruler is adamant. Andrugio, now in the city under a disguise, sees his sister's unhappiness and resolves to surrender himself to the King at the risk of being put to death. Promos makes a sincere confession of his misdeeds and is led out to execution. Andrugio's boy enters with the news that his master is alive. The King pardons Andrugio, and then pardons Promos for the sake of Cassandra, exhorting Promos always to measure grace with justice. He restores him to the governorship of the city. "The lost sheep found, for joy the feast was made."

Whetstone's play has also a comic underplot, involving a courtesan, unscrupulous officers, informers, and bawds. With the corruption of the magistrates, all the city becomes corrupt.

The version in the *Heptameron* is substantially the same as that of the play. Andrugio is disguised as a hermit, and reveals himself after hearing the King say that Promos might be pardoned if Andrugio were alive. The entire story is narrated by one Isabella.

Summary

Measure for Measure is generally closer to Whetstone's versions than to *Epitia;* but it does show significant correspondences with Cinthio's play at certain points where Whetstone differs markedly. "The relation of *Measure for Measure* to Giraldi's *novella* is ambiguous, since some of the correspondences to that might have come through Whetstone, some through *Epitia*."[1] Among the similarities between *Measure for Measure* and *Epitia* may be mentioned the following: the secretary in *Epitia* protests to the podesta of the harshness of the law and the severity of its enforcement; in a soliloquy he comments on the rigor of those in power (compare Escalus' protests to Angelo in II.i); the criminal whose head is substituted for that of Vico is hopelessly evil (compare Ragozine, described as a notorious pirate); like Isabella, Epitia also distinguishes between act and intention. Some close verbal parallels have been noted by Kenneth Muir.[2]

---

[1] Madeleine Doran, *Endeavors of Art: A Study of Form in Elizabethan Drama.* Madison, Wisconsin: University of Wisconsin Press, 1954, pp. 386–387.

[2] *Shakespeare's Sources.* London: Methuen & Co., Ltd., 1957, I, 104–05.

Commentaries

WILLIAM HAZLITT

from *Characters of Shakespear's Plays*

This is a play as full of genius as it is of wisdom. Yet there is an original sin in the nature of the subject, which prevents us from taking a cordial interest in it. "The height of moral argument" which the author has maintained in the intervals of passion or blended with the more powerful impulses of nature, is hardly surpassed in any of his plays. But there is in general a want of passion; the affections are at a stand; our sympathies are repulsed and defeated in all directions. The only passion which influences the story is that of Angelo; and yet he seems to have a much greater passion for hypocrisy than for his mistress. Neither are we greatly enamored of Isabella's rigid chastity, though she could not act otherwise than she did. We do not feel the same confidence in the virtue that is "sublimely good" at another's expense, as if it had been put to some less disinterested trial. As to

From *Characters of Shakespear's Plays* by William Hazlitt. 2nd ed. London: Taylor & Hessey, 1818.

the Duke, who makes a very imposing and mysterious stage character, he is more absorbed in his own plots and gravity than anxious for the welfare of the state; more tenacious of his own character than attentive to the feelings and apprehensions of others. Claudio is the only person who feels naturally; and yet he is placed in circumstances of distress which almost preclude the wish for his deliverance. Mariana is also in love with Angelo, whom we hate. In this respect, there may be said to be a general system of cross purposes between the feelings of the different characters and the sympathy of the reader or the audience. This principle of repugnance seems to have reached its height in the character of Master Barnardine, who not only sets at defiance the opinions of others, but has even thrown off all self-regard—"one that apprehends death no more dreadfully but as a drunken sleep; careless, reckless, and fearless of what's past, present, and to come." He is a fine antithesis to the morality and the hypocrisy of the other characters of the play. Barnardine is Caliban transported from Prospero's wizard island to the forests of Bohemia or the prisons of Vienna. He is the creature of bad habits as Caliban is of gross instincts. He has however a strong notion of the natural fitness of things, according to his own sensations—"He has been drinking hard all night, and he will not be hanged that day"—and Shakespear has let him off at last. We do not understand why the philosophical German critic, Schlegel, should be so severe on those pleasant persons, Lucio, Pompey, and Master Froth, as to call them "wretches." They appear all mighty comfortable in their occupations, and determined to pursue them, "as the flesh and fortune should serve." A very good exposure of the want of self-knowledge and contempt for others, which is so common in the world, is put into the mouth of Abhorson, the jailor, when the Provost proposes to associate Pompey with him in his office—"A bawd, sir? Fie upon him, he will discredit our mystery." And the same answer will serve in nine instances out of ten to the same kind of remark, "Go to, sir, you weigh equally; a feather will turn the scale." Shakespear was in one sense the least moral of all writers; for morality (commonly so called) is made up of antipathies; and his talent consisted in sympathy with human nature, in all its shapes, degrees, depressions, and elevations. The object of the pedantic moralist is to find out the bad in everything: his was to show that "there is some soul of goodness in things evil." Even Master Barnardine is not left to the mercy of what others think of him; but when he comes in, speaks for himself, and pleads his own cause, as well as if counsel had been assigned him. In one sense, Shakespear was no moralist at all: in another, he was the greatest of all moralists. He was a moralist in the same sense in which nature is one. He taught what he had learnt from her. He showed the greatest knowledge of humanity with the greatest fellow-feeling for it.

WALTER PATER

"Measure for Measure"

In *Measure for Measure,* as in some other of his plays,
Shakespeare has remodeled an earlier and somewhat
rough composition to "finer issues," suffering much to
remain as it had come from the less skillful hand, and not
raising the whole of his work to an equal degree of intensity. Hence perhaps some of that depth and weighti-
ness which make this play so impressive, as with the true
seal of experience, like a fragment of life itself, rough and
disjointed indeed, but forced to yield in places its profounder meaning. In *Measure for Measure,* in contrast
with the flawless execution of *Romeo and Juliet,* Shakespeare has spent his art in just enough modification of the
scheme of the older play to make it exponent of this
purpose, adapting its terrible essential incidents, so that
Coleridge found it the only painful work among Shakespeare's dramas, and leaving for the reader of today more
than the usual number of difficult expressions; but infus-
ing a lavish color and a profound significance into it, so
that under his touch certain select portions of it rise far
above the level of all but his own best poetry, and working
out of it a morality so characteristic that the play might
well pass for the central expression of his moral judgments. It remains a comedy, as indeed is congruous with
the bland, half-humorous equity which informs the whole

From *Appreciations* (1889).

composition, sinking from the heights of sorrow and terror into the rough scheme of the earlier piece; yet it is hardly less full of what is really tragic in man's existence than if Claudio had indeed "stooped to death." Even the humorous concluding scenes have traits of special grace, retaining in less emphatic passages a stray line or word of power, as it seems, so that we watch to the end for the traces where the nobler hand has glanced along, leaving its vestiges, as if accidentally or wastefully, in the rising of the style.

The interest of *Measure for Measure,* therefore, is partly that of an old story told over again. We measure with curiosity that variety of resources which has enabled Shakespeare to refashion the original material with a higher motive; adding to the intricacy of the piece, yet so modifying its structure as to give the whole almost the unity of a single scene; lending, by the light of a philosophy which dwells much on what is complex and subtle in our nature, a true human propriety to its strange and unexpected turns of feeling and character, to incidents so difficult as the fall of Angelo, and the subsequent reconciliation of Isabella, so that she pleads successfully for his life. It was from Whetstone, a contemporary English writer, that Shakespeare derived the outline of Cinthio's "rare history" of *Promos and Cassandra,* one of that numerous class of Italian stories, like Boccaccio's *Tancred of Salerno,* in which the mere energy of southern passion has everything its own way, and which, though they may repel many a northern reader by a certain crudity in their coloring, seem to have been full of fascination for the Elizabethan age. This story, as it appears in Whetstone's endless comedy, is almost as rough as the roughest episode of actual criminal life. But the play seems never to have been acted, and some time after its publication Whetstone himself turned the thing into a tale, included in his *Heptameron of Civil Discourses,* where it still figures as a genuine piece, with touches of undesigned poetry, a quaint field-flower here and there of diction or sentiment, the whole strung up to an effective brevity, and with the fragrance of that admirable age of literature

all about it. Here, then, there is something of the original
Italian color: in this narrative Shakespeare may well have
caught the first glimpse of a composition with nobler
proportions; and some artless sketch from his own hand,
perhaps, putting together his first impressions, insinuated
itself between Whetstone's work and the play as we actually read it. Out of these insignificant sources Shakespeare's play rises, full of solemn expression, and with a
profoundly designed beauty, the new body of a higher,
though sometimes remote and difficult poetry, escaping
from the imperfect relics of the old story, yet not wholly
transformed, and even as it stands but the preparation
only, we might think, of a still more imposing design.
For once we have in it a real example of that sort of
writing which is sometimes described as *suggestive*, and
which by the help of certain subtly calculated hints only,
brings into distinct shape the reader's own half-developed
imaginings. Often the quality is attributed to writing
merely vague and unrealized, but in *Measure for Measure*,
quite certainly, Shakespeare has directed the attention of
sympathetic readers along certain channels of meditation
beyond the immediate scope of his work.

Measure for Measure, therefore, by the quality of these
higher designs, woven by his strange magic on a texture
of poorer quality, is hardly less indicative than *Hamlet*
even, of Shakespeare's reason, of his power of moral
interpretation. It deals, not like *Hamlet* with the problems
which beset one of exceptional temperament, but with
mere human nature. It brings before us a group of persons, attractive, full of desire, vessels of the genial, seed-
bearing powers of nature, a gaudy existence flowering
out over the old court and city of Vienna, a spectacle
of the fullness and pride of life which to some may seem
to touch the verge of wantonness. Behind this group of
people, behind their various actions, Shakespeare inspires
in us the sense of a strong tyranny of nature and circumstance. Then what shall there be on this side of it—on
our side, the spectators' side, of this painted screen, with
its puppets who are really glad or sorry all the time?
what philosophy of life, what sort of equity?

Stimulated to read more carefully by Shakespeare's own profounder touches, the reader will note the vivid reality, the subtle interchange of light and shade, the strongly contrasted characters of this group of persons, passing across the stage so quickly. The slightest of them is at least not ill-natured: the meanest of them can put forth a plea for existence—*Truly, sir, I am a poor fellow that would live!*—they are never sure of themselves, even in the strong tower of a cold unimpressible nature: they are capable of many friendships and of a true dignity in danger, giving each other a sympathetic, if transitory, regret—one sorry that another "should be foolishly lost at a game of tick-tack." Words which seem to exhaust man's deepest sentiment concerning death and life are put on the lips of a gilded, witless youth; and the saintly Isabella feels fire creep along her, kindling her tongue to eloquence at the suggestion of shame. In places the shadow deepens: death intrudes itself on the scene, as among other things "a great disguiser," blanching the features of youth and spoiling its goodly hair, touching the fine Claudio even with its disgraceful associations. As in Orcagna's fresco at Pisa, it comes capriciously, giving many and long reprieves to Barnardine, who has been waiting for it nine years in prison, taking another thence by fever, another by mistake of judgment, embracing others in the midst of their music and song. The little mirror of existence, which reflects to each for a moment the stage on which he plays, is broken at last by a capricious accident; while all alike, in their yearning for untasted enjoyment, are really discounting their days, grasping so hastily and accepting so inexactly the precious pieces. The Duke's quaint but excellent moralizing at the beginning of the third act does but express, like the chorus of a Greek play, the spirit of the passing incidents. To him in Shakespeare's play, to a few here and there in the actual world, this strange practical paradox of our life, so unwise in its eager haste, reveals itself in all its clearness.

The Duke disguised as a friar, with his curious moralizing on life and death, and Isabella in her first mood of

renunciation, a thing "ensky'd and sainted," come with
the quiet of the cloister as a relief to this lust and pride
of life: like some gray monastic picture hung on the wall
of a gaudy room, their presence cools the heated air of
the piece. For a moment we are within the placid conventual walls, whither they fancy at first that the Duke
has come as a man crossed in love, with Friar Thomas
and Friar Peter, calling each other by their homely, English names, or at the nunnery among the novices, with
their little limited privileges, where

> If you speak you must not show your face,
> Or if you show your face you must not speak.
>
> (I.iv.12–13)

Not less precious for this relief in the general structure
of the piece, than for its own peculiar graces is the episode
of Mariana, a creature wholly of Shakespeare's invention,
told, by way of interlude, in subdued prose. The moated
grange, with its dejected mistress, its long, listless, discon-
tented days, where we hear only the voice of a boy broken
off suddenly in the midst of one of the loveliest songs
of Shakespeare, or of Shakespeare's school,[1] is the pleas-
antest of many glimpses we get here of pleasant places—
the fields without the town, Angelo's gardenhouse, the
consecrated fountain. Indirectly it has suggested two of
the most perfect compositions among the poetry of our
own generation. Again it is a picture within a picture,
but with fainter lines and a grayer atmosphere: we have
here the same passions, the same wrongs, the same continuance of affection, the same crying out upon death,
as in the nearer and larger piece, though softened, and
reduced to the mood of a more dreamy scene.

Of Angelo we may feel at first sight inclined to say
only *guarda e passa!* or to ask whether he is indeed psychologically possible. In the old story, he figures as an
embodiment of pure and unmodified evil, like "Hyliogaba-
lus of Rome or Denis of Sicyll." But the embodiment of
pure evil is no proper subject of art, and Shakespeare,
in the spirit of a philosophy which dwells much on the

---

[1] Fletcher, in the *Bloody Brother*, gives the rest of it.

complications of outward circumstance with men's inclinations, turns into a subtle study in casuistry this incident
of the austere judge fallen suddenly into utmost corruption by a momentary contact with supreme purity. But the
main interest in *Measure for Measure* is not, as in *Promos
and Cassandra,* in the relation of Isabella and Angelo,
but rather in the relation of Claudio and Isabella.

Greek tragedy in some of its noblest products has taken
for its theme the love of a sister, a sentiment unimpas-
sioned indeed, purifying by the very spectacle of its pas-
sionlessness, but capable of a fierce and almost animal
strength if informed for a moment by pity and regret. At
first Isabella comes upon the scene as a tranquilizing influence in it. But Shakespeare, in the development of the
action, brings quite different and unexpected qualities out
of her. It is his characteristic poetry to expose this cold,
chastened personality, respected even by the worldly
Lucio as "something ensky'd and sainted, and almost
an immortal spirit," to two sharp, shameful trials, and
wring out of her a fiery, revealing eloquence. Thrown
into the terrible dilemma of the piece, called upon to
sacrifice that cloistral whiteness to sisterly affection, become in a moment the ground of strong, contending passions, she develops a new character and shows herself
suddenly of kindred with those strangely conceived women,
like Webster's Vittoria, who unite to a seductive sweetness something of a dangerous and tigerlike changefulness
of feeling. The swift, vindictive anger leaps, like a white
flame, into this white spirit, and, stripped in a moment
of all convention, she stands before us clear, detached,
columnar, among the tender frailties of the piece. Cassandra, the original of Isabella in Whetstone's tale, with
the purpose of the Roman Lucretia in her mind, yields
gracefully enough to the conditions of her brother's safety;
and to the lighter reader of Shakespeare there may seem
something harshly conceived, or psychologically impossible even, in the suddenness of the change wrought in
her, as Claudio welcomes for a moment the chance of
life through her compliance with Angelo's will, and he
may have a sense here of flagging skill, as in words less

inely handled than in the preceding scene. The play,
though still not without traces of nobler handiwork, sinks
down, as we know, at last into almost homely comedy,
and it might be supposed that just here the grander manner deserted it. But the skill with which Isabella plays
upon Claudio's well-recognized sense of honor, and endeavors by means of that to insure him beforehand from
the acceptance of life on baser terms, indicates no coming
laxity of hand just in this place. It was rather that there
rose in Shakespeare's conception, as there may for the
reader, as there certainly would in any good acting of the
part, something of that terror, the seeking for which is
one of the notes of romanticism in Shakespeare and his
circle. The stream of ardent natural affection, poured as
sudden hatred upon the youth condemned to die, adds
an additional note of expression to the horror of the
prison where so much of the scene takes place. It is not
here only that Shakespeare has conceived of such extreme
anger and pity as putting a sort of genius into simple
women, so that their "lips drop eloquence," and their
intuitions interpret that which is often too hard or fine
for manlier reason; and it is Isabella with her grand
imaginative diction, and that poetry laid upon the "prone
and speechless dialect" there is in mere youth itself, who
gives utterance to the equity, the finer judgments of the
piece on men and things.

From behind this group with its subtle lights and shades,
its poetry, its impressive contrasts, Shakespeare, as I said,
conveys to us a strong sense of the tyranny of nature and
circumstance over human action. The most powerful expressions of this side of experience might be found here.
The bloodless, impassible temperament does but wait for
opportunity, for the almost accidental coherence of
time with place, and place with wishing, to annul its long
and patient discipline, and become in a moment the very
opposite of that which under ordinary conditions it seemed
to be, even to itself. The mere resolute self-assertion of
the blood brings to others special temptations, temptations
which, as defects or overgrowths, lie in the very qualities
which make them otherwise imposing or attractive; the

very advantage of men's gifts of intellect or sentiment being dependent on a balance in their use so delicate that men hardly maintain it always. Something also must be conceded to influences merely physical, to the complexion of the heavens, the skyey influences, shifting as the stars shift; as something also to the mere caprice of men exercised over each other in the dispensations of social or political order, to the chance which makes the life or death of Claudio dependent on Angelo's will.

The many veins of thought which render the poetry of this play so weighty and impressive unite in the image of Claudio, a flowerlike young man, whom, prompted by a few hints from Shakespeare, the imagination easily clothes with all the bravery of youth, as he crosses the stage before us on his way to death, coming so hastily to the end of his pilgrimage. Set in the horrible blackness of the prison, with its various forms of unsightly death, this flower seems the braver. Fallen by "prompture of the blood," the victim of a suddenly revived law against the common fault of youth like his, he finds his life forfeited as if by the chance of a lottery. With that instinctive clinging to life, which breaks through the subtlest casuistries of monk or sage apologizing for an early death, he welcomes for a moment the chance of life through his sister's shame, though he revolts hardly less from the notion of perpetual imprisonment so repulsive to the buoyant energy of youth. Familiarized, by the words alike of friends and the indifferent, to the thought of death, he becomes gentle and subdued indeed, yet more perhaps through pride than real resignation, and would go down to darkness at last hard and unblinded. Called upon suddenly to encounter his fate, looking with keen and resolute profile straight before him, he gives utterance to some of the central truths of human feeling, the sincere, concentrated expression of the recoiling flesh. Thoughts as profound and poetical as Hamlet's arise in him; and but for the accidental arrest of sentence he would descend into the dust, a mere gilded, idle flower of youth indeed, but with what are perhaps the most eloquent of all Shakespeare's words upon his lips.

As Shakespeare in *Measure for Measure* has refashioned, after a nobler pattern, materials already at hand, so that the relics of other men's poetry are incorporated into his perfect work, so traces of the old "morality," that early form of dramatic composition which had for its function the inculcating of some moral theme, survive in it also, and give it a peculiar ethical interest. This ethical interest, though it can escape no attentive reader, yet, in accordance with that artistic law which demands the predominance of form everywhere over the mere matter or subject handled, is not to be wholly separated from the special circumstances, necessities, embarrassments, of these particular dramatic persons. The old "moralities" exemplified most often some rough-and-ready lesson. Here the very intricacy and subtlety of the moral world itself, the difficulty of seizing the true relations of so complex a material, the difficulty of just judgment, of judgment that shall not be unjust, are the lessons conveyed. Even in Whetstone's old story this peculiar vein of moralizing comes to the surface: even there, we notice the tendency to dwell on mixed motives, the contending issues of action, the presence of virtues and vices alike in unexpected places, on "the hard choice of two evils," on the "imprisoning" of men's "real intents." *Measure for Measure* is full of expressions drawn from a profound experience of these casuistries, and that ethical interest becomes predominant in it: it is no longer *Promos and Cassandra,* but *Measure for Measure,* its new name expressly suggesting the subject of *poetical justice.* The action of the play, like the action of life itself for the keener observer, develops in us the conception of this poetical justice, and the yearning to realize it, the true justice of which Angelo knows nothing, because it lies for the most part beyond the limits of any acknowledged law. The idea of justice involves the idea of rights. But at bottom rights are equivalent to that which really is, to facts; and the recognition of his rights therefore, the justice he requires of our hands, or our thoughts, is the recognition of that which the person, in his inmost nature, really is; and as sympathy alone can discover that which really is in matters of feeling and thought, true justice is in its essence a finer knowledge through love.

> 'Tis very pregnant:
> The jewel that we find we stoop and take it,
> Because we see it; but what we do not see
> We tread upon, and never think of it.
>
> (II.i.23–26)

It is for this finer justice, a justice based on a more delicate appreciation of the true conditions of men and things, a true respect of persons in our estimate of actions, that the people in *Measure for Measure* cry out as they pass before us; and as the poetry of this play is full of the peculiarities of Shakespeare's poetry, so in its ethics it is an epitome of Shakespeare's moral judgments. They are the moral judgments of an observer, of one who sits as a spectator, and knows how the threads in the design before him hold together under the surface: they are the judgments of the humorist also, who follows with a half-amused but always pitiful sympathy, the various ways of human disposition, and sees less distance than ordinary men between what are called respectively great and little things. It is not always that poetry can be the exponent of morality; but it is this aspect of morals which it represents most naturally, for this true justice is dependent on just those finer appreciations which poetry cultivates in us the power of making, those peculiar valuations of action and its effect which poetry actually requires.
[1874]

G. WILSON KNIGHT

"Measure for Measure" and the Gospels

In *Measure for Measure* we have a careful dramatic pattern, a studied explication of a central theme: the moral nature of man in relation to the crudity of man's justice, especially in the matter of sexual vice. There is, too, a clear relation existing between the play and the Gospels, for the play's theme is this:

> Judge not, that ye be not judged. For with what judgment ye judge, ye shall be judged: and with what measure ye mete, it shall be measured to you again.
>
> (Matthew 7:1–2)

The ethical standards of the Gospels are rooted in the thought of *Measure for Measure*. Therefore, in this analysis we shall, while fixing attention primarily on the play, yet inevitably find a reference to the New Testament continually helpful, and sometimes essential.

Measure for Measure is a carefully constructed work. Not until we view it as a deliberate artistic pattern of certain pivot ideas determining the play's action throughout shall we understand its peculiar nature. Though there is consummate psychological insight here and at least one

From *The Wheel of Fire* by G. Wilson Knight. 4th ed. rev. London: Methuen & Co., Ltd.; New York: British Book Centre, 1949. Reprinted by permission of Methuen & Co., Ltd.

person of most vivid and poignant human interest, we must first have regard to the central theme, and only second look for exact verisimilitude to ordinary processes of behavior. We must be careful not to let our human interest in any one person distort our single vision of the whole pattern. The play tends towards allegory or symbolism. The poet elects to risk a certain stiffness, or arbitrariness, in the directing of his plot rather than fail to express dramatically, with variety and precision, the full content of his basic thought. Any stiffness in the matter of human probability is, however, more than balanced by its extreme fecundity and compacted significance of dramatic symbolism. The persons of the play tend to illustrate certain human qualities chosen with careful reference to the main theme. Thus Isabella stands for sainted purity, Angelo for Pharisaical righteousness, the Duke for a psychologically sound and enlightened ethic. Lucio represents indecent wit, Pompey and Mistress Overdone professional immorality. Barnardine is hardheaded, criminal insensitiveness. Each person illumines some facet of the central theme: man's moral nature. The play's attention is confined chiefly to sexual ethics: which in isolation is naturally the most pregnant of analysis and the most universal of all themes. No other subject provides so clear a contrast between human consciousness and human instinct; so rigid a distinction between the civilized and the natural qualities of man; so amazing, yet so slight, a boundary set in the public mind between the foully bestial and the ideally divine in humanity. The atmosphere, purpose, and meaning of the play are throughout ethical. The Duke, lord of this play in the exact sense that Prospero is lord of *The Tempest,* is the prophet of an enlightened ethic. He controls the action from start to finish, he allots, as it were, praise and blame, he is lit at moments with divine suggestion comparable with his almost divine power of foreknowledge, and control, and wisdom. There is an enigmatic, otherworldly mystery suffusing his figure and the meaning of his acts: their results, however, in each case justify their initiation; wherein we see the allegorical nature of the play, since the plot is so arranged that each person receives his deserts in the light of the Duke's—which is really the Gospel—ethic.

The poetic atmosphere is one of religion and critical morality. The religious coloring is orthodox, as in *Hamlet*. Isabella is a novice among "the votarists of St. Clare" (I.iv.5); the Duke disguises himself as a Friar, exercising the divine privileges of his office towards Juliet, Barnardine, Claudio, Pompey. We hear of "the consecrated fount a league below the city" (IV.iii.99). The thought of death's eternal damnation, which is prominent in *Hamlet*, recurs in Claudio's speech:

> Ay, but to die and go we know not where;
> To lie in cold obstruction and to rot;
> This sensible warm motion to become
> A kneaded clod; and the delighted spirit
> To bathe in fiery floods, or to reside
> In thrilling region of thick-ribbed ice;
> To be imprison'd in the viewless winds,
> And blown with restless violence round about
> The pendant world; or to be worse than worst
> Of those that lawless and incertain thoughts
> Imagine howling: 'tis too horrible!
> The weariest and most loathed worldly life
> That age, ache, penury, and imprisonment
> Can lay on nature is a paradise
> To what we fear in death.

(III.i.118–32)

So powerful can orthodox eschatology be in *Measure for Measure*: it is not, as I shall show, all-powerful. Nor is the play primarily a play of death philosophy: its theme is rather that of the Gospel ethic. And there is no more beautiful passage in all Shakespeare on the Christian redemption than Isabella's lines to Angelo:

> Alas! Alas!
> Why, all the souls that were, were forfeit once;
> And He, that might the vantage best have took
> Found out the remedy. How would you be,
> If He which is the top of judgment, should

But judge you as you are? O, think on that;
And mercy then will breathe within your lips,
Like man new made.

(II.ii.72–79)

This is the natural sequence to Isabella's earlier lines:

Well, believe this,
No ceremony that to great ones 'longs,
Not the king's crown, nor the deputed sword,
The marshal's truncheon, nor the judge's robe,
Become them with one half so good a grace
As mercy does.   (II.ii.58–63)

These thoughts are a repetition of those in Portia's famous "mercy" speech. There they come as a sudden, gleaming, almost irrelevant beam of the ethical imagination. But here they are not irrelevant: they are intrinsic with the thought of the whole play, the pivot of its movement. In *The Merchant of Venice* the Gospel reference is explicit:

. . . we do pray for mercy;
And that same prayer doth teach us all to render
The deeds of mercy.   (IV.i)

And the central idea of *Measure for Measure* is this:

And forgive us our debts as we forgive our debtors.
(Matthew 6:12)

Thus "justice" is a mockery: man, himself a sinner, cannot presume to judge. That is the lesson driven home in *Measure for Measure*.

The atmosphere of Christianity pervading the play merges into the purely ethical suggestion implicit in the inter-criticism of all the persons. Though the Christian ethic be the central theme, there is a wider setting of varied ethical thought, voiced by each person in turn, high or low. The Duke, Angelo, and Isabella are clearly obsessed with such ideas and criticize freely in their dif-

ferent fashions. So also Elbow and the officers bring in
Froth and Pompey, accusing them. Abhorson is severely
critical of Pompey:

> A bawd? Fie upon him! He will discredit our mystery.
> (IV.ii.28–29)

Lucio traduces the Duke's character, Mistress Overdone
informs against Lucio. Barnadine is universally despised.
All, that is, react to each other in an essentially ethical
mode: which mode is the peculiar and particular vision
of this play. Even music is brought to the bar of the
ethical judgment:

> ... music oft hath such a charm
> To make bad good, and good provoke to harm.
> (IV.i.14–15)

Such is the dominating atmosphere of this play. Out of it
grow the main themes, the problem and the lesson of
Measure for Measure. There is thus a pervading atmosphere of orthodoxy and ethical criticism, in which is cen-
tered the mysterious holiness, the profound death-philoso-
phy, the enlightened human insight and Christian ethic
of the protagonist, the Duke of Vienna.

The satire of the play is directed primarily against self-
conscious, self-protected righteousness. The Duke starts
the action by resigning his power to Angelo. He addresses
Angelo, outspoken in praise of his virtues, thus:

> Angelo,
> There is a kind of character in thy life,
> That to the observer doth thy history
> Fully unfold. Thyself and thy belongings
> Are not thine own so proper, as to waste
> Thyself upon thy virtue, they on thee.
> Heaven doth with us as we with torches do;
> Not light them for themselves; for if our virtues
> Did not go forth of us, 'twere all alike
> As if we had them not. Spirits are not finely touch'd,
> But to fine issues, nor Nature never lends

> The smallest scruple of her excellence,
> But, like a thrifty goddess, she determines
> Herself the glory of a creditor,
> Both thanks and use.   (I.i.26–40)

The thought is similar to that of the Sermon on the Mount:

> Ye are the light of the world. A city that is set on an
> hill cannot be hid. Neither do men light a candle, and
> put it under a bushel, but on a candlestick; and it giveth
> light unto all that are in the house.
>
> (Matthew 5:14–15)

Not only does the Duke's "torch" metaphor clearly recall
this passage, but his development of it is vividly paralleled
by other of Jesus' words. The Duke compares "Nature"
to "a creditor," lending qualities and demanding both
"thanks and use." Compare:

> For the Kingdom of Heaven is as a man traveling
> into a far country, who called his own servants, and
> delivered unto them his goods.
> And unto one he gave five talents, to another two,
> and to another one; to every man according to his sev-
> eral ability; and straightway took his journey.
>
> (Matthew 25:14–15)

The sequel needs no quotation. Now, though Angelo
modestly refuses the honor, the Duke insists, forcing it on
him. Later, in conversation with Friar Thomas, himself
disguised as a Friar now, he gives us reason for his strange
act:

> We have strict statutes and most biting laws,
> The needful bits and curbs to headstrong steeds,
> Which for this nineteen years we have let slip;
> Even like an o'ergrown lion in a cave,
> That goes not out to prey. Now, as fond fathers,
> Having bound up the threatening twigs of birch,
> Only to stick it in their children's sight
> For terror, not to use, in time the rod
> Becomes more mock'd than fear'd; so our decrees,

Dead to infliction, to themselves are dead;
And liberty plucks justice by the nose;
The baby beats the nurse, and quite athwart
Goes all decorum.
                                        (I.iii.19–31)

Therefore he has given Angelo power and command to
"strike home." Himself he will not exact justice, since he
has already, by his laxity, as good as bade the people sin
by his "permissive pass": the people could not readily
understand such a change in himself—with a new governor it would be different. But these are not his only reasons. He ends:

                 Moe reasons for this action
     At our more leisure shall I render you;
     Only, this one: Lord Angelo is precise;
     Stands at a guard with envy; scarce confesses
     That his blood flows, or that his appetite
     Is more to bread than stone: hence shall we see
     If power change purpose, what our seemers be.
                                        (I.iii.48–54)

The rest of the play slowly unfolds the rich content of the
Duke's plan, and the secret, too, of his lax rule.
Escalus tells us that the Duke was

     One that, above all other strifes, contended especially to
     know himself.   (III.ii.235–36)

But he has studied others, besides himself. He prides himself on his knowledge:

     There is written in your brow, provost, honesty and
     constancy: if I read it not truly, my ancient skill be-
     guiles me . . .
                                        (IV.ii.156–58)

Herein are the causes of his leniency. His government
has been inefficient, not through an inherent weakness or
laxity in him, but rather because meditation and self-
analysis, together with profound study of human nature,
have shown him that all passions and sins from other men

have reflected images in his own soul. He is no weakling:
he has been "a scholar, a statesman, and a soldier"
(III.ii.148). But to such a philosopher government and
justice may begin to appear a mockery, and become ab-
horrent. His judicial method has been original: all crimi-
nals were either executed promptly or else freely released
(IV.ii.135–37). Nowhere is the peculiar modernity of the
Duke in point of advanced psychology more vividly apparent. It seems, too, if we are to judge by his treatment
of Barnadine (IV.iii.65–82), that he could not tolerate
an execution without the criminal's own approval! The
case of Barnadine troubles him intensely:

> A creature unprepared, unmeet for death;
> And to transport him in the mind he is
> Were damnable.   (IV.iii.68–70)

The Duke's sense of human responsibility is delightful
throughout: he is like a kindly father, and all the rest are
his children. Thus he now performs the experiment of
handing the reins of government to a man of ascetic purity
who has an hitherto invulnerable faith in the rightness and
justice of his own ideals—a man of spotless reputation
and self-conscious integrity, who will have no fears as to
the "justice" of enforcing precise obedience. The scheme
is a plot, or trap: a scientific experiment to see if extreme
ascetic righteousness can stand the test of power.

The Duke, disguised as the Friar, moves through the
play, a dark figure, directing, watching, moralizing on the
actions of the other persons. As the play progresses and
his plot on Angelo works he assumes an ever-increasing
mysterious dignity, his original purpose seems to become
more and more profound in human insight, the action
marches with measured pace to its appointed and logical
end. We have ceased altogether to think of the Duke as
merely a studious and unpractical governor, incapable
of office. Rather he holds, within the dramatic universe,
the dignity and power of a Prospero, to whom he is
strangely similar. With both, their plot and plan is the
plot and plan of the play: they make and forge the play,

and thus are automatically to be equated in a unique sense with the poet himself—since both are symbols of the poet's controlling, purposeful, combined, movement of the chessmen of the drama. Like Prospero, the Duke tends to assume proportions evidently divine. Once he is actually compared to the Supreme Power:

> O my dread lord,
> I should be guiltier than my guiltiness,
> To think I can be undiscernible,
> When I perceive your grace, like power divine,
> Hath look'd upon my passes.
>
> (V.i.369–73)

So speaks Angelo at the end. We are prepared for it long before. In the rhymed octosyllabic couplets of the Duke's soliloquy in III.ii there is a distinct note of supernatural authority, forecasting the rhymed mystic utterances of divine beings in the Final Plays. He has been talking with Escalus and the Provost, and dismisses them with the words:

> Peace be with you!

They leave him and he soliloquizes:

> He who the sword of Heaven will bear
> Should be as holy as severe;
> Pattern in himself to know
> Grace to stand and virtue go;
> More nor less to other paying
> Than by self-offenses weighing.
> Shame to him whose cruel striking
> Kills for faults of his own liking!
> Twice treble shame on Angelo,
> To weed my vice and let his grow!
> O what may man within him hide,
> Though angel on the outward side!
> How may likeness made in crimes,
> Making practice on the times,
> To draw with idle spiders' strings
> Most ponderous and substantial things!

Craft against vice I must apply:
With Angelo tonight shall lie
His old betrothed but despised;
So disguise shall, by the disguised,
Pay with falsehood false exacting,
And perform an old contracting.

(III.ii.264–85)

This fine soliloquy gives us the Duke's philosophy: the philosophy that prompted his original plan. And it is important to notice the mystical, prophetic tone of the speech.

The Duke, like Jesus, is the prophet of a new order of ethics. This aspect of the Duke as teacher and prophet is also illustrated by his cryptic utterance to Escalus just before this soliloquy:

Escalus. Good even, good father.

Duke. Bliss and goodness on you.

Escalus. Of whence are you?

Duke. Not of this country, though my chance is now
To use it for my time: I am a brother
Of gracious order, late come from the See
In special business from his Holiness.

Escalus. What news abroad i' the world?

Duke. None, but that there is so great a fever on goodness, that the dissolution of it must cure it: novelty is only in request; and it is as dangerous to be aged in any kind of course, as it is virtuous to be constant in any undertaking. There is scarce truth enough alive to make societies secure; but security enough to make fellowships accursed: much upon this riddle runs the wisdom of the world. This news is old enough, yet it is every day's news. I pray you, sir, of what disposition was the Duke?

Escalus. One that, above all other strifes, contended especially to know himself.

(III.ii.217–36)

This remarkable speech, with its deliberate, incisive, cryptic sentences, has a profound quality and purpose which reaches the very heart of the play. It deserves exact attention. Its expanded paraphrase runs thus:

No news, but that goodness is suffering such a disease that a complete dissolution of it (goodness) is needed to cure it. That is, our whole system of conventional ethics should be destroyed and rebuilt. A change (novelty) never gets beyond request, that is, is never actually put in practice. And it is as dangerous to continue indefinitely a worn-out system or order of government, as it is praiseworthy to be constant in any individual undertaking. There is scarcely enough knowledge of human nature current in the world to make societies safe; but ignorant self-confidence (i.e., in matters of justice) enough to make human intercourse within a society a miserable thing. This riddle holds the key to the wisdom of the world (probably, both the false wisdom of the unenlightened, and the true wisdom of great teachers). This news is old enough, and yet the need for its understanding sees daily proof.

I paraphrase freely, admittedly interpreting difficulties in the light of the recurring philosophy of this play on the blindness of men's moral judgments, and especially in the light of the Duke's personal moral attitude as read from his other words and actions. This speech holds the poetry of ethics. Its content, too, is very close to the Gospel teaching, the insistence on the blindness of the world, its habitual disregard of the truth exposed by prophet and teacher:

And this is the condemnation, that light is come into the world, and men loved darkness rather than light, because their deeds were evil.   (John 3:19)

The same almost divine suggestion rings in many of the Duke's measured prose utterances. There are his supremely beautiful words to Escalus (IV.ii.206–09):

Look, the unfolding star calls up the shepherd. Put

not yourself into amazement how these things should
be: all difficulties are but easy when they are known.

The first lovely sentence—a unique beauty of Shakespearean prose, in a style peculiar to this play—derives
part of its appeal from New Testament associations, and
the second sentence holds the mystic assurance of Matthew 10:26:

> . . . for there is nothing covered, that shall not be re-
> vealed; and hid, that shall not be known.

The Duke exercises the authority of a teacher throughout
his disguise as a friar. He speaks authoritatively on repentance to Juliet:

> *Duke.*   . . . but lest you do repent,
> As that the sin hath brought you to this shame,
> Which sorrow is always towards ourselves, not Heaven,
> Showing we would not spare Heaven as we love it,
> But as we stand in fear——
>
> *Juliet.* I do repent me as it is an evil,
> And take the shame with joy.
>
> *Duke.* There rest . . .   (II.iii.30–36)

After rebuking Pompey the bawd very sternly but not
unkindly, he concludes:

> Go mend, go mend.   (III.ii.28)

His attitude is that of Jesus to the woman taken in adultery:

> Neither do I condemn thee: go, and sin no more.
>   (John 8:11)

Both are more kindly disposed towards honest impurity
than light and frivolous scandalmongers, such as Lucio,
or Pharisaic self-righteousness such as Angelo's.

The Duke's ethical attitude is exactly correspondent

with Jesus': the play must be read in the light of the
Gospel teaching, if its full significance is to be apparent.
So he, like Jesus, moves among men suffering grief at
their sins and deriving joy from an unexpected flower of
simple goodness in the deserts of impurity and hardness.
He finds softness of heart where he least expects it—in
the Provost of the prison:

> *Duke.* This is a gentle provost: seldom when
>   The steeled jailer is the friend of men.   (IV.ii.88–89)

So, too, Jesus finds in the centurion,

> a man under authority, having soldiers under me . . .
>   (Matthew 8:9)

a simple faith where he least expects it:

> . . . I say unto you, I have not found so great faith,
> no, not in Israel.

The two incidents are very similar in quality. Now, in that
he represents a perfected ethical philosophy joined to
supreme authority, the Duke is, within the dramatic universe, automatically comparable with Divinity; or we may
suggest that he progresses by successive modes, from
worldly power through the prophecy and moralizing of
the middle scenes, to the supreme judgment at the end,
where he exactly reflects the universal judgment as suggested by many Gospel passages. There is the same apparent injustice, the same tolerance and mercy. The Duke
is, in fact, a symbol of the same kind as the Father in the
Parable of the Prodigal Son (Luke 15) or the Lord in that
of the Unmerciful Servant (Matthew 18). The simplest
way to focus correctly the quality and unity of *Measure
for Measure* is to read it on the analogy of Jesus' parables.
   Though his ethical philosophy is so closely related to
the Gospel teaching, yet the Duke's thoughts on death
are devoid of any explicit belief in immortality. He addresses Claudio, who is to die, and his words at first appear
vague, agnostic: but a deeper acquaintance renders their

profundity and truth. Claudio fears death. The Duke comforts him by concentrating not on death, but on life. In a series of pregnant sentences he asserts the negative nature of any single life-joy. First, life is slave to death and may fail at any chance moment; however much you run from death, yet you cannot but run still towards it; nobility in man is inextricably twined with "baseness" (this is, indeed, the moral of *Measure for Measure*), and courage is ever subject to fear; sleep is man's "best rest," yet he fears death which is but sleep; man is not a single independent unit, he has no solitary self to lose, but rather is compounded of universal "dust"; he is always discontent, striving for what he has not, forgetful of that which he succeeds in winning; man is a changing, wavering substance; his riches he wearily carries till death unloads him; he is tortured by disease and old age. The catalogue is strong in unremittent condemnation of life:

> Thou hast nor youth nor age,
> But, as it were, an after-dinner's sleep,
> Dreaming on both; for all thy blessed youth
> Becomes as aged, and doth beg the alms
> Of palsied eld; and when thou art old and rich,
> Thou hast neither heat, affection, limb, nor beauty,
> To make thy riches pleasant. What's yet in this
> That bears the name of life? Yet in this life
> Lie hid moe thousand deaths: yet death we fear,
> That makes these odds all even.   (III.i.32–41)

Life is therefore a sequence of unrealities, strung together in a time succession. Everything it can give is in turn killed. Regarded thus, it is unreal, a delusion, a living death. The thought is profound. True, the Duke has concentrated especially on the temporal aspect of life's appearances, regarding only the shell of life and neglecting the inner vital principle of joy and hope; he has left deeper things untouched. He neglects love and all immediate transcendent intuitions. But since it is only this temporal aspect of decayed appearances which death is known to end, since it is only the closing of this very time-succession which Claudio fears, it is enough to prove this succession

valueless. Claudio is thus comforted. The death of such
a life is indeed not death, but rather itself a kind of life:

> I humbly thank you.
> To sue to live, I find I seek to die;
> And seeking death, find life: let it come on.
>
> (III.i.41–43)

Now he "will encounter darkness as a bride," like Antony
(III.i.84). The Duke's death philosophy is thus the philosophy of the great tragedies to follow—of *Timon of
Athens,* of *Antony and Cleopatra.* So, too, his ethic is the
ethic of *King Lear.* In this problem play we find the profound thought of the supreme tragedies already emergent
and given careful and exact form, the Duke in this respect
being analogous to Agamemnon in *Troilus and Cressida.*
Both his ethical and his death thinking are profoundly
modern. But Claudio soon reverts to the crude time-
thinking (and fine poetry) of his famous death speech,
in which he regards the afterlife in terms of orthodox
eschatology, thinking of it as a temporal process, like
Hamlet:

> Ay, but to die, and go we know not where . . .
>
> (III.i.118)

In the Shakespearean mode of progressive thought it is
essential first to feel death's reality strongly as the ender
of what we call "life": only then do we begin to feel the
tremendous pressure of an immortality not known in
terms of time. We then begin to attach a different meaning to the words "life" and "death." The thought of this
scene thus wavers between the old and the new death
philosophies.

The Duke's plot pivots on the testing of Angelo. Angelo
is a man of spotless reputation, generally respected. Escalus says

> If any in Vienna be of worth
> To undergo such ample grace and honor,
> It is Lord Angelo.
>
> (I.i.22–24)

Angelo, hearing the Duke's praise, and his proposed trust, modestly declines, as though he recognizes that his virtue is too purely idealistic for the rough practice of state affairs:

> Now, good my lord,
> Let there be some more test made of my metal,
> Before so noble and so great a figure
> Be stamp'd upon it.   (I.i.47–50)

Angelo is not a conscious hypocrite: rather a man whose chief faults are self-deception and pride in his own right-eousness—an unused and delicate instrument quite useless under the test of active trial. This he half-recognizes, and would first refuse the proffered honor. The Duke insists: Angelo's fall is thus entirely the Duke's responsibility. So this man of ascetic life is forced into authority. He is

> A man whose blood
> Is very snow-broth; one who never feels
> The wanton stings and motions of the sense,
> But doth rebate and blunt his natural edge
> With profits of the mind, study and fast.
>   (I.iv.57–61)

Angelo, indeed, does not know himself: no one receives so great a shock as he himself when temptation overthrows his virtue. He is no hypocrite. He cannot, however, be acquitted of Pharisaical pride: his reputation means much to him, he "stands at a guard with envy" (I.iii.51). He "takes pride" in his "gravity" (II.iv.10). Now, when he is first faced with the problem of Claudio's guilt of adul-tery—and commanded, we must presume, by the Duke's sealed orders to execute stern punishment wholesale, for this is the Duke's ostensible purpose—Angelo pursues his course without any sense of wrongdoing. Escalus hints that surely all men must know sexual desire—how then is Angelo's procedure just? Escalus thus adopts the Duke's ethical point of view, exactly:

> Let but your honor know

(Whom I believe to be most strait in virtue),
That, in the working of your own affections,
Had time cohered with place, or place with wishing,
Or that the resolute acting of your blood
Could have attain'd the effect of your own purpose,
Whether you had not, some time in your life,
Err'd in this point, which now you censure him,
And pull'd the law upon you.

(II.i.8–16)

Which reflects the Gospel message:

Ye have heard that it was said by them of old time,
Thou shalt not commit adultery:
But I say unto you, that whosoever looketh on a
woman to lust after her hath committed adultery with
her already in his heart.

(Matthew 5:27–28)

Angelo's reply, however, is sound sense:

'Tis one thing to be tempted, Escalus,
Another thing to fall.

(II.i.17–18)

Isabella later uses the same argument as Escalus:

. . . Go to your bosom;
Knock there, and ask your heart what it doth know
That's like my brother's fault: if it confess
A natural guiltiness, such as is his,
Let it not sound a thought upon your tongue
Against my brother's life.

(II.ii.136–41)

We are reminded of Jesus' words to the Scribes and Phari-
sees concerning the woman "taken in adultery":

He that is without sin among you, let him first cast a
stone at her.

(John 8:7)

Angelo is, however, sincere: terribly sincere. He feels no
personal responsibility, since he is certain that he does
right. We believe him when he tells Isabella:

It is the law, not I, condemn your brother:

> Were he my kinsman, brother, or my son,
> It should be thus with him.   (II.ii.80–82)

To execute justice, he says, is kindness, not cruelty, in the long run.

Angelo's arguments are rationally conclusive. A thing irrational breaks them, however: his passion for Isabella. Her purity, her idealism, her sanctity enslave him—she who speaks to him of

> true prayers
> That shall be up at heaven and enter there
> Ere sunrise, prayers from preserved souls,
> From fasting maids whose minds are dedicate
> To nothing temporal.   (II.ii.151–55)

Angelo is swiftly enwrapped in desire. He is finely shown as falling a prey to his own love of purity and asceticism:

> What is't I dream on?
> O cunning enemy, that, to catch a saint,
> With saints dost bait thy hook!   (II.ii.178–80)

He "sins in loving virtue"; no strumpet could ever allure him; Isabella subdues him utterly. Now he who built so strongly on a rational righteousness, understands for the first time the sweet unreason of love:

> Ever till now,
> When men were fond, I smiled and wonder'd how.
>   (II.ii.185–86)

Angelo struggles hard: he prays to Heaven, but his thoughts "anchor" on Isabel (II.iv.4). His gravity and learning—all are suddenly as nothing. He admits to himself that he has taken "pride" in his well-known austerity, adding "let no man hear me"—a pathetic touch which casts a revealing light both on his shallow ethic and his honest desire at this moment to understand himself. The violent struggle is short. He surrenders, his ideals all toppled over like ninepins:

Blood, thou art blood:
Let's write good angel on the Devil's horn,
'Tis not the Devil's crest.   (II.iv.15–17)

Angelo is now quite adrift: all his old contacts are irrevocably severed. Sexual desire has long been anathema to him, so his warped idealism forbids any healthy love. Good and evil change places in his mind, since this passion is immediately recognized as good, yet, by every one of his stock judgments, condemned as evil. The Devil becomes a "good angel." And this wholesale reversion leaves Angelo in sorry plight now: he has no moral values left. Since sex has been synonymous with foulness in his mind, this new love, reft from the start of moral sanction in a man who "scarce confesses that his blood flows," becomes swiftly a devouring and curbless lust:

I have begun,
And now I give my sensual race the rein.
(II.iv.159–60)

So he addresses Isabella. He imposes the vile condition of Claudio's life. All this is profoundly true: he is at a loss with this new reality—embarrassed as it were, incapable of pursuing a normal course of love. In proportion as his moral reason formerly denied his instincts, so now his instincts assert themselves in utter callousness of his moral reason. He swiftly becomes an utter scoundrel. He threatens to have Claudio tortured. Next, thinking to have had his way with Isabella, he is so conscience-stricken and tortured by fear that he madly resolves not to keep faith with her: he orders Claudio's instant execution. For, in proportion as he is nauseated at his own crimes, he is terror-struck at exposure. He is mad with fear, his story exactly pursues the Macbeth rhythm:

This deed unshapes me quite, makes me unpregnant
And dull to all proceedings. A deflower'd maid!
And by an eminent body that enforced
The law against it! But that her tender shame
Will not proclaim against her maiden loss,

How might she tongue me! Yet reason dares her no:
For my authority bears so credent bulk,
That no particular scandal once can touch
But it confounds the breather. He should have lived,
Save that his riotous youth, with dangerous sense,
Might in the times to come have ta'en revenge,
By so receiving a dishonor'd life
With ransom of such shame. Would yet he had lived!
Alack, when once our grace we have forgot,
Nothing goes right: we would, and we would not.
                                        (IV.iv.22–36)

This is the reward of self-deception, of pharisaical pride,
of an idealism not harmonized with instinct—of trying,
to use the Duke's pregnant phrase:

> To draw with idle spiders' strings
> Most ponderous and substantial things. (III.ii.278–79)

Angelo has not been overcome with evil. He has been
ensnared by good, by his own love of sanctity, exquisitely
symbolized in his love of Isabella: the hook is baited with
a saint, and the saint is caught. The cause of his fall is this
and this only. The coin of his moral purity, which flashed
so brilliantly, when tested does not ring true. Angelo is
the symbol of a false intellectualized ethic divorced from
the deeper springs of human instinct.

The varied close-inwoven themes of *Measure for
Measure* are finally knit in the exquisite final act. To that
point the action—reflected image always of the Ducal
plot—marches

> By cold gradation and well-balanced form.
>   (IV.iii.101)

The last act of judgment is heralded by trumpet calls:

> Twice have the trumpets sounded;
> The generous and gravest citizens
> Have hent the gates, and very near upon
> The Duke is entering.   (IV.vi.12–15)

So all are, as it were, summoned to the final judgment.
Now Angelo, Isabella, Lucio—all are understood most
clearly in the light of this scene. The last act is the key
to the play's meaning, and all difficulties are here resolved. I shall observe the judgment measured to each,
noting retrospectively the especial significance in the play
of Lucio and Isabella.

Lucio is a typical loose-minded, vulgar wit. He is the
product of a society that has gone too far in condemnation of human sexual desires. He keeps up a running
comment on sexual matters. His very existence is a condemnation of the society which makes him a possibility.
Not that there is anything of premeditated villainy in him:
he is merely superficial, enjoying the unnatural ban on
sex which civilization imposes, because that very ban
adds point and spice to sexual gratification. He is, however, sincerely concerned about Claudio, and urges Isabella to plead for him. He can be serious—for a while.
He can speak sound sense, too, in the full flow of his
vulgar wit:

> Yes, in good sooth, the vice is of a great kindred; it is well
> allied: but it is impossible to extirp it quite, friar, till eat-
> ing and drinking be put down. They say this Angelo was
> not made by man and woman after this downright way of
> creation: is it true, think you?   (III.ii.103–08)

This goes to the root of our problem here. Pompey has
voiced the same thought (II.i.238–54). This is, indeed,
what the Duke has known too well: what Angelo and
Isabella do not know. Thus Pompey and Lucio here at
least tell downright facts—Angelo and Isabella pursue impossible and valueless ideals. Only the Duke holds the
balance exact throughout. Lucio's running wit, however,
pays no consistent regard to truth. To him the Duke's
leniency was a sign of hidden immorality:

> Ere he would have hanged a man for getting a hundred
> bastards, he would have paid for the nursing of a thou-
> sand: he had some feeling of the sport; he knew the
> service, and that instructed him to mercy. (III.ii.119–23)

He traduces the Duke's character wholesale. He does not
pause to consider the truth of his words. Again, there is
no intent to harm—merely a careless, shallow, truthless
wit-philosophy which enjoys its own sex chatter. The type
is common. Lucio is refined and vulgar, and the more
vulgar because of his refinement; whereas Pompey, because of his natural coarseness, is less vulgar. Lucio can
only exist in a society of smug propriety and self-deception: for his mind's life is entirely parasitical on those
insincerities. His false—because fantastic and shallow—
pursuit of sex, is the result of a false, fantastic denial of
sex in his world. Like so much in *Measure for Measure*
he is eminently modern. Now Lucio is the one person the
Duke finds it all but impossible to forgive:

> I find an apt remission in myself;
> And yet here's one in place I cannot pardon.
>   (V.i.501–02)

All the rest have been serious in their faults. Lucio's condemnation is his triviality, his insincerity, his profligate
idleness, his thoughtless detraction of others' characters:

> You, sirrah, that knew me for a fool, a coward,
> One all of luxury, an ass, a madman;
> Wherein have I so deserved of you,
> That you extol me thus?   (V.i.503–06)

Lucio's treatment at the close is eminently, and fittingly,
undignified. He is threatened thus: first he is to marry
the mother of his child, about whose wrong he formerly
boasted; then to be whipped and hanged. Lucio deserves
some credit, however: he preserves his nature and answers with his characteristic wit. He cannot be serious.
The Duke, his sense of humor touched, retracts the sentence:

> *Duke.* Upon mine honor, thou shalt marry her.
> Thy slanders I forgive; and therewithal
> Remit thy other forfeits. Take him to prison;
> And see our pleasure herein executed.

Lucio. Marrying a punk, my lord, is pressing to death, whipping, and hanging.

Duke. Slandering a prince deserves it.   (V.i.521–27)

Idleness, triviality, thoughtlessness receive the Duke's strongest condemnation. The thought is this:

> But I say unto you, That every idle word that men shall speak, they shall give account thereof in the day of judgment.
> (Matthew 12:36)

Exactly what happens to Lucio. His wit is often illuminating, often amusing, sometimes rather disgusting. He is never wicked, sometimes almost lovable, but terribly dangerous.[1]

Isabella is the opposite extreme. She is more saintly than Angelo, and her saintliness goes deeper, is more potent than his. When we first meet her, she is about to enter the secluded life of a nun. She welcomes such a life. She even wishes

> a more strict restraint
> Upon the sisterhood, the votarists of Saint Clare.
> (I.iv.4–5)

Even Lucio respects her. She calls forth something deeper than his usual wit:

> I would not—though 'tis my familiar sin
> With maids to seem the lapwing and to jest,
> Tongue far from heart—play with all virgins so:
> I hold you as a thing ensky'd and sainted,
> By your renouncement an immortal spirit,
> And to be talk'd with in sincerity,
> As with a saint.
> (I.iv.31–37)

Which contains a fine and exact statement of his shallow behavior, his habitual wit for wit's sake. Lucio is throughout a loyal friend to Claudio: truer to his cause, in fact, than Isabella. A pointed contrast. He urges her to help.

[1] For Lucio, see also *The Imperial Theme*, p. 20.

She shows a distressing lack of warmth. It is Lucio that
talks of "your poor brother." She is cold:

> *Lucio.*   Assay the power you have.
>
> *Isabella.* My power; Alas, I doubt——
>
> *Lucio.*   Our doubts are traitors
> And make us lose the good we oft might win,
> By fearing to attempt.   (I.iv.76–79)

Isabella's self-centered saintliness is thrown here into
strong contrast with Lucio's manly anxiety for his friend.
So, contrasted with Isabella's ice-cold sanctity, there are
the beautiful lines with which Lucio introduces the matter to her:

> Your brother and his lover have embraced:
> As those that feed grow full, as blossoming time
> That from the seedness the bare fallow brings
> To teeming foison, even so her plenteous womb
> Expresseth his full tilth and husbandry.   (I.iv.40–44)

Compare the pregnant beauty of this with the chastity of
Isabella's recent lisping line:

> Upon the sisterhood, the votarists of Saint Clare.
>   (I.iv.5)

Isabella lacks human feeling. She starts her suit to Angelo
poorly enough. She is lukewarm:

> There is a vice that most I do abhor,
> And most desire should meet the blow of justice;
> For which I would not plead but that I must;
> For which I must not plead, but that I am
> At war 'twixt will and will not.   (II.ii.29–33)

Lucio has to urge her on continually. We begin to feel
that Isabella has no real affection for Claudio; has stifled
all human love in the pursuit of sanctity. When Angelo at
last proposes his dishonorable condition she quickly
comes to her decision:

> Then, Isabel, live chaste and, brother, die.
> More than our brother is our chastity.
>
> (II.iv.184–85)

When Shakespeare chooses to load his dice like this—which is seldom indeed—he does it mercilessly. The Shakespearean satire here strikes once, and deep: there is no need to point it further. But now we know our Isabel. We are not surprised that she behaves to Claudio, who hints for her sacrifice, like a fiend:

> Take my defiance!
> Die, perish! Might but my bending down
> Reprieve thee from thy fate, it should proceed:
> I'll pray a thousand prayers for thy death,
> No word to save thee.
>
> (III.i.143–47)

Is her fall any less than Angelo's? Deeper, I think. With whom is Isabel angry? Not only with her brother. She has feared this choice—terribly: "O, I do fear thee, Claudio," she said (III.i.74). Even since Angelo's suggestion she has been afraid. Now Claudio has forced the responsibility of choice on her. She cannot sacrifice herself. Her sex inhibitions have been horribly shown her as they are, naked. She has been stung—lanced on a sore spot of her soul. She knows now that it is not all saintliness, she sees her own soul and sees it as something small, frightened, despicable, too frail to dream of such a sacrifice. Though she does not admit it, she is infuriated not with Claudio, but with herself. "Saints" should not speak like this. Again, the comment of this play is terribly illuminating. It is significant that she readily involves Mariana in illicit love: it is only her own chastity which assumes, in her heart, universal importance.[2]

Isabella, however, was no hypocrite, any more than Angelo. She is a spirit of purity, grace, maiden charm: but all these virtues the action of the play turns remorselessly against herself. In a way, it is not her fault. Chastity is hardly a sin—but neither, as the play emphasizes, is it

[2] I now doubt if Isabella's attitude to Mariana should be held against her (1955).

the whole of virtue. And she, like the rest, has to find a
new wisdom. Mariana in the last act prays for Angelo's
life. Confronted by that warm, potent, forgiving, human
love, Isabella herself suddenly shows a softening, a sweet
humanity. Asked to intercede, she does so—she, who was
at the start slow to intercede for a brother's life, now im-
plores the Duke to save Angelo, her wronger:

> I partly think
> A due sincerity govern'd his deeds,
> Till he did look on me.   (V.i.448–50)

There is a suggestion that Angelo's strong passion has
itself moved her, thawing her ice-cold pride. This is the
moment of her trial: the Duke is watching her keenly, to
see if she has learnt her lesson—nor does he give her any
help, but deliberately puts obstacles in her way. But she
stands the test: she bows to a love greater than her own
saintliness. Isabella, like Angelo, has progressed far during the play's action: from sanctity to humanity.

Angelo, at the beginning of this final scene, remains
firm in denial of the accusations leveled against him. Not
till the Duke's disguise as a friar is made known and he
understands that deception is no longer possible, does he
show outward repentance. We know, however, that his
inward thoughts must have been terrible enough. His earlier agonized soliloquies put this beyond doubt. Now, his
failings exposed, he seems to welcome punishment:

> Immediate sentence then and sequent death
> Is all the grace I beg.   (V.i.376–77)

Escalus expresses sorrow and surprise at his actions. He
answers:

> I am sorry that such sorrow I procure:
> And so deep sticks it in my penitent heart
> That I crave death more willingly than mercy;
> 'Tis my deserving and I do entreat it.   (V.i.477–80)

To Angelo, exposure seems to come as a relief: the hor-

ror of self-deception is at an end. For the first time in his
life he is both quite honest with himself and with the
world. So he takes Mariana as his wife. This is just: he
threw her over because he thought she was not good
enough for him,

> Partly for that her promised proportions
> Came short of composition, but in chief
> For that her reputation was disvalued
> In levity.
> (V.i.219–22)

He aimed too high when he cast his eyes on the sainted
Isabel: now, knowing himself, he will find his true level
in the love of Mariana. He has become human. The union
is symbolical. Just as his supposed love-contact with
Isabel was a delusion, when Mariana, his true mate, was
taking her place, so Angelo throughout has deluded himself. Now his acceptance of Mariana symbolizes his new
self-knowledge. So, too, Lucio is to find his proper level
in marrying Mistress Kate Keepdown, of whose child he
is the father. Horrified as he is at the thought, he has to
meet the responsibilities of his profligate behavior. The
punishment of both is this only: to know, and to be,
themselves. This is both their punishment and at the same
time their highest reward for their sufferings: self-knowledge being the supreme, perhaps the only, good. We re-
remember the parable of the Pharisee and the Publican
(Luke 18).

So the Duke draws his plan to its appointed end. All,
including Barnadine, are forgiven, and left, in the usual
sense, unpunished. This is inevitable. The Duke's original
leniency has been shown by his successful plot to have
been right, not wrong. Though he sees "corruption boil
and bubble" (V.i.319) in Vienna, he has found, too,
that man's sainted virtue is a delusion: "judge not that
ye be not judged." He has seen an Angelo to fall from
grace at the first breath of power's temptation, he has
seen Isabella's purity scarring, defacing her humanity. He
has found more gentleness in "the steeled jailer" than in
either of these. He has found more natural honesty in

Pompey the bawd than in Angelo the ascetic; more humanity in the charity of Mistress Overdone than in Isabella condemning her brother to death with venomed words in order to preserve her own chastity. Mistress Overdone has looked after Lucio's illegitimate child:

> ... Mistress Kate Keepdown was with child by him in the Duke's time; he promised her marriage; his child is a year and a quarter old, come Philip and Jacob: I have kept it myself ...

> (III.ii.202–05)

Human virtue does not flower only in high places: nor is it the monopoly of the pure in body. In reading *Measure for Measure* one feels that Pompey with his rough humor and honest professional indecency is the only one of the major persons, save the Duke, who can be called "pure in heart." Therefore, knowing all this, the Duke knows his tolerance to be now a moral imperative: he sees too far into the nature of man to pronounce judgment according to the appearances of human behavior. But we are not told what will become of Vienna. There is, however, a hint, for the Duke is to marry Isabel, and this marriage, like the others, may be understood symbolically. It is to be the marriage of understanding with purity; of tolerance with moral fervor. The Duke, who alone has no delusions as to the virtues of man, who is incapable of executing justice on vice since he finds forgiveness implicit in his wide and sympathetic understanding—he alone wins the "enskied and sainted" Isabel. More, we are not told. And we may expect her in future to learn from him wisdom, human tenderness, and love:

> What's mine is yours and what is yours is mine.
> (V.i.540)

If we still find this universal forgiveness strange—and many have done so—we might observe Mariana, who loves Angelo with a warm and realistically human love. She sees no fault in him, or none of any consequence:

> O my dear lord,
> I crave no other nor no better man.
>
> (V.i.428–29)

She knows that

> best men are molded out of faults,
> And, for the most, become much more the better
> For being a little bad.   (V.i.442–44)

The incident is profoundly true. Love asks no questions, sees no evil, transfiguring the just and unjust alike. This is one of the surest and finest ethical touches in this masterpiece of ethical drama. Its moral of love is, too, the ultimate splendor of Jesus' teaching.

Measure for Measure is indeed based firmly on that teaching. The lesson of the play is that of Matthew 5:20:

> For I say unto you, That except your righteousness shall exceed the righteousness of the scribes and Pharisees, ye shall in no case enter into the Kingdom of Heaven.

The play must be read, not as a picture of normal human affairs, but as a parable, like the parables of Jesus. The plot is, in fact, an inversion of one of those parables—that of the Unmerciful Servant (Matthew 18); and the universal and level forgiveness at the end, where all alike meet pardon, is one with the forgiveness of the Parable of the Two Debtors (Luke 7). Much has been said about the difficulties of *Measure for Measure*. But, in truth, no play of Shakespeare shows more thoughtful care, more deliberate purpose, more consummate skill in structural technique, and, finally, more penetrating ethical and psychological insight. None shows a more exquisitely inwoven pattern. And, if ever the thought at first sight seems strange, or the action unreasonable, it will be found to reflect the sublime strangeness and unreason of Jesus' teaching.

MARY LASCELLES

from *Shakespeare's "Measure for Measure"*

. . . The Duke himself does not engage our concern
by what he does, or suffers. How, we may fairly ask, does
he—or should he—engage it? Criticism has for some while
inclined towards the opinion that here is one of those
persons in Shakespearean drama who should be regarded
as important in respect rather of function than of character, and are to be interpreted as we should interpret
the principal persons in allegory.[1] Now, the language of
allegory is at least approximately translatable. These persons, therefore, must stand for something that can be
expressed in other than allegorical terms, and the concept
for which the Duke stands be capable of formulation in
such terms as criticism may employ. What is this concept?

This is not an easy question to answer, nor are the
answers so far proposed easy to discuss. Since those that
suggest a religious allegory, and hint at a divine analogy,
are shocking to me, and cannot be anything of the sort
to those who have framed them, it must follow that my
objections are all too likely to shock in their turn. This
offense is apt to be mutual; for, where reverence is concerned, there is even less hope of reaching agreement by

From *Shakespeare's "Measure for Measure"* by Mary Lascelles. London: The Athlone Press, University of London, 1953; New York: John
De Graff, Inc., 1954. Reprinted by permission of the Athlone Press.
1. This opinion is shared by those who find in the play an explicitly
Christian meaning. See p. 41 above. [The number refers to Miss Lascelles'
earlier allusion to G. Wilson Knight and R. W. Chambers.]

argument than in matters of taste. I would not willingly offend; but there is not room for compromise.

Let me recall the burden of the popular tale of the monstrous ransom: the situation in which the woman, the judge, and the ruler confronted one another signified power, exerted to its full capacity against weakness, and weakness (reduced to uttermost misery) gathering itself up to appeal beyond power to authority. Expressed thus, in simple and general terms, it seems indeed analogous with that allegory of divine might invoked to redress abuse of human inequality which is shadowed in Browning's *Instans Tyrannus*. But it should be remembered that such simplification obliterates one particular which, if fairly reckoned with, might forbid religious analogy: in the old tale, the ruler was distant, ignorant, brought to intervene only by uncommon exertion on the part of those whom his absence had exposed to oppression;[2] and none of the amplifications designed to make the tale more acceptable had done anything to shift or reduce this untoward circumstance. Indeed, by magnifying the whole, they made the part more obvious.

Lupton's *Siuqila* beyond the rest develops that element in the story which draws us to think about the maintenance of justice, not merely in the version it gives of this tale but also in the similar tales surrounding it. And it is notable that, whereas this one tale is told by the wretched Siuqila to show that even in his own country one who has no longer anything to lose will tell all and thus bring about retribution, Omen's tales are told to illustrate the happier state of Mauqsun. The theme of three of them is the success of the good ruler who goes about his domain incognito to discover and redress wrong. In one, a judge who waylays and interrogates suitors is able to rescue a woman from oppression. In both of the others, the king himself is shown using disguise and similar subterfuge, not only to obtain truth but also to make it publicly apparent. In one, he learns by means of his "privie Espials," who ride about the country at his com-

2. For this absence, a reason is usually given—seemingly, to forestall censure.

mand in the character of private gentlemen, the plight of
a woman who has been ill used by her stepson. He hides
her at court and lets it be rumored that she is dead; and,
after much handling of witnesses, confronts the offender
with his victim, and delivers sentence. The other tells how
he "changed his apparell, making himselfe like a
Servingmā, and went out at a privie Posterngate, and so
enquired in the prisons, what prisoners were there," and
was able to confute the cunning oppressor by bringing
him face to face with the oppressed.

Now, in all these variations on a single theme, the
activity of some magistrate or ruler—going about or send-
ing out his agents, in disguise—*assists* in bringing smoth-
ered truth to light. Reflecting on opportune intervention
in one,[3] Siuqila sums up the moral of all: "It was only the
Lords working, that putte it into his heart" to speak with
the woman who was secretly oppressed, and into hers
to tell this stranger what she has hitherto forborne to
utter; for "God works al this by marvellous means, if we
would consider it, for the helping of the innocent and
godly." Even under an ideal system of justice, that is,
the discovery of wrong might well be impossible were it
not for the intervention of divine providence, which, on
some particular occasion, puts it into the heart of this or
that human agent to make a pertinent inquiry. Now, this
is in keeping with popular thought, which comes very
near to supposing an element of caprice in divine government,[4] because it does not look ahead, but complacently
descries pieces of pattern in particular events, without
considering the ugly unreason of the total design which
such parts must compose. But, how fearfully the distance
between this false start and its logical conclusion diminishes, if the ruler is regarded not as agent but as emblem
of divine providence! It is difficult to believe that those
who would have us interpret the Duke's part so can have
followed the implied train of thought all the way.

3. The story of the ill-used stepmother.
4. This is well exemplified by the speech of Whetstone's compassionate jailer, after he has released Andrugio (In *Promos and Cassandra,*
IV.v).

The center of gravity for this interpretation is the
passage in which Angelo capitulates to the alliance of
knowledge and power in the reinstated Duke:

> Oh, my dread Lord,
> I should be guiltier than my guiltinesse,
> To thinke I can be undiscerneable,
> When I perceive your grace, like powre divine,
> Hath look'd upon my passes.[5]

On this Professor Wilson Knight comments:

> Like Prospero, the Duke tends to assume proportions
> evidently divine. Once he is actually compared to the
> Supreme Power.[6]

So to argue is surely to misunderstand the nature and
usage of imagery—which does not liken a thing to itself.
Yet this argument has been widely accepted; if not un-
reservedly, yet with reservations which do not reach the
real difficulty. To suggest that the comparison may have
been made "unconsciously" by Shakespeare, and to admit
that "both the Duke in *Measure for Measure,* and Prospero, are endowed with characteristics which make it
impossible for us to regard them as direct representatives
of the Deity, such as we find in the miracle plays . . .
Prospero, at least, [having] human imperfections"[7]—this
is not enough. There will, of course, be human imperfections in any human representation, most plentiful where
least desired, for what we ourselves are is most evident
when we declare what we would be, in the endeavor to
represent ideal beings. But observe where the prime fault
occurs, in the character of this ruler: he is to blame in

5. V.i.369–73.
6. *The Wheel of Fire* (1949), p. 79.
7. S. L. Bethell, *Shakespeare and the Popular Dramatic Tradition*
(1944), pp. 106–07. See also Leavis, "The Greatness of *Measure for
Measure,*" and Traversi, "*Measure for Measure*" (*Scrutiny,* January and
Summer 1942). V. K. Whitaker ("Philosophy and Romance in Shakespeare's 'Problem' Comedies" in *The Seventeenth Century* by R. F. Jones
and others, Stanford University Press, 1951, p. 353) suggests that this
passage approaches as nearly to a reference to God "as Shakespeare
could come under the law of 1605 against stage profanity"—an explanation which raises many more questions than it answers.

respect of the performance of that very function in virtue
of which he is supposedly to be identified with Divine
Providence. Read the sentence

> . . . I perceive your grace, like powre divine,
> Hath look'd upon my passes

as the figurative expression which its syntax proclaims it—
that is, as a comparison proposed between distinct, even
diverse, subjects in respect of a particular point of resemblance—and it yields nothing at odds with the accepted
idea of a ruler who, despite the utmost exertion of human
good will, must still be indebted to a power beyond his
own for any success in performance of that duty which
is entailed on him as God's vice-regent, and who, when
such success visits his endeavors, will transiently exemplify
the significane of that vice-regency. But, exact from that
same sentence more than figurative expression has to
give, and you are confronted with the notion of a divine
being who arrives (like a comic policeman) at the scene
of the disaster by an outside chance, and only just in time.

Treat the whole story as fairy tale, and you are not
obliged to challenge any of its suppositions. Treat it as
moral apologue, expressed in terms proper to its age, and
it will answer such challenge as may fairly be offered. The
Duke's expedients will then serve to illustrate the energy
and resources of a human agent. But, suppose him other
than human,[8] and the way leads inescapably to that conclusion which Sir Edmund Chambers reaches, when he
reflects on this play: "Surely the treatment of Providence
is ironical."[9] Unless *Measure for Measure* is to be accepted, and dismissed, as simple fairy tale—and what
fairy tale ever troubled so the imagination?—the clue to
this central and enigmatic figure must be sought in repre-
sentations of the good ruler as subjects of a Tudor sovereign conceived him; about all, in those illustrative anec-

8. For the extreme form of this supposition, see Battenhouse, *"Measure for Measure* and Christian Doctrine of the Atonement" (*Publications
of the Modern Language Association of America,* December 1946).
9. *Shakespeare: A Survey* (1925), p. 215.

dotes which writers (popular and learned alike) were glad to employ, and content to draw from common sources.

A number of these are to be found associated with the name and reputation of the Emperor Alexander Severus.[10] Developing on a course similar to that taken by Guevara's Marcus Aurelius romance, this curious legend was for a spell popular in England. Its fullest, most circumstantial, and most influential exemplar I take to be Sir Thomas Elyot's *Image of Governance*.[11] Here the salient features of the ideal portrait are these: inheriting a legacy of disorder and corruption, the good emperor is zealous in the reform of manners by means of social legislation and the careful appointment and assiduous supervision of his ministers of justice. To ensure a just outcome he will intervene in a case by subterfuge, not merely employing spies but acting in that capacity himself, and, when he has detected wrongdoing, not content merely to bring the accused to trial, he will handle the witnesses, cause false information to be put about, and trick the culprit into pronouncing his own sentence.[12] One after another, Tudor and Stuart sovereigns were addressed obliquely through anecdotes of Alexander Severus, congratulated on resemblance to him in respect of those virtues which the writer most desired in a ruler, and delicately invited to put to opportune employment those powers and qualities of which the country stood in need.[13] These pseudo-historical anecdotes, of which more than one bears a resemblance to those in Lupton's *Siuqila*, are many of them commonplaces of popular fiction; but, used by writers whose main

10. For an account of this legend, its development in England and range of application, see my article: "Sir Thomas Elyot and the Legend of Alexander Severus" (*Review of English Studies*, October 1951).

11. *The Image of Governance Compiled of the Acts and Sentences notable, of the moste noble Emperour Alexander Severus* (1541). This purports to be a translation from a Greek work by the Emperor's secretary, supplemented from other sources.

12. See particularly Chapters VIII to XIX, XXIV, XXXVIII, and XXXIX.

13. For an illustration of the adaptability of Elyot's anecdotes, see Whetstone's *Mirour for Magestrates of Cyties*, apparently a free version of those that Whetstone found congenial to his own times, and temper.

intention was not to tell a story (either historical or fictitious), they illustrate an idea of the business of government which could then be seriously canvassed by men
involved in that very business, or eager to advise those
so involved. They chart the tides and currents that a
writer for an Elizabethan audience must have reckoned
with, and remind us how far the direction of these habitual
sympathies and antipathies has since altered: thus remov-
ing some of the obstacles to a fair estimate of the Duke's
conduct. . . .

Isabel is the chief of those characters who are themselves engaged, and engage us, by the opportunity and
capacity they are given for suffering; of whose sentient
core we are keenly aware. And yet our consciousness
of it is not constant. From the moment when she presents herself before Angelo to that of the Duke's intervention between her and Claudio, she holds our imagination subject by her alternations of hope and fear.
Then she seems to abdicate. Her reaction to the one
subsequent event which should reinstate her, the news
of Claudio's death, is, as the text stands, hardly more
than squirrel's chatter, "anger insignificantly fierce." From
the moment of her submission to the Duke, until that in
which she pleads for Angelo against his express injunc-
tion, she *is* insignificant. We may usefully recall, here,
the comparison afforded by *The Heart of Midlothian*:
whereas Jeanie takes matters into her own hands and,
at severe cost to herself, wins her sister's pardon, Isabel
appears to relinquish initiative and, under another's direction, to follow a course at once easier and less admirable.
Out of her seeming subservience the opinion has arisen
that Shakespeare wearied of her; had never (perhaps)
intended that she should fill so big a place, or else, had
designed her to perform a particular task and had now no
further use for her. And yet, in the estimation of many,
a full tide of significance flows back into her even in that
instant of recovered independence. Here is an extreme,
if not a singular, instance of a character fluctuating between two and three dimensions.

I believe that the explanation must be sought through

scrutiny of a greater anomaly, within the character. Isabel's chief activity in the play springs from the passions generated by a personal relationship—and yet this *source of all she does* is very strangely treated. The conventions of poetic drama bear hard on minor personal relationships; but *this* is of major importance. It is, besides, almost the only such relationship explicit in the play. Escalus' recollection of Claudio's father hardly alters this strangely *un-familied* world; and, though he is seen entering the prison, we do not see him with the prisoner. As for Claudio and Juliet, the extant text leaves me in doubt whether they are ever seen together. More surprising still, Claudio seems never to speak of Juliet, after that single reference in talk with Lucio. Shakespeare's *improvers*, mindful of those proprieties which are rather social than literary, attempt a remedy: Davenant making Claudio commit Juliet to Isabella's care, and introducing a letter to him from Juliet; Gildon adding a scene between these two.[14] Their officiousness is at least understandable: Claudio's silence must appear an oversight, unless we suppose that Shakespeare was deliberately flattening this part of his composition in order to throw into relief another relationship—and what should this be but the relationship between brother and sister? It is as Claudio's sister that Isabel comes into the play: as the woman who is drawn by a personal attachment into a dire predicament. And yet in her pleading on his behalf this personal relationship is faintly expressed. Many times, in her most moving passages, it would be possible to substitute "neighbor" for "brother," and hardly wake a ripple. Not that her pleading is passionless—to suppose so is to fall into Lucio's error. The very incandescence of her fiery compassion transcends the personal occasion, carrying her to a height at which, if she would plead for one man, she must plead for all. By contrast, the sense of personal relationship is sharply, even intolerably, explicit in the

14. Juliet committed to Isabella's care: Davenant, *The Law against Lovers*, p. 161; Gildon, *Measure for Measure, or Beauty the Best Advocate*, p. 24. Juliet's letter, Davenant, *op. cit.*, p. 185; Gildon's scene between Claudio and Juliet, *op. cit.*, pp. 34–36.

scene of her conflict with Claudio—the only scene in which they speak together. It puts an edge on her anger and fear; and it is in terms of their common heritage, and what it entails of participation in shame, that she denounces him. Thus this personal connection, which is the pivot of the play's action, is presented in its full significance only at the instant of its apparent dislocation.

Suppose we should find a single explanation valid for these, and all those other apparent anomalies in this character which have emerged from the foregoing examination of the play: it would surely be a master key. Let me briefly recapitulate the perplexities that have to be taken into account. When Isabel first hears of Claudio's predicament, her thought follows that course taken by Epitia's and Cassandra's: "Oh, let him marry her."[15] But, when she intercedes with Angelo, she does not urge, as they had done, and as all Vienna is ready to do, that the law is at fault if it demands the life of an offender who is able and willing to repair the wrong he has done. Nevertheless, when the Duke proposes to her a course of action whose justification is that it will commit Angelo to an act for which he may be compelled to make similar reparation, she acquiesces; and this, although she has reiterated to him her abhorrence of Claudio's act. And, if we explain this compliance in terms of her anxiety on her brother's behalf, we are reminded of strange fluctuations in her relationship with that very brother—and even, in the *density* of her own substance.

To understand what has happened, we must take into consideration something that emerges from a comparison between Giraldi's various developments of this theme, of a woman confronted with an abominable choice. Where this woman is sister to the condemned man and herself unmarried, it is assumed that any wrong done and suffered, in her surrender to his adversary, can be repaired by marriage.[16] But the situation that this assumption yields is fundamentally undramatic: there is no real con-

15. I.iv.49.
16. Whetstone, despite national and religious differences, is in accord with Giraldi here.

flict between characters, nor within any character; merely such a show of opposition as suffices for a slight story. The sister has only to say on her brother's behalf: "Since he can, and will, make good the wrong done, your sentence is too severe." And to say this costs her nothing. Likewise, when her opponent—bearing down this acknowledged right by might—tempts her to obtain what she asks by consenting to an offense the counterpart of her brother's, the two of them agree that she has but to stipulate for the same reparation, marriage. Thus, the whole cause of her distress is the advantage which strength takes of weakness: the double breach of faith by a man whose will is—for the time being—law. It is a piteous tale. It does not yield the stuff of a play. In those other versions of this theme, however, which make the woman wife to the condemned man, dramatic tension is developed through her abhorrence of the act required of her as injurious to that very relationship by force of which she is brought to consent: she must buy his life at the price of an infamy in which he is to be sharer. This is a dilemma such as we associate with tragedy, because it presents a choice of courses from which there can be no good issue. (Hence, such versions as those of Roilletus, Lupton and Belleforest.) Now, in Giraldi's variations on this theme, still in his favorite mood of tragicomedy, his tales of Dorothea and Gratiosa, romance and comedy are respectively invoked and given power to challenge the assumption that a choice must be made between two bad ways. And, in both, this favorable intervention forestalls any possible distress, and so prevents painful engagement of our sympathies: for, no sooner is the wicked proposal made than something points to the existence of a third door.

Shakespeare accepted the version in which the woman is the condemned man's sister, and unmarried. As an experienced dramatist, however, he could not but recognize the dramatic insufficiency of this situation. It offered him an unhitched rope, one of which the slack would never be taken up; and the only means of making it taut was to give Isabel a motive for reluctance equivalent to that which forbade the wife's surrender. He gave her the convent.[17] So much may be common knowledge; but, like a troublesome debtor, I must still ask more patience of the reader, before I can show any return on what I have already borrowed. In making this one alteration, Shakespeare found himself committed to a number of others. As to plot, he must prevent the violation of her person; or else a happy ending would be repugnant to moral sentiment. As to character, she is marked at the outset by her sense of separateness: she cannot plead in the terms others use; and no shadow of comparison between Juliet or Mariana and herself ever crosses her mind. What, then, has become of her isolation when, with no apparent consciousness of doing anything questionable, she publishes her fictitious shame, and incurs suspicion of which she cannot count on being cleared?

I suggest that the dramatic center of the play, until the Duke intervenes, is an abhorrence of unchastity which carries the force of the original situation in which a wife faces a tragic dilemma. The form is changed, Shakespeare having taken (deliberately or no) that one of Giraldi's two channels for carrying the story away from tragedy which necessitates a change of relationship between the woman and the condemned man; but it is the old current which flows between these new banks. The pressure which we feel comes, as in a stream dammed up, from such a reluctance on the woman's part as neither Epitia nor Cassandra had fully known. But this dam does not hold. Once the responsibility for choosing has been lifted from Isabel's shoulders, the obstacle to choice begins to lose its significance. In the situation as it is refashioned by the Duke, it is no longer a factor. Presently it vanishes from recollection. In a world rapidly becoming secular; on a stage which was (by force of tacit agreement as well as censorship) the most secular institution in that world; and in the hands of a dramatist who

17. By the same means, he fastens guilt upon Angelo's inclination, barring the way to love and marriage.

>   in matters of conscience adhered to two rules,
>   To advise with no bigots, and jest with no fools,

it did not offer itself to free and familiar expression. An
Elizabethan dramatist of far less than Shakespeare's power
could far more easily have conveyed to an Elizabethan
audience, within the conventions both understood, the
reluctance, say, of Lucrece.

When a storyteller has to devise an equivalent for something in his story, as he originally knew or conceived it,
which has proved intractable to his purpose, this new
constituent is liable to remain imperfectly substantiated,
perhaps because he unconsciously reckons on its retaining
the potency which his imagination still associates with
that which it replaces. Here it may signify all that he
requires, and there, dwindle into insignificance. An echo
of this story as it may first have visited Shakespeare's
imagination seems to reverberate in that antagonism which
develops between brother and sister, when she perceives
that he does not participate in her sense of the infamy of
consent. But that very sense, and its justification, are so
little evident in the part of the play which follows that
Isabel's account of herself as one "in probation of a sisterhood,"[18] seems but a reminder of something lost by
the way. It is only when she stands alone again, opposed
even to the Duke, that her former separateness seems
for an instant to recover its importance.

18. V.i.72.

MARCIA RIEFER POULSEN

"Instruments of Some More Mightier Member": The Constriction of Female Power in Measure for Measure

Isabella has recently been called Measure for Measure's "greatest problem."[1] She has not always been taken so seriously. Coleridge dismissed her by saying simply that Isabella "of all Shakespeare's female characters, interests me the least."[2] Criticism of her character has been cyclical and paradoxical, in part because critics have tended to focus on one implicit question: is she or is she not an exemplar of rectitude? On the one hand Isabella has been idealized as a paragon of feminine virtue; on the other hand she has been denigrated as an example of frigidity. Over the centuries, Isabella has been labeled either "angel" or "vixen," as if a judgment of her moral nature were the only important statements to be made about her.[3]

Reprinted by permission from Shakespeare Quarterly, 35 (1984), 157–69, where the author's name is given as Marcia Riefer. Copyright © 1984 by Marcia Riefer.

1. George L. Geckle, "Shakespeare's Isabella," Shakespeare Quarterly, 22 (1971), 163.
2. Samuel Taylor Coleridge, Coleridge's Miscellaneous Criticism, ed. Thomas Middleton Raysor (Cambridge, Mass.: Harvard Univ. Press, 1936), p. 49.
3. Among those who idealize Isabella are Anna Jameson (Shakespeare's Heroines: Characteristics of Women, Moral, Poetical, and Historical [London: G. Bell, 1913], p. 66) and George Geckle, who call her, respectively, an "angel of light" and a "heroine of superior moral qualities." Taking the opposite stance are Sir Arthur Quiller-Couch ("Introduction" to Measure for Measure, ed. Quiller-Couch and J. Dover Wilson [Cambridge: Cambridge Univ. Press, 1922], p. xxx), who

When not idealizing or denigrating Isabella, critics have generally ignored her.[4]

I

The debate over Isabella's virtue obscures a more important point, namely that through her one can explore the negative effects of patriarchal attitudes on female characters and on the resolution of comedy itself.[5] In the course of the play, Isabella changes from an articulate, compassionate woman during her first encounter with Angelo (II.ii), to a stunned, angry, defensive woman in her later confrontations with Angelo and with her imprisoned brother (II.iv and III.i), to, finally, a shadow of her former articulate self, on her knees before male authority in Act V. As the last and one of the most problematic of the pre-romance comedies, *Measure for*

calls Isabella a "bare procuress" who "is something rancid in her chastity"; Charlotte Lennox (*Shakespear Illustrated*, I [London, 1753], p. 32), who calls her a "Vixen in her Virtue"; and Una Mary Ellis-Fermor (*The Jacobean Drama: An Interpretation* [London: Methuen, 1936], p. 262), who refers to her as "Hard as an icicle." I am grateful to George Geckle for several of these references.

4. Frank Harris (*Women of Shakespeare* [New York: Mitchell Kennerley, 1912]) ignores Isabella, presumably because he could not identify a correlative for her in Shakespeare's life. A book by "An Actress" (*The True Ophelia and Other Studies of Shakespeare's Women* [New York: Putnam, 1914]) similarly excludes Isabella, as does Helena Faucit, Lady Martin's *On Some of Shakespeare's Female Characters* (Edinburgh and London: William Blackwood, 1887). Even recent feminist critics slight Isabella. In *The Woman's Part: Feminist Criticism of Shakespeare* (eds. Carolyn Ruth Swift Lenz, Gayle Greene, Carol Thomas Neely [Urbana: Univ. of Illinois Press, 1980]), only two articles make significant mention of her, pointing out that Isabella is one of the few female characters in Shakespeare to confront men without benefit of men's garments. (See Paula S. Berggren, "Female Sexuality as Power in Shakespeare's Plays," p. 22, and Clara Claiborne Park, "As We Like It: How a Girl Can Be Smart and Still Popular," p. 109.) Two other recent books written from a feminist perspective—Irene Dash, *Wooing, Wedding, and Power: Women in Shakespeare's Plays* (New York: Columbia Univ. Press, 1981), and Linda Bamber, *Comic Women, Tragic Men: A Study of Gender and Genre in Shakespeare* (Stanford: Stanford Univ. Press, 1982)—have little more to say about Isabella, relegating her to footnotes or oblique references.

5. For a discussion of patriarchy as a destructive force in Shakespeare's tragedies, see Madelon Gohlke, " 'I wooed thee with my sword': Shakespeare's Tragic Paradigms" in *The Woman's Part*.

Measure traces Isabella's gradual loss of autonomy and ultimately demonstrates, among other things, the incompatibility of sexual subjugation with successful comic dramaturgy.

The kind of powerlessness Isabella experiences is an anomaly in Shakespearean comedy.[6] Most of the heroines in whose footsteps Isabella follows have functioned as surrogate dramatist figures who are generally more powerful, in terms of manipulating plot, than the male characters in the same plays. One need only recall the Princess of France and her ladies in *Love's Labor's Lost*, Portia in *The Merchant of Venice*, Mistresses Page and Ford in *The Merry Wives of Windsor*, Beatrice in *Much Ado About Nothing*, Viola in *Twelfth Night*, Helena in *All's Well That Ends Well*, and, of course, Rosalind in *As You Like It*. Those heroines who have not actually been in control of the comic action have at least participated in it more actively than Isabella ever does. In *A Midsummer Night's Dream*, for instance, Helena and Hermia, while admittedly acting within Oberon's master plot, still take the initiative in pursuing their loves, which is certainly not true of Isabella. Even Kate in *The Taming of the Shrew* exercises dramaturgical skills. In her final "tour de force" she employs those very tactics which Petruchio has taught her, reversing them subtly on him and indicating through loving "opposites—as he has done in his "taming" of her—that she may have some taming of her own in store for him.[7] Her "obedience" to Petruchio's dramatic manipulation is far more playful and even assertive than Isabella's obedience to Vincentio. Besides, as Richard Wheeler points out, Petruchio's long-range significance is that the model of love by male conquest he embodies very soon

6. See Linda Bamber's *Comic Women, Tragic Men* for an articulate recent analysis of the centrality of women in Shakespeare's comedies.
7. Note the similarity between Kate's descriptions of the ideal husband—far from Petruchio's shrewish behavior thus far—(a "prince," a man "that cares for thee and for thy maintenance," someone who is "loving" and "honest," and who "commits his body to painful labor" for his wife's sake, V.ii.147–60) and Petruchio's earlier descriptions of the ideal Kate—far from her behavior at that time—(her "mildness prais'd in every town," her "virtues spoke of," and her "beauty sounded," II.i.185–94).

drops out of the maturing world of Shakespeare's comedy, to be replaced by such forceful, loving heroines as Portia and Rosalind.[8]

It is hardly incidental that in *Measure for Measure* Shakespeare places dramaturgical control almost exclusively in the hands of a male character—Duke Vincentio —who is, in effect, a parody of his more successful, mostly female, predecessors. An understanding of Vincentio's function in this play is essential background for exploring Isabella's character and dramatic function, so it is to him that we must turn our attention first.

II

As a dramatist figure, the Duke perverts Shakespeare's established comic paradigm in that he lacks certain essential dramaturgical skills and qualities previously associated with comic dramatist figures—qualities necessary for a satisfying resolution of comedy—especially (1) a consistent desire to bring about sexual union, what Northrop Frye calls "comic drive," [9] and (2) a sensitivity to "audience."[10] The prime victim of the Duke's flawed dramaturgy is, of course, Isabella, who, more than any of Shakespeare's heroines so far, is excluded from the "privileges of comedy," namely the privileges of exercising control over the events of the plot—privileges from which, Linda Bamber claims, it is Shakespeare's men who are typically excluded.[11] Deprived of her potential for leadership, Isabella succumbs

8. Richard Wheeler, *Shakespeare's Development and the Problem Comedies: Turn and Counter-Turn* (Berkeley: Univ. of California Press, 1981), p. 141.

9. Northrop Frye, *A Natural Perspective: The Development of Shakespearean Comedy and Romance* (New York: Harcourt-Brace, 1965), p. 73.

10. The merry wives, for example, must correctly gauge their "audience's"—Falstaff's—vanity in order for their plots to succeed. Viola demonstrates a similar sensitivity to audience response when, disguised as Cesario, she explains to Olivia the way a man should present himself if he wants to elicit a woman's love (*Twelfth Night*, I.v.266–74). In *As You Like It*, the splendidly dramatic Rosalind is not only astute about her own audience, but she teaches Orlando to be more sensitive to *his* as well (see, for example, IV.i.41–46).

11. Bamber, p. 120.

to the control of a man she has no choice but to obey—a man whose orders are highly questionable—and as a consequence her character is markedly diminished.

That the Duke's actions are questionable is apparent from the beginning, when he unexpectedly appoints Angelo to rule in his place instead of Escalus, who, as the opening scene establishes, is clearly the logical choice. Throughout the play, the Duke continues to undermine his credibility as a dramatist figure by making decisions strictly according to his own desires without considering the responses of those he is attempting to manipulate. For instance, his lofty tone in lecturing Claudio on how to make himself "absolute for death" (III.i.5–41)* is far from sensitive to the condemned man's situation. Not surprisingly, his effort fails; within a hundred lines Claudio is begging, "Sweet sister, let me live" (1. 132). Similarly unsympathetic, and similarly unsuccessful, is the Duke's attempt to convince the recalcitrant Barnardine to offer his head in place of Claudio's. This attempt results in the ridiculous appearance of a head whose owner, Ragozine, has no other purpose in the play than to cover for (even while calling attention to) Vincentio's insensitivity to the exigencies of motivation. The Duke's ineptitude as a playwright surrogate lies partly in his failure, in Viola's words, to "observe their mood on whom he jests" (*Twelfth Night*, III.i.63)—a failure which will prove especially detrimental to Isabella.

Another way in which the Duke perverts the Shakespearean comic paradigm is in his unusual antagonistic relationship to the "normal action" of comedy, which Frye defines as the struggle of the main characters to overcome obstacles in order to achieve sexual union.[12] The Duke *appears* to be possessed by a comic drive toward union when he proposes the bed-trick (dubious as it is) or when he arranges what Anne Barton refers to as the "outbreak

---

* All quotations from *Measure for Measure* are from the Signet Classic paperback edition, ed. S. Nagarajan (New York: New American Library, 1964, rev. ed. 1988); all other quotations from Shakespeare are from *The Complete Signet Classic Shakespeare*, ed. Sylvan Barnet (New York: Harcourt, Brace, Jovanovich, 1972).

12. Frye, *A Natural Perspective*, p. 72.

of that pairing-off disease"[13] in Act V. But his explicit denial that he has anything in common with those sinners and weaklings who allow themselves to be struck by the "dribbling dart of love" (I.iii.2)—along with his implicit condoning of Angelo's revival of obsolete sexual restrictive policies ("I have on Angelo imposed the office, / Who may, in th' ambush of my name, strike home" [I.iii.40–41])—sets him apart from earlier comic dramatists, predominantly women, whose desire was to escape, rather than to impose, sexual restriction. As Wheeler says, *Measure for Measure* is guided to its comic conclusion by a character whose essence is the denial of family ties and sexuality, the denial, that is to say, of the essence of comedy."[14] Vincentio represents not love's facilitator but its "blocking" agent. In this play, the hero and the "alazon" figure—the main obstacle to resolution in a typical comedy[15]—are, ironically, identical. Thus, the Duke, as protagonist, also embodies those traits characteristic of a comic antagonist. The "savior" in *Measure for Measure* turns out to be a villain as well. (Vincentio even allies himself with the play's more obvious antagonist, announcing that Angelo can "my part in him advertise" [I.i.41] and inviting Angelo, in his absence, to be "at full ourself" [I.i.43]. The Duke's intent may be to flatter Angelo with these phrases, but by positing this unity of their characters, he leaves himself open to suspicion.)

Part of what is comically "villainous" in the Duke is his excessive self-interest. Thomas Van Laan is among those critics who point out the Duke's egotism, arguing that he "cares about his image above all else." Van Laan describes the Duke as writer/producer/director of his own "carefully devised playlet," a man who is "like some film star more interested in his own virtuosity than ideal representation of the script." Indeed, the Duke's purpose for relinquishing his public responsibilities—a purpose he

13. Anne Barton, Introduction to *Measure for Measure* in *The Riverside Shakespeare*, p. 548.
14. Wheeler, p. 149.
15. Frye, *Anatomy of Criticism: Four Essays* (Princeton Univ. Press, 1957), pp. 164–65, 172.

himself admits is "grave and wrinkled" (I.iii.5)—is remi-
niscent of Tom Sawyer's reason for playing dead: he
wants to find out what people will say about him when
he's gone.[16]

While some may argue that such an evaluation of the
Duke as selfishly motivated is unduly harsh, there is much
in this play to support it, especially in those scenes in
which the Duke's actions seem well-intentioned. During
the opening scene, for example, Vincentio lavishes praise
on Angelo in an unnecessarily long and rhetorically elaborate passage (I.i.26–41), all the while knowing that Angelo has abandoned Mariana, an act which the Duke later
calls "unjust" (III.i.244). Far from having Vienna's best
interests in mind as he claims—and as many critics accept
—the Duke is actually setting up Angelo for a fall while
protecting himself ("my nature never in the fight / To do
in slander" [I.iii.42–43]), and at the same time betraying
the public as well, a public whom he admits he has effectively "bid" to be promiscuous through his permissiveness
(ll. 36–38). His ultimate intention seems to be setting
the stage for his final dramatic saving of the day—a day
which would not need saving except for his contrivances
in the first place. Vincentio's brand of dramaturgy is not
as well-meaning as it first appears, and it should make us
apprehensive about the Duke's potential to warp the experiences of those involved in his plots.

III

The female characters in this play, Mariana and Isabella, are the prime victims of the Duke's disturbing
manipulativeness—a significant reversal of the roles wom-
en have played in earlier comedies. While both male and
female characters serve to some extent as the Duke's

16. See Thomas F. Van Laan, *Role-Playing in Shakespeare* (Toronto:
Univ. of Toronto Press, 1978), pp. 98–100. See also Wheeler,
pp. 130–32.

"puppets,"[17] only the men resist his orders; the women are bound to be "directed" by him (IV.iii.138), "advised" by him (IV.vi.3), "ruled" by him (IV.vi.4). As Jean E. Howard points out, Barnardine, Lucio, and Angelo, even though punished in the end, do at times "refuse to be pawns in someone else's tidy playscript": Barnardine refuses to die, Angelo refuses to pardon Claudio, Lucio refuses to shut up.[18] Neither Mariana nor Isabella ever exhibits such defiance. Thus this play creates a disturbing and unusual sense of female powerlessness. But far from prescribing female reticence, *Measure for Measure* serves to reveal contingencies that make it difficult for women, even strong-willed women like Isabella, to assert themselves in a patriarchal society like Vienna—contingencies that do not impinge in the same way on the men. By allowing such contingencies to dominate the action, Shakespeare throws into question both the play's status as a comedy and the legitimacy of the prevailing social standards it portrays.

When we judge Isabella, we must consider, as Wheeler does, that she is surrounded by "the threat of sexual degradation"—a threat which, in this play, is "moved to the very center of the comic action," while in the festive comedies that threat is "deflected by wit and subordinated to the larger movements" of those plays.[19] More than any comic heroine thus far, Isabella has reason to take sexual degradation seriously. Whereas in most Shakespearean comedies the patriarchal world is peripheral to the main action, thereby allowing female characters exceptional latitude, in this play the expansiveness of a "green world" is inconceivable. Isabella has no Arden to retreat to. As Frye suggests, the green world in *Measure for Measure*,

---

17. William Empson (*The Structure of Complex Words* [London: Chatto and Windus, 1951], p. 283) sees the Duke as a character who manipulates "his subjects as puppets for the fun of seeing them twitch."
18. Jean E. Howard, "*Measure for Measure* and the Restraints of Convention," *Essays in Literature*, 10 (1983), 151–52. Dr. Howard has provided immeasurable support to me in my preparation of this study.
19. Wheeler, p. 102.

if present at all, has shrunk to the size of Mariana's all
but inconsequential moated grange.[20]

The constriction of the heroine's power throughout the
course of Shakespeare's pre-romance comedies has been
noted by Anthony Dawson, but only with regard to Portia, Rosalind, and Helena.[21] Isabella represents the logical
extension of this trend. The restrictiveness of Isabella's
environment in *Measure for Measure* is evident in her
doubts about her effectiveness ("My power? Alas, I
doubt—" [I.iv.77]) in the world as it must appear to her
—a Vienna in which lust is rampant and in which even
fiancées and wives are referred to in the same terms as
whores. Elbow's speeches, for instance, denigrate, if inad-
vertently, his own wife: "My wife, sir, whom I detest
before heaven and your honor—" (II.i. 68–69), and
"Marry, sir, by my wife, who, if she had been a woman
cardinally given, might have been accused in fornication,
adultery, and all uncleanliness there" (ll. 78–80). Of the
female characters who appear in this play, none are actually wives, and the one who is betrothed, Juliet, is called
a "fornicatress" (II.ii.23). Otherwise, one of the women
has been wronged (Mariana), one is a nun who has with-
drawn from this lust-infected Vienna, one is trying to
withdraw (Isabella), and the last is a whore (Mistress
Overdone, nicknamed Madam Mitigation) whose customers are all sent to jail, leaving her to fret over her lost
income. Sex in this Vienna is to be either punished or be-
littled. While Claudio, the true lover, sits in prison, the
rakish Lucio roams the streets, joking about getting
caught at a game of "tick-tack" (I.ii.194–95). The word
"healthy" could hardly be associated with female sexuality
in such an environment, no matter how positively a woman saw herself.

What Isabella is afraid of, synonymous with her loss of

20. Frye, *A Natural Perspective*, pp. 141–45, and *Anatomy of Criticism*, pp. 182–83. See also Bamber, pp. 36–38, on the relationship
between the world of "holiday brilliance" (the green world) and that
of "political hegemony" (the patriarchal world) in Shakespeare's
comedies.
21. Anthony Dawson, *Indirections: Shakespeare and the Art of Illusion* (Toronto: Univ. of Toronto Press, 1978), p. 87.

virginity, is her loss of respect, both her own self-respect and the respect of the community. Her desire for "a more strict restraint / Upon the sisterhood" (I.iv.4–5) must be linked with a strong fear of the consequences of integrating herself into a society dominated by exploitative men. In Irene Dash's terms, "In *Measure for Measure* Shakespeare again raises the question of women's personal autonomy —her right to control her body."[22] For Isabella, in light of the Vienna facing her, sexuality and self-esteem are mutually exclusive options. She has made her choice before she ever sets foot on stage. A woman in her position would not make such a decision without difficulty, even resentment. Isabella realizes that her "prosperous art," her ability to "play with reason and discourse" (I.ii.188–89), would be wasted in the city. So she attempts to withdraw to the protective cloister—an option much missed by women in post-Reformation England.[23] Just as Kate has taken "perverse refuge" behind the role of Shrew,[24] Isabella tries to take refuge behind the role of Nun.

But just as Isabella is on the brink of forswearing the company of men, Lucio arrives to pull her back into it. Reluctantly she returns to Vienna, where, gradually, her character dissolves, her spirit erodes, and she becomes an obedient follower of male guidance: an actress in a male-dominated drama.

IV

If we examine Isabella's development in this play, we can see how her sense of self is undetermined and finally destroyed through her encounters with patriarchal authority represented emphatically, but not exclusively, by the insensitive Duke. Her dilemma initially becomes apparent when she appears, a mere nun, before the Duke's appoint-

22. Dash, p. 251.
23. English convents, offering "a haven and a vocation for gentlewomen," were closed at the Reformation (Ian Watt, *The Rise of the Novel* [Berkeley: Univ. of California Press, 1957], p. 145). According to Watt, "What was most needed, it was generally thought, was a substitute for the convents."
24. Wheeler, p. 140.

ed deputy. At first she is hesitant to assert herself against Angelo and is ready, at the slightest resistance, to give up her task of persuading him to free Claudio. But with Lucios' prompting, her "prosperous art" with words becomes evident. More and more masterfully she develops her argument, pleading eloquently for her brother's life:

> Go to your bosom,
> Knock there, and ask your heart what it doth know
> That's like my brother's fault; if it confess
> A natural guiltiness such as is his,
> Let it not sound a thought upon your tongue
> Against my brother's life.
>
> (II.ii.136–41)

Even though at this early point in the play Isabella is already acting according to male direction, namely Lucio's, her integrity, which she so adamantly desires to protect, is still intact. Her voice remains, impressively, her own.

But Angelo assaults that integrity when he forces Isabella to choose between her brother's life and her maidenhood. He commands her, "Be that you are, / That is a woman," defining a woman's "destined livery" in no uncertain terms (II.iv.134 ff.). As hard as she has tried to avoid understanding Angelo earlier in this scene, Isabella can now no longer claim to be ignorant of his "pernicious purpose" (l. 150). When the deputy finally departs, leaving Isabella in the wake of his promise to torture her brother if she doesn't yield up her body to his will ("thy unkindness shall his death draw out / To ling'ring sufferance" [II.iv.166–67]), she cries out in exasperation, "To whom shall I complain?" Her only hope for compassion lies with Claudio: "I'll to my brother," she declares, assured that there is at least one man in the world possessed of "a mind of honor" (ll. 171–79).

Naturally, when Claudio echoes Angelo's demands, arguing that Isabella's surrendering her virginity in this case would be a virtue, her frustration is exacerbated. She reacts the way a woman might if she had been raped and had found those closest to her unsympathetic; she feels isolated, hurt, terrified, enraged. Loss of virginity, after all, is never a light matter for Shakespeare's calumniated, or potentially calumniated, women. In *Much Ado About Nothing,* the perception of Hero as sexually tainted corresponds directly with the illusion of her as dead. For Isabella, too, the prospect of giving herself to Angelo is tantamount to dying: "Better it were a brother died at once, / Than that a sister . . . / Should die for ever" (II.iv.106–8). If we understand how high the stakes are, we can hardly justify labeling Isabella a "vixen" when her strong will, until now subdued, gets the better of her and she swears,

> O you beast!
> O faithless coward! O dishonest wretch!
> . . . . .
> Take my defiance!
> Die, perish! Might but my bending down
> Reprieve thee from thy fate, it should proceed.
> I'll pray a thousand prayers for thy death,
> No word to save thee.

> (III.i.137–47)

Her oaths here are far from endearing. But what they expose is neither rigidity nor coldness but a deeply rooted fear of exploitation, a fear justified by the attitudes toward women prevalent in this Vienna. Claudio's urging Isabella to give up her virginity, understandable as it is from his point of view, compounds her increasing sense of vulnerability and helplessness.

Our experience of Isabella's being "thwarted here, there, and everywhere"[25] is reinforced by the intervention of the Duke at precisely this troublesome point in the play. Although his intentions appear honorable at first, in his own way he replicates Angelo's and Claudio's indifference to Isabella's desire to remain true to herself. Like

---

25. Sarojini Shintri, *Woman In Shakespeare* (Dharwad: Karnatak Univ., 1977), p. 276.

Angelo and Claudio before him, Vincentio sees in Isabella a reflection of his own needs. Consider his surprising endorsement of her attack on her brother. Rather than recoil at the harshness of her attack (as most of the play's critics have done), the Duke responds with delight: "The hand that hath made you fair hath made you good; the goodness that is cheap in beauty makes beauty brief in goodness; but grace, being the soul of your complexion, shall keep the body of it ever fair" (III.i.182–86). The Duke's perceptions of Isabella here reveal more about his character than about hers. What the Duke sees at this moment is the ideal woman that Hamlet never found: a woman who combines beauty and honesty; a woman who doesn't need to be told to get herself to a nunnery; a woman who represents the opposite of Frailty. Unfortunately for Isabella, the Duke is so taken by his Hamletian fantasies that he fails to see the woman she really is—a woman in distress, who fears the very thing he will eventually require: the sacrifice of her autonomy.

Isabella's willingness to cooperate with the Duke's unscrupulous plot—and so to forfeit her autonomy—is clearly related to his choice of disguises. Vincentio, wearing Friar Francis' robe, has become the very thing he accuses Angelo of being: an "angel on the outward side" (III.ii.275).[26] Lucio is right to call him the "Duke of dark corners" (IV.iii.159).[27] But whatever "crotchets" the Duke has in him (III.ii.130), his disguise represents an authority that Isabella, as a nun, can hardly repudiate. When he invites her to fasten her ear on his advisings, she agrees to follow his direction. But like the Provost, who protests that the Duke's orders will force him to break an

26. Christopher Marlowe (*The Tragical History of the Life and Death of Doctor Faustus* [Oxford: Clarendon Press, 1950], p. 9, I.iii.25–26) supplies a literary precedent for Vincentio's hypocritical disguise when he has Faustus assert that the "holy shape" of a Franciscan friar "becomes a devil best."

27. Calvin S. Hall (*A Primer of Freudian Psychology* [New York: New American Library, 1979], p. 92) could be describing Duke Vincentio when he explains "reaction formation" (caused by a repressed wish to possess something): "Romantic notions of chastity and purity may mask crude sexual desires, altruism may hide selfishness, and piety may conceal sinfulness."

oath (IV.ii.185), Isabella makes it clear that she does not want to play any part that would require her to violate her personal sense of truth: "I have spirit to do any thing that appears not foul in the truth of my spirit" (III.i.208–10). She does not want to have to sacrifice her own voice.

But by the time the fourth act closes, the Duke has imposed on Isabella a role which goes against her wishes. As she explains to Mariana in the last scene of that act, "To speak so indirectly I am loath: I would say the truth" (ll. 1–2). However, because a supposed religious superior has instructed her to "veil full purpose" (l. 4), she denies her personal inclinations and obeys the Duke without questioning. Neither green world nor cloister is available to Isabella now; she can neither subvert nor avoid the distorted value system which Vienna represents. She has no alternative but to submit to the Duke's authority. The Church, which was originally to function as Isabella's protector, has become her dictator.[28] Even though she was able to resist both Angelo's attempt to ravish her body and Claudio's attempt to change her mind, Isabella is unable, finally, to resist the Duke's demands on her spirit.

V

This negation of Isabella's essentially self-defined character becomes complete upon the Duke's taking control of the action in Act III. Critics have noted this change variously. Richard Fly, for example, says that Isabella, "formerly an independent and authentic personality with a voice of her own," is "suddenly reduced to little more than a willing adjunct to the Duke's purpose."[29] Clara

28. Church-supported witch hunts were still a reality in Shakespeare's England. The playwright could hardly have been unaware of the sexual oppressiveness, latent and actual, in religious doctrine of his day. For information on the involvement of both Catholic and Protestant churches in the witch hunts, see Barbara Ehrenreich and Deirdre English, *For Her Own Good: 150 Years of the Experts' Advice to Women* (New York: Doubleday, 1978), pp. 35–39, or their booklet *Witches, Midwives, and Nurses: A History of Women Healers* (Old Westbury, N.Y.: The Feminist Press, 1971), pp. 6–15.
29. Richard Fly, *Shakespeare's Mediated World* (Amherst: Univ. of Massachusetts Press, 1976), p. 59.

Claiborne Park refers to Isabella as losing center stage.[30] Whatever autonomy Isabella possessed in the beginning of the play, whatever "truth of spirit" she abided by, disintegrates once she agrees to serve in the Duke's plan. As soon as this "friar" takes over, Isabella becomes an actress whose words are no longer her own. There are no more outbursts. In complying with the role Vincentio has created for her, Isabella becomes his creation in a way that the male character never do. When he presents her with the irreverent idea of the bed-trick, Isabella simply answers, "Show me how, good father" (III.i.242) and "The image of it gives me content already" (l. 264). She cooperates with the Duke throughout the last act, in spite of her preference for "saying truth." When Angelo says that he perceives these "poor informal women" as "instruments of some more mightier member / That sets them on" (V.i.236–38), he doesn't know how truly he speaks.

The Duke claims, of course, to be acting in Isabella's best interest, just as he has claimed to be acting in the best interests of Vienna. He professes to be withholding the news that Claudio is alive in order to make Isabella "heavenly comforts of despair, / When it is least expected" (IV.iii.111–12). But the relationship between his professed intentions and the scenario he asks Isabella to act out is tenuous. In reward for her cooperation, Isabella has to kneel and swear in public that she, a recognized member of a local convent, "did yield" to the learned deputy (V.i.101)—a humiliating position to be forced into, no matter how cleverly the Duke may be intending to redeem her reputation.[31] In retrospect, the Duke's promise to comfort Isabella—what Frye calls a "brutal lie"[32]—appears to be a veiled justification for perpetuating his control over her. The passage in which the Duke urges Isabella to "pace" her wisdom "In that good path that [he] would wish it go"—a passage densely packed with imperatives (IV.iii.119–50)—is followed, significantly,

30. Claiborne Park, p. 109.
31. See Wheeler, p. 129.
32. Frye, *A Natural Perspective*, p. 11.

by the entrance of the ego-puncturing Lucio. This juxta-
position of scenes should warn us not to take the Duke's
proclaimed altruism at face value—just as the Duke's proclaimed aversion to staging himself to the people's eyes
(I.i.68) belies *its* face value. Vincentio's grand opus, Act
V—complete with trumpets to announce his entrance—is
so conspicuously dramaturgical that it divides into a five-
part structure.[33] Clearly we are not to rest easy with this
man's proclamations, nor should we be comfortable with
the role he is asking Isabella to play.

Isabella's last words reveal just how far this imposed
role diminishes her character. To those who argue that
rather than depriving Isabella of autonomy the Duke is
actually releasing her from moral rigidity by arranging for
her to plead for Angelo's life, I answer that Isabella's final
speech, often accepted as representing character growth,
in fact represents the opposite.[34] Ostensibly, Isabella is
once again displaying her "prosperous art," using rhetoric
to reveal a new-found capacity for mercy. But the quality
of mercy here is strained:

> Most bounteous sir,
> Look, if it please you, on this man condemned
> As if my brother lived. I partly think
> A due sincerity governèd his deeds,
> Till he did look on me. Since it is so,
> Let him not die. My brother had but justice,
> In that he did the thing for which he died;
> For Angelo,
> His act did not o'ertake his bad intent,
> And must be buried but as an intent
> That perished by the way. Thoughts are no subjects,
> Intents but merely thoughts.

> (V.i.446–57)

This speech lacks the integrity of Isabella's earlier speeches

33. See Josephine Bennett, *"Measure for Measure" as Royal Entertainment* (New York: Columbia Univ. Press, 1966), pp. 131–33.
34. See Fly, p. 69, Dawson, p. 114, and Geckle, p. 168, for discussions of the problematic nature of this passage.

in which she pleaded with Angelo to ask his heart what it
knew that was like her brother's fault. Logic, used so con-
vincingly in the earlier speeches, has become twisted. For
example, Isabella argues that since Claudio did "the thing
for which he died" but Angelo did not commit the sin he
thought he had, Angelo should not be punished. This
argument is illogical because it wrongfully implies that
evil actions, when carried out under mistaken circumstances, are harmless. If the crime had been misdirected
murder, by this logic Isabella would have claimed that the
act was no crime since the intended victim was still alive.
Not only the laws of logic, but the concept of justice is
twisted here. Isabella claims—as she need not—that her
brother's supposed execution was, in fact, just. Her mode
of argument is unsettling, not only because she sounds
indifferent to Claudio's death, but also because she resorts
to specious legalism where one would expect her to appeal
to her faith, as she did when pleading for Claudio's salva-
tion in II.ii.75–77:

> How would you be,
> If He, which is the top of judgment, should
> But judge you as you are?

In comparison with this earlier speech, Isabella's final appeal represents not an increased but a stunted capacity for
mercy. Her "prosperous art," subjected to the Duke's
perverted dramaturgical efforts, has itself become perverted. Vincentio's charge—"trust not my holy Order, /
If I pervert your course" (IV.iii.149–50)—becomes retrospectively ominous.

With the conclusion of her final speech, Isabella is immediately confronted with a series of overwhelming
events: a living Claudio appears, the Duke proposes marriage, and Angelo is pardoned. All of Isabella's main
assumptions—that Angelo was condemned, that the Duke
was a committed celibate, that her brother was dead, and
that she herself would remain chaste for life—are chal-
lenged, if not negated, in the space of five lines. She remains speechless, a baffled actress who has run out of

lines. The gradual loss of her personal voice during the course of the play has become, finally, a literal loss of voice. In this sense, *Measure for Measure* is Isabella's tragedy. Like Lavinia in *Titus Andronicus,* the eloquent Isabella is left with no tongue.

VI

If we see Isabella as a victim of bad playwriting, we can compare her bewilderment at the end of *Measure for Measure* with our own. She has trusted the Duke, as we've trusted our playwright, to pattern events as he has led her to expect events to be patterned—and the Duke, sharing Shakespeare's affinity for surprises in this play, pulls those expectations out from under her.[35] But by using Ragozine's head, for example—*caput ex machina*—to call attention to the ridiculousness of the Duke's machinations, Shakespeare simultaneously calls attention to his own superior skills. With this play Shakespeare has moved from comedy's romantic pole to its opposite, ironic, pole.[36] What he has created in *Measure for Measure* is not a poorly written play, but, to some extent, a model for

35. Surprise is an important element of the plot—both for the characters and for us as audience. Among the bewildered audiences that *Measure for Measure* leaves in its wake are Angelo and Escalus at the end of I.i, just after the Duke's sudden exit; Mistress Overdone in the following scene ("But shall all our houses of resort in the suburbs be pulled down?" I.ii.104–05); Friar Thomas, not quite grasping the Duke's partial explanation for his abdication ("It rested in your Grace / To unloose this tied-up Justice when you pleased," I.iii.31–32); Isabella, hearing of her brother's imprisonment ("Woe me! For what?" I.iv.26); Escalus and Angelo, confounded by the bumbling protestations of Pompey, Elbow, and Froth (II.i.); Angelo, surprised at his awakened lust (II.ii.162); Isabella, hearing of Angelo's mistreatment of Mariana ("Can this be so? Did Angelo so leave her?" III.i. 228); the Duke, shocked at Angelo's order for Claudio's immediate execution (IV.ii.122–29); the Provost, "amazed" when the disguised Duke miraculously produces a letter with the Duke's seal on it (IV.ii.212); the Duke, surprised by Barnardine's resistance and by Ragozine's conveniently appearing head (IV.iii.77); Escalus and Angelo, confused by the Duke's "uneven and distracted" letters (IV.iv.1–7); and, of course, Isabella, stupefied at the Duke's proposal of marriage, along with Angelo and Lucio, distressed at their suddenly ordered couplings.
36. Frye, *Anatomy of Criticism,* pp. 177–79.

poor playwriting.[37] (Such a model, clearly of abiding interest to Shakespeare, is less subtly depicted in the rustics' production of "Pyramus and Thisby" in *A Midsummer Night's Dream*.) By creating in Duke Vincentio a model third-rate playwright—one whose mind-set Jean Howard calls "confining, inelastic, dangerously reductive," one who has no qualms about "[draining] the life out of previously vital characters such as Isabella"[38]—Shakespeare calls into question the ethics of his own craft, including the ethics involved in handling characters of the opposite sex. However, the intent to which Shakespeare transcends the Duke's limitations is not clear, especially with regard to the treatment of female characters. It is in this area that the comparison between the playwright and his surrogate becomes most murky.

Vincentio's sexual double standard is hardly subtle. Ever oblivious to female experience, Vincentio tells Juliet that because she returns Claudio's affection—because the "most offenseful act" is "mutually committed"—her sin is therefore "of heavier kind" than Claudio's (II.iii.26–28). Such chauvinism, while present in Shakespeare's previous comedies, has almost always eventually been subverted in favor of mutuality.[39] It would be tempting to claim that because the expected subversion of chauvinistic values does not occur in *Measure for Measure*, therefore Shakespeare must be consciously critiquing the Duke's double standard, once again—as in the case of Ragozine's

37. Those who view the play as exemplifying some lapse on Shakespeare's part include Philip Edwards (*Shakespeare and the Confines of Art* [London: Methuen, 1968], pp. 108–10), who deems the play a "failure" because of its "insistence on a happy ending in spite of the evidence." On the other hand, critics like Howard and Fly credit Shakespeare with having purposefully created a disruptive audience experience—an argument prefigured by Michael Goldman's appendix on *Measure for Measure* in *Shakespeare and the Energies of Drama* (Princeton: Princeton Univ. Press, 1972), p. 164, in which he suggests that in *Measure for Measure*, as in *Hamlet* and *Lear*, audience experience is "turned against itself to produce a comment on the action."

38. Howard, pp. 155 and 151, respectively.

39. See, for example, Marianne L. Novy, "Giving, Taking, and the Role of Portia in *The Merchant of Venice*," *Philological Quarterly*, 58 (1979), 137–54 for a discussion of mutuality in relationships in Shakespearean comedy.

head—showing himself to be the superior craftsman. But this claim would be ill-founded, considering that Shakespeare's own treatment of female characters at this point in his career becomes less than generous. As Vincentio "drains" life out of Isabella and Mariana, so Shakespeare drains life out of Gertrude and Ophelia, giving them scarcely any character at all. Joel Fineman's well-documented discussion of Shakespeare's "not uncommon defensive gynophobia," which erupts in certain tragedies, would support such an argument.[40] If Shakespeare can be credited with critiquing Vincentio's treatment of female "characters," which seems unlikely, then he must also be said to be critiquing his treatment of some of his own.

But regardless of the playwright's intention, *Measure for Measure*, more than any of his previous plays, exposes the dehumanizing effect on women of living in a world dominated by powerful men who would like to re-create womanhood according to their fantasies. Duke Vincentio's distorted interpretation of Isabella's outrage in the prison scene is only one example of this kind of dehumanizing mind-set. His tampering with Isabella's character in Act V —which she must endure, according to religious edict—is no less a violation than Angelo's attempt to possess her body. As Hans Sachs puts it, the Duke succeeds in committing "in a legitimate and honorable way, the crime which Angelo attempted in vain."[41]

This play reveals, among other things, the price women pay in order for male supremacy to be maintained. That price for Isabella is, precisely, a mandatory denial of her personal standards. But Isabella's plight is only one element in a larger pattern. As a whole, *Measure for Measure* explores the incompatibility of patriarchal and comic structures. The world of patriarchy, antithetical to the world of comedy throughout Shakespeare's works, comes closest here to overthrowing the comic world. Far from

40. Joel Fineman, "Fratricide and Cuckoldry: Shakespeare's Doubles," *The Psychoanalytic Review*, 64 (1977), 426.
41. Hans Sachs, "The Measure in *Measure for Measure*," in *The Design Within*, ed. M. Faber (New York: Science House, 1970), pp. 495–96.

the one-dimensional representative of morality that critics have perceived her to be, Isabella is a key part of a dramatic environment in which the forces of patriarchy and comedy clash. In this context, her dramaturgical powerlessness becomes a variable in an equation in which the pervasiveness of chauvinism and the possibility of comic resolution are indirectly proportional. In other words, the stronger the forces of patriarchy, the less likely—or at least less convincing—comic resolution becomes.

Generically, Isabella is Shakespeare's pivotal female figure. She simultaneously links the dramatically effective early comic women to the victimized tragic women, even while her sympathetic portrayal anticipates the revival of influential women in the later plays. If Isabella's voice is lost in *Measure for Measure*—to remain mute throughout Shakespeare's tragedies, in which male misfortune and misogyny explode into significantly linked central issues[42] —that voice is rediscovered in the romances, Shakespeare's most mature creations, in which patriarchal and misogynistic values, if present at all, are, as in the early comedies, subverted, and in which the imaginative environment once again allows female characters, like Paulina in *The Winter's Tale*, for example, to exert a powerful, positive force in shaping dramatic action.

42. Bamber, p. 15.

S. NAGARAJAN

Measure for Measure on Stage and Screen

The earliest evidence of a performance of the play is an entry in the Revels Accounts, which says that *"Mesur for Mesur"* by "Shaxberd" was acted at Whitehall on December 26, 1604, St. Stephen's Night, by His Majesty's Players. We next hear of a performance in 1662 in Sir William Davenant's adaptation *The Law Against Lovers.* Davenant's sweeping changes in the plot and characterizations reduce greatly the seriousness of Shakespeare's play. He introduced characters from *Much Ado About Nothing,* and rewrote many speeches to suit Restoration ideas of decorum and clarity of expression. Samuel Pepys, who characterized this adaptation as "a good play" when he saw it at The Duke's House in Lincoln Inn's Fields on February 18, 1662, singled out for praise the dancing and singing of the girl who played one of the new roles created by Davenant.

The next recorded performance is of another adaptation, Charles Gildon's *Measure for Measure, or Beauty the Best Advocate,* in 1700, at Lincoln's Inn Fields. This version, with Thomas Betterton playing Angelo and Mrs. Bracegirdle as Isabella, was performed eight times during the season of 1699–1700. There is a little more of Shakespeare in Gildon than in Davenant, but substantial alterations still make this bear only a remote resemblance to Shakespeare's play. Gildon omitted the bawdry of the play, and introduced in its place an operatic interlude by Henry Purcell, *The Loves of Dido and Aeneas* with

libretto by Nahum Tate. He gave a love speech to the
Duke to reduce the abruptness of his proposal of marriage
to Isabella.

Between 1701 and 1750 the play (or an adaptation)
was enacted 69 times, being, according to C. B. Hogan
(cited in the *New Variorum* edition p. 468), "the sixth
most frequent among Shakespeare's comedies." (The
1720 performance restored Shakespeare's text to the
stage.) In 1737 Mrs. Cibber appeared as Isabella and
remained unchallenged in the role till she retired in 1759.
We do not hear of the play on the London stage again
till 1770, although it was occasionally played in the prov-
inces and in Dublin. Between 1751 and 1800 there were
sixty-four performances in London. After Mrs. Cibber
had retired, the role of Isabella was played by Mrs. Siddons at David Garrick's Drury Lane. (She was later
joined by her brothers, John Philip Kemble and Charles
Kemble.) Mrs. Siddons's Isabella was "noble, high-
principled, idealistic and even fierce, but understandable
and lovable as well. It was the sort of part [she] loved to
play and people raved about it" (K. Mackenzie, *The
Great Sarah,* 1968, p. 70). Her style was somewhat de-
clamatory, but she could feel her way into the part, and
make it sympathetic. She was seen for the last time in
1812 when she was so weak with age (although she was
only 57) and ill health that she had to be helped up in the
last act after kneeling to the Duke. (To hide the fact,
Mariana was also helped up.) After Mrs. Siddons, the
role passed on to Elizabeth O'Neill at the Covent Garden.
Regarded as a worthy successor, she was praised for adding the grandeur of lofty declamation to the pathos of
intense feeling and harmonizing sublimity of expression
with tenderness of thought.

In the nineteenth century there were (according to the
New Variorum) only twenty-two performances. In 1824
Macready played the Duke at Drury Lane; the richness
of the costumes was particularly remarked. But the usual
nineteenth-century emphasis on spectacle, including illu-
sionistic sets that took considerable time to erect and to

strike, meant that the text had to be cut. Samuel Phelps, who in 1846 produced *Measure for Measure* at Sadler's Wells with himself as the Duke, especially deserves to be remembered, because he did more than any one else before William Poel to restore Shakespeare's text.

Poel produced *Measure for Measure* in 1893 at the Royalty and again in 1908 at the Gaiety in Manchester. A pioneer in his insistence that Shakespeare could be appreciated only on the unlocalized stage for which he wrote and that dramatic speech should be both swift and musical, Poel declared that if the actor "got the tunes right" and observed certain principles of deportment, the rest would follow. (It did not do so always.) He coached his cast in the art of rhythmic speech and the value of the word to be emphasized. C. E. Montagu has described how in Poel's productions the short scenes and the long ones flowed into one another and the stage arrangement never froze the imagination as reconstructed scholarship often does. The dresses were quaint but rich and some attempt was made to achieve historical accuracy. As for the scenery, one simply did not think about it. Scenes were changed by the drawing of a curtain. Because the settings were simple, the full text could be given in the original sequence of the scenes, revealing Shakespeare's art of construction. At the production of 1893 gentlemen in Elizabethan costume sat on the sides of the stage, as in some theaters in Shakespeare's day, and during the intervals they smoked Elizabethan claypipes. In 1908, at the end of the performance, the company made a great impression when they knelt in line on the stage and recited the King's Prayer from the pre-Shakespearean play of *Ralph Roister Doister*. Poel had his faults, of course. He was still sufficiently Victorian to bowdlerize the text. In the line "By yielding up thy body to my will," "body" became "self," though the line became unmetrical thereby; "He has got a wench with child" became "He will shortly be a father." (The bawdry of the play has always been objected to till recently.) Poel sometimes carried his dislike of elaborate scenery too far, and his emphasis on

natural intonation led him to ignore the variations demanded by different circumstances. Nevertheless our debt
to Poel remains great. We owe the swiftness and continu-
ity of modern productions to him.

Poel, who took the part of Angelo in both of the productions, argued that Angelo should not be seen as a
moral reprobate, for he had, after all, won the heart of
Mariana. He was the one instance in Shakespeare of a
man who fell while contemplating virtue. In the Manchester production Sara Allgood played Isabella as a
character of passionate truth. She did not wear any religious habit because if she did, argued Poel, the Duke could
not very well offer to marry her. Poel cast the Duke
(James Hearne, in 1908) as a man of about forty, alert,
full of resource and energy, adored for his kindly ways
and far too witty and wise for anyone to feel bored in his
company. Poel insisted that his speech to Claudio on
death should be given with ease and spirit, for in Poel's
view the Duke was not a conventional religious man.
(Samuel Johnson, it will be recalled, thought that the description of death as sleep is impious in the Friar, foolish
in the reasoner, and trite and vulgar in the poet.)

With Poel begins the modern stage history of the play,
characterized by the determined attempts of producers to
give a modern reading of the characters and of the general
significance of the play. The play is seen either in modern
psychological terms or in theological (or anti-theological)
terms. The division of critical opinion that the play has
occasioned is seen in the theater also, for instance, in the
interpretation of the characters of the Duke and Isabella.
The play itself is read sometimes either as a dramatic
enactment of Christian charity, or, at the other extreme,
as a satire on the arbitrary ways of human and divine
authority. Isabella's response to the Duke's proposal of
marriage is also variously interpreted.

Passing over productions in 1924 (in one of which
Ernest Milton played a memorable Angelo) and 1925, we
may consider Tyrone Guthrie's production at the Old Vic
in 1933. (He had produced the play earlier, in 1930, at

Cambridge.) This production was remarkable for Charles Laughton's Angelo as an outright sensualist, a precisian dressed in a black water-silk robe who paced the stage in restless torment and spoke his lines "as if," said one reviewer, "he were drawing a garden-rake across intractable soil." Guthrie himself has written that Laughton's Angelo was "a cunning oleaginous monster whose cruelty and lubricity could have surprised no one, least of all himself" (*A Life in the Theatre* [1960], pp. 109–110). Flora Robson as Isabella gave a moving performance, although Guthrie himself thought she made the character too pure. James Agate saw in her acting sensuality under tempestuous restraint (*First Nights*, p. 236). Roger Livesey, Guthrie wrote, made "a glittering and commanding Duke suggesting glamor and the sinister power of absolute authority."

Guthrie came back to the play in 1937, again at the Old Vic, with Emlyn Williams now as a proud, pale, and disturbed deputy struggling to keep his sensuality down. Although his movements betrayed his lust for power, the agony of his temptation was real, and Williams made both the struggle and remorse moving. Isabella was played by Marie Ney. While Agate found her a scold (*The Amazing Theatre* [1939], p. 41), Audrey Williamson admired the intensity of her feeling and the intellectual maturity and poise of her bearing (*Old Vic Drama* [1948], p. 72). (The latter qualities lapsed, however, in her conduct with her brother.) Stephen Murray played a middle-aged Duke, and Sylvia Coleridge presented a Mariana whose forgiveness of Angelo struck many reviewers as truly sublime.

Departing from chronology, we may note that Guthrie produced the play again in 1966 at the Bristol Old Vic. But there was a difference, for he had come to accept the Christian interpretation of the play. (This is chiefly associated with the essay of Professor Wilson Knight included in the Signet Classic edition, but as early as 1908 Charlotte Porter had advanced a similar interpretation in a First Folio edition by herself and Helen A. Clarke.)

Guthrie made the Duke the central figure of the production now, describing him in the program note as a figure of Almighty God and even comparing him to the Heavenly Bridegroom in the last scene. "Shakespeare is permitting himself," wrote Guthrie, "a theological comment upon an all-wise, merciful Father-God who permits the frightful and apparently meaningless disasters which unceasingly befall his children." The theme of the play was justice tempered by mercy and authority tempered by love. (Nevertheless the production did not lack an element of fun.) John Franklyn Robbins played the part in a habit and manner that evoked the popular image of Christ. Not everyone was impressed; one critic irreverently said that the Duke was a vulgar-minded man gratifying himself by playing Christ in a water-spaniel wig. However, the comedy was enjoyable, and the tension of the Angelo (Richard Pascoe)–Isabella (Barbara Leigh-Hunt) debates was realized.

There were productions of the play at Stratford in 1940 (by Iden Payne) and in 1946 (by Frank McMullan of the Yale Department of Drama). (For differing views of McMullan's production, see Professor Wilson Knight's *Shakespearian Production* [1964], pp. 255–58 and T. C. Kemp and J. C. Trewin in *The Stratford Festival* [1953]). The play was again seen at Stratford in 1947 produced by Ronald Giffen with Beatrix Lehmann as Isabella, Paul Scofield as Lucio, and Michael Golden as the Duke.

Nineteen fifty saw what many regard as the best production of the play: Peter Brook's at Stratford in England. Derek Granger, reviewing Anthony Quayle's 1956 production in *The Financial Times*, recalled that Brook's production had the effect of an important discovery, as if "a dark and rarely seen canvas had been suddenly stripped of dirty varnish and newly presented with unexpectedly brilliant highlights."

Brook believes that desiging the stage and directing the play are inseparable responsibilities. With the assistance of Michael Northen and Kegan Smith he devised an adaptable set consisting of a circle of gray stone pillars and arches. Downstage on either side stood a heavy postern gate. This permanent set gave coherence to the production and permitted the action to flow swiftly and continuously. It could be an image both of the material prosperity of Vienna and the severity of its penal system. Even the little details were significant. There was, for instance, a tarboosh on a prisoner's head suggesting that Turkey was not far away. This simple setting allowed the actors and the text to assume their rightful importance. In the stage business Brook made a distinction between the religious and the comic parts. Brook recognized that the play was religious in thought and suggested a morality play in its symmetrical pattern and balance. Although the director was free to improvise stage action for the comedy, which is in prose, he did not have the same freedom in the poetic part of the play, which deals with the weightier themes. Thus, Brook's Pompey distributed advertisements for Mistress Overdone's establishment, a piece of business for which there is no authority in the text. But in the noncomic scenes Brook was very restrained. Brook has said that the meanings of the play will emerge only if the comic and the serious—the Rough and the Holy, as he calls them —are both accepted in good faith. (Whether Brook himself did so has been questioned by Professor Herbert Weil in *Shakespeare Survey 25*, 1972. Weil argues that in Brook's text the ambivalence of the play was significantly diminished. Later directors have fully played up this ambivalence.)

Brook's Angelo was played as a repressed, sensual Puritan by John Gielgud, who had not somehow played that role at all in his long and distinguished Shakespearean career. Wearing a close-fitting black cap that made him look "spiritually clean-shaven, unromantic and very strict," he brought what one observer called a "thin-lipped hauteur" to the part. His Angelo was not a hypocrite, but a self-ignorant man who thought himself incorruptible till he met Isabella and discovered how unscrupulous he could be under the impulse of sudden lust. Gielgud made him a near-tragic figure, for whom one felt some pity when he said in the last scene, "Immediate sentence then, and sequent death, is all the grace I beg." Barbara Jefford, who was only nineteen and was making her debut, played Isabella, proving equal to the double challenge of the role and her place opposite Gielgud. Her Isabella was an emotionally restrained and innocent young novice for whom it was entirely natural to prefer chastity to the life of her brother. She conveyed Brook's own conviction (reported in *The Times* March 10, 1950), that Isabella's preference was consistent with the tradition of the age, her calling, and her faith. She spoke the "proud man" speech with an air of discovery rather than in cynical denunciation. Several times she stopped Angelo from leaving the chamber by kneeling to him and clutching his arm. At one point Gielgud showed subtly the response of the awakened Angelo. His voice became ever so slightly less sure and steady. The audience was aware of the change, but Isabella was not. Her attractiveness had begun to work on him, though of course she had not set out to exploit it. The scenes of Angelo's attempted seduction of Isabella were highly effective. The actress Gwen Watford has described the first meeting as follows: "It was a purely mental process, he made no physical movement at all, but seemed as if a tremendous force had suddenly gripped every muscle in his body and numbed his brain. There was a timeless pause as the shock lessened and he found sufficient strength to move down to the table and sit. And then the tremendous relief when he heard his own voice speaking steadily and under control. I must confess I found myself gasping under the impact." At the difficult line, "More than our brother is our chastity," Isabella turned toward the wall, as if "she was herself ashamed that her intellect could find no more adequate expression of her heart's certainty" (Richard David, in *Shakespeare Survey 4* [1951], pp. 136–137). There was an agonized excitement in her voice. Her anger against her brother was not the hysterical outburst of a sexually repressed woman, as in many productions, but "anger with her own failure as a witness to truth, her own inability to communicate it to others" (David, p. 137). The most memorable moment of the performance came when she had to plead for Angelo. After the Duke's definitive-sounding "He dies for Claudio," there was a long pause, for two minutes. (Brook had instructed Miss Jefford to prolong the pause till she felt the audience could take it no longer.) Then she slowly moved across the stage and knelt before the Duke. "Her words came quiet, and as their full import of mercy reached Angelo, a sob broke from him" (David, p. 137). Robert Speaight felt that this Angelo deserved to be pardoned, and Brook himself has said in *The Empty Space* (p. 89) that in the silence of the long pause the abstract notion of mercy became concrete to all those who were present.

But it was the Duke who held the central place in Brook's production. Harry Andrews presented him, says Richard David, as the Friar turned Duke rather than as the Duke turned Friar. He maintained an exact measure of aloofness and conveyed Authority and Benevolence without any supernatural overtones. When his proposal was accepted by Isabella the audience did not feel any sense of incongruity in the characters. Maxine Audley presented Mariana as a woman who might honestly love and admire Angelo. The comic characters (Leon Quartermaine as a sprightly Lucio, George Rose as an amiable vigorous spiv with his own brand of integrity, Rosalind Atkinson as Mistress Overdone) were all played as natural English characters. Alan Badel made a genuinely terrified Claudio. Brook's production has become a classic of the stage and a landmark in the stage history of the play.

In 1951 the Berliner Ensemble of Brecht (who regarded *Measure for Measure* as Shakespeare's most progressive play) staged a version under a title that translates as "Round Heads and Pointed Heads." Juliet is made an Aryan girl whom Claudio (renamed Guzman) has seduced. He is condemned to death. His sister Isabella agrees to the Police Chief's proposal, which is the same as Angelo's. When she goes to a prostitute for advice on how to conduct herself during the assignation, the brothel-

keeper is shocked that a lady should take this job upon
herself and for a handsome payment deputes one of her
girls. The girl is, however, paid her usual time-rate while
Madam pockets the difference. Margot Heinemann explains that Brecht's point is that "the gentry can usually
find someone else to suffer the unpleasant experiences for
them" (Jonathan Dollimore and Alan Sinfield: *Political
Shakespeare* [1985], p. 220). This, according to Ms.
Heinemann, is hinted at in Shakespeare's play. Mariana
is vulnerable because she has lost the dowry, and the
Duke seeks to substitute Barnardine or Claudio. "Beneath
the surface of Shakespeare's reassuringly happy ending
lurks a very nasty underworld of sexual and commercial
exploitation of inferiors which is never cleaned up, only
played down and obscured. In Brecht's rewriting this side
of the contradiction becomes the central impression"
(Heinemann). A similar political interpretation was given
to a Polish production in 1956 in which a parallel was
drawn between Vienna under Angelo and Poland on the
eve of the Poznan riots.

In 1954 the play was produced by Cecil Clarke at the
Ontario Stratford festival as an exploration into the com-
plexities and inconsistencies of human nature. But perhaps
the production in 1956 at the English Stratford by Anthony Quayle is better known. Quayle made the Duke the
central figure of his production, with Anthony Nicholls
playing him as a human figure, forceful, noble and reassur-
ing. (Quayle cut out lines that could be interpreted against
this interpretation.) Emlyn Williams played Angelo again,
but his performance this time was considered inferior to
his earlier one of 1937 with Guthrie, for now he made
Angelo too obviously a hypocrite, with only occasional
glimpses of the tortured soul, and in the central scenes his
restlessness was too self-conscious. Isabella, played by
Margaret Johnston, was a girl utterly dedicated to the
religious life. (This made her acceptance of the Duke's
proposal rather out of character.) In the scene with her
brother (Emrys Jones), she conveyed the impression that
her denunciation of him reflected her own moral agony.

Alan Badel's Lucio made corruption attractive and venial, and conveyed the view that man's instincts represented the basic truth of human nature. Patrick Wymark's Pompey was a Cockney with a music-hall touch in his gestures and miming. The sets (of Tanya Moisewitsch) showed a permanent vault which suited the play's moods in many of the scenes, but they did not capture the corrupt Vienna of the play.

In 1957 Margaret Webster produced the play at the Old Vic. Miss Webster saw a Heaven-Earth-Hell pattern in the play, with the characters having a threefold identity: as they liked to appear; as they liked to think they were; and as they really were (*Don't Put Your Daughter on the Stage,* New York [1972], pp. 303–305). The play was concerned, in her reading, with the use and abuse of power. She postponed the second Isabella-Angelo encounter in order not to lose sight of Angelo for too long. Barry Kay designed a unit set for her with the Duke entering at the highest level and "Hell" being the dungeons. Angelo first wore a scholar's black gown; then the robes of public office; and at the end he was stripped. (Miss Webster would have liked to strip him completely.) Lucio's wig of golden hair came off when he was arrested, revealing a bald, scabrous skull. Anthony Nicholls again played the Duke as a human figure. Miss Webster believed that the character could be humanized and given a variety of thought and feeling by the actor. John Nevill's Angelo was a precisian swept off his feet by temporary lust. Isabella was again played by Barbara Jefford as a warm-blooded young woman devoted to chastity and possessing a strong sense of right. She accepted the Duke's proposal.

In 1962 the allegorical Duke reappeared in John Blatchley's production at the English Stratford. Blatchley felt that the preference for chastity could not be made the main theme in a modern production of the play. Nor sex; Brook had already done that. He chose the problem of evil as his cohesive idea: how to reconcile the existence and prevalence of evil in a world created by an omnipotent, omniscient, and good God. The Duke (Tom Fleming) was the pivot of the performance. He was omnipresent. He knew all about Angelo, and like a schoolmaster who has conceived a dislike for the clever boy of the form, set a trap for him (*The* (London) *Times*, April 11, 1962). But the star performance was Marius Goring's Angelo. Goring presented Angelo as a neurotic, though sincere, Puritan who happened to make a sudden and appalling discovery of his own corruption. He became hysterical; scourged himself; fell prone on the ground; and writhed at Isabella's feet in the second meeting. Isabella, played by Judi Dench, was too robust a figure for some reviewers. She did not make her passion, her sense of vocation, or the agony of her dilemma convincing. (Incidentally, her dress, an uncommonly low-cut gown, remained secular throughout the performance.) The set consisted of a backwall made of large pieces of stone, a slightly raised platform that filled more than half the stage, and a section of cobblestones. This bare setting agreed with the central conception of the production.

It is probably an index of the improved critical and theatrical fortunes of the play that Michael Elliott should have selected it for the last night of the Old Vic on April 3, 1963 before that theater closed down. The program notes were prepared by Professor Nevill Coghill of Oxford, who had earlier written on the underlying medieval comic form of the play (*Shakespeare Survey 8*, 1955) and had himself produced it in 1956 for the Bristol University Union. James Maxwell made a severe but just Duke, dignified, saintly, and aloof. He was a mysterious, semidivine personage, and there was a strong suggestion that the final scene was a kind of Day of Judgment. Dilys Hamlet played Isabella as a fiery-tempered and passionate girl suddenly confronted with a reality different from what she had expected. She screamed at her brother for exposing her to one more glimpse of ugly reality. Lee Montagu played a nonascetic, virile-looking Angelo, unbuttoned to his chest hair in his second meeting with Isabella.

There were interesting productions in 1965 by John Neville (who had earlier played Angelo) at the Notting-

ham Playhouse and in 1969 by David Giles in Stratford
in Canada, but the landmark of 1970 was John Barton's
controversial production at Stratford in England. Barton
made some cuts in the text and shifted some scenes and
speeches. He recognized that the background of the play
was religious, but he opted for a human Duke. Barton
thinks that allegorical, symbolical, or metaphysical interpretations are not easy to realize in stage terms; besides,
the acting tradition in England has always favored the
exploration of character ("Directing the Problem Plays:
John Barton Talks to Gareth Lloyd Evans," in *Shakespeare Survey 25* [1972], pp. 63–71). Although very well-
informed about the criticism of the play, Barton did not
wish to illustrate any particular critical view of the play
in his production. For instance, many critics (e.g., Tillyard) think that the play breaks up or changes its characters in the middle. Barton disagrees. If the actors bring
the characters to life in the first part of the play, the so-
called division of the play is hardly apparent in the
theater. There is a change of emphasis with the entry of
Mariana, but that is a different matter. The play is open-
ended, and an honest production must also be open-ended.
The controversy was whether Barton's own production
was open-ended.

Barton's Duke, played by Sebastian Shaw, was a philosopher statesman—his dusty table was piled with books—
but he was an ineffectual ruler. Shaw captured all aspects
of the Duke except his authority. Juliet was indignant
when he questioned her, and Claudio went on with his
prison meal without paying any attention to the Duke-
Friar's consolation. (On the first night there was an unnecessarily vulgar piece of stage business when Barnardine
threw the crucifix given to him into a chamber pot and
noisily urinated into it. The audience was not amused, and
the business was dropped after a few performances.) His
proposal of marriage evoked a shocked silence from Isabella. "After a long pause of silence, he uttered a resigned
'So,' put on his glasses, and departed with all others
leaving a bewildered Isabella alone on the stage looking

out of the audience" (Jane Williamson, "The Duke and
Isabella on the Modern Stage," in *The Triple Bond*, ed.
Joseph G. Price, University Park, Pa. [1975], pp. 149–
169). From the heights of royalty and divinity (says Ms.
Williamson), the character had slid down in Barton's
production into a pathetic, ineffective bumbler, lost and
confused in the real world of men and affairs.

Barton's Angelo was played by Ian Richardson, handsome and physically well cast for the part. He portrayed
Angelo as rather nervous to begin with, but once installed
in office, he became proud, arrogant, and cold. His im-
patience and superciliousness were shown when he pulled
a chair with his foot for Isabella. He looked at the Duke's
dusty table with obvious distaste, and when *he* came to sit
at it, it was spotlessly clean. He was constantly wiping his
hands. He was a hypocrite, aware of all things sexual.
When Isabella entered his presence, he was busy with
papers. Then he lifted up his head and saw her, and there
was a small pause. It conveyed much. In the second meeting he left the table and went toward her while she moved
into action, reversing roles, as it were. When he proposed
his condition, he grabbed her by the hair, pulled her over
the table, and caressed her body. (This piece of violence,
suggested by the actress herself, helped her to utter the
difficult line, "More than our brother is our chastity.")
Barton also improvised a scene in which the Provost
silently showed Angelo the head of Claudio in a bag.
Angelo broke down and wept, unable to confront the consequences of his own cruelty.

In Barton's view the play was Isabella's. His Isabella
was played by Estelle Kohler, a very youthful actress.
There was an air of uncertainty about her performance,
and it was hard to make out whether it belonged to the actress or to her interpretation of the character. The program
note (written by Professor Anne Barton of Cambridge)
spoke of Isabella's purity as concealing an hysterical fear
of sex. When she spoke the line about chastity, she flung
her arm out, like a general waving his troops on into
action, said Harold Hobson. And in "the proud man"

speech, she stressed the word "man," intimating that women were different. When her brother accepted the sentence, she sat by his side, but when he showed signs of weakening, she leaped away to denounce him. When the Duke proposed to her, she stared at him. Was it incredulity, dislike, or disgust? She remained on the stage after all the others had left, pondering the strange ways of men, perhaps recalling what she had told Angelo—that men always try to take advantage of a woman's weakness at the slightest chance. She seemed to have realized the power of sex, that everything goes down before it— authority, justice, piety, even decency. The whole business of concealing the fact that her brother was alive had only one aim: to rush her into marriage in a freshet of gratitude. Barton made the ending ambiguous in this way. Sara Kestelman played Mariana and was the dominant presence in the last act. (The program note said that she was the only character in the play who existed in "an uncriticized absolute.") She was portrayed as "a pale, auburn-haired pre-Raphaelite beauty whose dejection [had] produced in her no hesitancy" (Peter Thomson in *Shakespeare Survey* 24 [1971], p. 124). The lower characters were, in general, not well realized, though Terence Hardman made a ratlike Lucio. Timothy O'Brien's sets of wall blocks of paneled wood, with semiparquet flooring and wooden ceiling, conveyed claustrophobic puritanical cleanliness, but not the corruption of Vienna.

Peter Thomson in *Shakespeare Survey* 24 summed up the difference between Brook and Barton in the following way: Barton looked for ways of revealing the text while Brook preferred to make his crucial discoveries in rehearsal, believing that theatrical revelation must not be anticipated but "risked." On this interpretation Brook's approach was more open-ended than Barton's.

The next production, Dr. Jonathan Miller's in February 1974 for the National Theatre, was equally interesting. Miller set the play in the pleasure-loving Vienna of Freud, who was the invisible, brooding presence of the production. The society of the play was characterized by bureaucratic rule and petty bourgeois professionalism. The performance was intended to throw light on the history that followed the 'thirties. Miller has argued in *Subsequent Performances* that a great play has an "after-life"; each performance is incomplete in itself but contributes to the development of the play. "If works of art are discovered after a long period of being lost or neglected, it is as if they are perceived and valued for reasons so different from those held originally that they virtually change their character and identity. There comes a point in the life of any cultural artefact, whether a play or a painting, when the continued existence of the physical token that represents it does not necessarily mean that the original identity of the work survives." It is this aesthetic that has guided many recent productions of the play.

The stage for Miller's production was designed by Bernard Culshaw, who set a long corridor with a row of doors nailed together without any stretches of wall to separate them. Miller has explained (in *Subsequent Performances*) that at the moment when any one door in the facade represented a door, none of the others did so. Though these doors were representational, referring to exits and entrances mentioned in the text, the overall style was dictated by the now-familiar idiom of an empty (rather than highly localized) space within which an action can occur without having to be slavishly pictorial. The only furniture was a table. Carl Davis's imitation classical music helped to realize the Viennese setting.

Angelo, played by Julian Curry, was angular, pear-faced, bespectacled, and went about always with a brief-case. He constantly referred to the lawbook on the table even while he was fondling Isabella's "holy-knee." Gillian Barge's Isabella was a highly professional Sister who had sacrificed her emotions for the sake of her calling. She shared Angelo's disgust at what her brother (played by David Bradley) had done. Angelo rather than the Duke was her man, and she cast a series of "furtive, longing" glances at him. Alan Macnaughten as the Duke projected the ambiguities of the character, principally his "meddlesome cruelty" (Miller's own phrase) and pleasure in other men's miseries. His disregard of Bernardine was brutal, and he stage-managed the denouement in a bluff and callous way. He did not reenter the city with the traditional fanfare, but slipped in after giving an oily handshake to the persons gathered around him (Peter Ansorge in *Plays and Players,* March 1974, p. 45). He looked like a 'thirties politician whose dirty deeds were to plunge the world soon into a world war. When he proposed to Isabella, she drew back in horror.

This interpretation was taken further in the production that followed: Keith Hack's at Stratford in England, in 1974. Hack followed Edward Bond's reading of the play, printing it in the program note: the play is an arraignment of all authority; Angelo is a lying self-deceiving fraud; the Duke is a vain, face-saving hypocrite; and the saintly Isabella is a vicious sex-hysteric. As Michael Billington pointed out in his *Guardian* review (September 5, 1974), the production became dull because such a reading does not permit any psychological growth. Michael Pennington presented a virile Angelo who, at the second meeting with Isabella, dropped to his knees, supplicating her and trembling with lust. This was the only scene which proved acceptable in the production. Otherwise it was regarded as a dismal failure. A charitable judgment was that it had the negative virtue of demonstrating that *Measure for Measure* cannot be treated as Jonsonian satire, only more nihilistic.

Hack's attempt at updating the play was put in the shade by the adaptation of Charles Marowitz produced at the Open Space in London in 1975. Marowitz omitted characters, rearranged scenes, and rewrote the plot. For instance, in Marowitz's version Isabella goes to bed (not altogether unwillingly) with Angelo.

In a modern-dress production in 1975 at the Ontario Stratford festival Robin Phillips saw the core of the play as consisting of sex, misuse of power, and the exploitation of women. It was the least Elizabethan of Shakespeare's plays, requiring a place where both low-life gaiety and

freedom and sophisticated upper-class life obtained and
outward piety went hand in hand with unspoken sexuality.
Venereal disease was a widespread problem, indicating
massive sexual repression. The Vienna of 1912 was the
obvious choice. (Besides, one could also think of a Duke
as Head of State in 1912.) In Phillips's production the
Duke (William Hutt), more a monster than a sage, was
totally insensitive to others and thought only of himself.
Isabella (Martha Henry) was dressed in the white costume of her order, but the soft jersey of her dress revealed
clearly the female form underneath. The costume gave the
clue to her character: sexuality overlaid with its transpar-
ent negation. She was aware of the contradiction, and the
awar. ı ess gave a touch of sorrow and self-contempt to
her tone and behavior. After Angelo had stated his condition aı d left, she dipped her hand in a water jug and
splashed the cold water on her forehead. At the end, after
the Duke had left with the other characters, she remained
on the stage, turned around, removed her headdress and
her steel-rimmed glasses, and placed the back of her hand
on her forehead. Her face showed her revulsion and
anguish at the prospect of marriage to the Duke. Some
reviewers received the impression that she accepted the
Duke's proposal in a spirit of fatalistic resignation, but
the director himself told Professor Ralph Berry that she
neither accepted nor rejected the proposal (*On Directing
Shakespeare* [1977], p. 103). Angelo (Brian Bedford)
welcomed the office bestowed on him with a self-satisfied
smirk on his face as a belated recognition of his merit.
When self-discovery overtook him, he was horrified at
himself. Richard Monette made a brash, cynical Lucio,
and Lewis Gordon made a hearty Pompey.

   The play was produced in 1978 at the English Stratford
by Barry Kyle. Kyle saw *Measure for Measure* not as a
parable of justice but as an essay on appearance and reality. The key image was that of dissembling. The stage
showed a black box with numerous exits and entrances
suggesting corridors and a warren of offices. The box
flattened out at the back to display cubicles where the

whores carried on their brisk business. The cubicles also served as prison cells. The walls swung inward to enclose Angelo and Isabella during their second interview. The sword of justice rested conspicuously on Angelo's knee while he was examining Pompey, and after he left, Escalus leaned it against the table. Angelo wore a long white robe decorated with red motifs that looked like tiny leaping flames. These motifs were also seen on the uniforms worn by the prison staff and the prisoners. Both Escalus and the Justice removed their robes of office after Pompey had left as if they were glad to be rid of them. Isabella arrived at the convent with a suitcase. She wore her nun's habit when going to meet Angelo.

The central figure in Kyle's production also was the Duke, played by Michael Pennington. He saw him neither as *deus ex machina* nor as a Christ figure. He was not much older than Isabella, for a marriage proposal from him would otherwise be incongruous. Pennington believed that the Duke not only guided Isabella but traveled in the play toward self-discovery, achieving humility. Pennington praised the Duke's relationship with Isabella as a real one, different from what is found in Romantic comedy. In the finale he was testing Isabella. Wearing his Friar's robes with arms outstretched, and looking at Isabella all the while, he delivered his "measure for measure" speech in a voice of authority. He ended the play on a note of harmony and self-knowledge. Angelo was played by Jonathan Pryce as a symbol of "emergent lust" (J. C. Trewin, *Shakespeare Quarterly*, Spring 1979, p. 154). He was an efficient career man, who knew nothing of his own sexuality. Nervous and fidgety, he was always plaiting his fingers. When he had to state the vile condition for saving Claudio, he turned toward the wall as if he was afraid of facing Isabella. The scenes of Isabella (Paola Dionisetti) with Angelo lacked the necessary element of erotic tension, but she successfully suggested that she had also undergone a gradual process of self-awakening. She felt drawn to the Duke and accepted his proposal with alacrity. Majorie Bland played Mariana with very few senti-

mental overtones. Richard Griffiths made an excellent
Pompey who lectured the officers on civic morality, and
John Nettles was "an unctuously unsnubbable" Lucio
(Irving Wardle, *The Times,* June 28, 1978). Kyle repeated the production in 1979 at the Aldwych. David Suchet
played Angelo as a precise man of affairs suddenly overcome by temptation. Pennington was the Duke in full
control of his part, giving the impression in the final scene
that he was enjoying it as the sequel to his masquerade.
Miss Sinead Cusack made a rather light Isabella.

In 1981 Michael Rudman produced the play for the
National Theatre. The cast was all West Indian because,
said Rudman, there were plenty of very good West Indies
actors available. According to Rudman, all the leading
characters behave very oddly, and he wanted to devise a
political context that would explain such behavior. He
chose a mythical Caribbean island that has just attained
independence and that has not yet learned how to govern
itself. A leader can be changed overnight, for instance.
High-minded laws have been passed that cannot be put
into practice. There is no distinction between private and
public behavior because everybody knows everybody.
Warm friendliness jostles with physical cruelty. The action
of the play began during an official reception at what had
obviously been the governor's place before independence.
The new regime had two connections with the old, a
worldly Escalus (Leslie Sands) and the Provost in khaki
(Anthony Brown). Eileen Diss had erected colonnades to
represent the marketplace where the local population
sang, danced and drank (hardly a picture of corruption,
was the wry comment of Roger Warren in *Shakespeare
Survey 35,* 1982). Stefan Kalipha as the Duke tended to
bury the emotion while Yvette Harris as Isabella merely
stated it. Norman Beaton made an uncompromising Angelo (a bishop in this production) brooding over his temptation without any inner turmoil—like a bureaucrat. Oscar
James played Pompey as a Lord of Misrule. Peter Strak-
er's Lucio sang an interpolated song describing how Angelo's repressive measures had led to increased pimping.

The verse was treated with excessive reverence. In general, opinion on the production was divided.

The next production in Stratford, England, took place in 1983. Adrian Noble saw the play as a comedy in its structure with a situation that could have come from a Bunuel film or from the Surrealists. The challenge of the play was that it had characters like Isabella as well as Mistress Overdone, and then there was the whole discussion about the development of government and autocracy. These features of the play indicated that it should be set in a recognizable period and have a clear social definition. Noble set the play in a Vienna of gilt mirrors, white wigs, and brocade coats, but underneath this seventeenth-century elegance seethed a world of moral anarchy. With the aid of Bob Crowley he set the stage to bring out the contrast between the secluded, opulent court and the teeming city. Two bisecting white carpets formed a crucifix pattern on the floor with a tottering, baroque campanile encrusted with candles, crosses, and legal scales suggesting a world gone awry. The carpeted strip was used for scenes in which a choice had to be made: Angelo's acknowledgment of his desires, or Isabella's response to his condition. It was also used for passages where characters from different strands of the play passed each other, almost touching each other but in reality oblivious of each other's existence. The music of Ilona Sekacz, sensuously blending with the setting, sounded like the deformed echo of some classical piece. The play opened to a woman's singing of sacred music which had a vague suggestion that she was simultaneously enjoying sexual pleasure. Daniel Massey played the Duke as a ruler who is aware of his authority but who still has to learn that self-knowledge is essential to a ruler. Angelo was presented by David Schofield as a repressed personality whose moral equilibrium is upset by sudden unsuspected passion. His knees buckled and his fingers began to flex and unflex involuntarily. Juliet Stevenson, whose emotional directness and vocal range were praised by many reviewers, portrayed Isabella as a moral absolutist who learns that compassion is superior to cloistered virtue. Her final acceptance of the Duke seemed right and proper. Noble repeated the production at the Barbican in 1984.

David Thacker produced the play twice (in modern dress on both occasions) at the Young Vic. in 1985 and in 1987. He projected the court of the Duke as a banker's boardroom where nothing counted but economics, and men with serious flaws of character encouraged dogma and repression in the name of sound and sensible administration. In 1985 Peter Guinness played a "grouchy and saturnine" Duke while in 1987 he was played by Matthew Marsh. John Gillett's 1985 Angelo was a figure of frigid virtue and serious demeanor, while in 1987 Corin Redgrave played the part with impressive control and precision, his torment when he realized his corruption being eloquent. Joanna Foster's Isabella in 1985 displayed a sincere belief in the value of chastity. (She accepted the Duke's proposal.) Saskia Reeves's 1987 Isabella showed a "rising passion of spiritual self-righteousness, flat-footed grace and awkward innocence of the world" (John Vidal in the *Guardian, London Theatre Record*, VII, 10, 609). Rod Edwards played Lucio on both occasions, though in 1987 there was less fun. Margaret Leicester was Mariana on both occasions. She sang her own song, and in general appeared as a forsaken middle-aged woman. The sober Escalus was given an affair with his secretary.

The play was also seen in 1985 at the Canadian Stratford festival directed by Michael Bogdanov with designs by Chris Dyer. The general aim of this production was to convey the disturbing qualities of the play to our more open society whose extremely relaxed attitude in sexual matters makes the audience somewhat shockproof. The director therefore introduced many innovations, such as a cabaret scene. In the same year Robert Egan produced *Measure for Measure* at the Mark Taper Forum in Los Angeles. He found that the play illustrated Freud's concepts of acquisitive, violent, and sexually aggressive instincts as well as Jung's archetypes. Its wholesome moral was that the "instinctual drives must be confronted, brought to consciousness and controlled" to achieve harmony and survival. Egan made the play into a psychodrama of the Duke (Ken Ruta) with Lucio (Kelsey Grammer) being a part of his own personality. The production suggested that all the women who were married at the end were victims of exploitation by men who were using marriage as a respectable form of whoredom.

The next production at Stratford took place in 1987 when Nicholas Hytner made his debut as producer with a competent (but not particularly remarkable) production. Roger Allam presented the Duke as a human character who has to find instant solutions to unexpected developments. He conveyed the impression that as Friar he was discovering the city he had long governed, or rather, failed to govern. Sean Baker played Angelo as a close-cropped, white-faced precisian, cast in marble. Isabella was played by a black actress, Josette Simon, who made the preference for chastity credible. When the Duke proposed to her, she stared at him—without actually rejecting him.

The play has been seen on the European stage also (at Peter Brook's theater in Paris, for instance) in translations that have been often described as excellent. There was also a Chinese production at the Beijing People's Art Theatre in 1981, described by Carolyn Wakeman in *Shakespeare Quarterly,* Winter 1982. (This may be supplemented by the following information provided by Consulting British Director of the production, Mr. Toby Robertson and by Mr. Charles Aylmer of Cambridge University, who kindly translated from the Chinese an article by the director, Ying Ruo Cheng.) The director himself translated and adapted the play for the stage. Some 500 lines containing references to God, prostitution, and beliefs that were inadmissible in 1981 were omitted. A new title was given: *Please Step into the Pot,* which recalled a well-known Chinese folktale about a corrupt official who was asked to enter a red-hot pot, which he had himself indicated was the proper punishment for corrupt officials. The Chinese director saw the play as a

realistic portrait of a society in transition, though the
characterization is not based on actuality. In the production the principal features of the Shakespearean stage
were adopted: no drop curtain, close contact between
actors and audience, swift and continuous action and a
quick tempo of speech. The Chinese players had to
change their style of acting to adopt these innovations.
They did so with great success. The stage setting (of Alan
Barrett) showed an old broken-down gray wall symbol-
izing decadent Vienna, while a large lace doily at the rear
suggested the refinement of the court. There were different hangings for the different locales of action. At the
rear, painted in red on a panel of white cloth, a leering,
frowning face looked down on the audience. One eye
looked up at the sky and another downward. A wavy line
at the neck suggested the Puritan's ruffled collar. This face
was the emblem of the play's contradictions and duality,
and it warned the Chinese audience not to expect straight
lessons. Sound and lighting also contributed to the tragic-
comic conception of the production. At the beginning and
at intervals "a ghoulish, maniacal, demonic" laugh (Wakeman) echoed across the stage. It faded into the mirth of
the disguised Duke as he explained to the Friar why he
had disguised himself. The shadow of a cross sometimes
loomed large on the stage, suggesting judgment. Throughout there were menacing shadows on the stage that dis-
appeared only at the end, replaced by "a warm red-tinged
glow that bathed the characters in a mellow golden light
and assured the audience that the threat to happiness and
to harmony had finally been extinguished" (Wakeman,
p. 501).

The Duke (Yu Shizhi) was lavishly costumed in ocher
velvet when he was the Duke and in plain black sack cloth
when he played the Friar. (Originally the company had
hoped to use modern dress, but this was almost the first
production of Shakespeare in Chinese after 1940, and it
was felt that there were many other innovative features
for the cast and the audience to get used to.) The Duke
was cunning and insinuating, genial and benevolent, as

occasion demanded. Angelo (Ren Baoxian) wore a black doublet, white ruff, and silver-cross pendant. He was stern and arrogant, and his tone was uniformly unyielding. Li Rong played Isabella in a simple gray surplice and appeared pure and innocent. When the Duke proposed to her, she stood silent on the platform stage with her back to the spectators. Then she turned and walked with graceful steps toward them, her face serene and unreadable. Finally she went up to the Duke and accepted his proffered hand. The tension-filled silence erupted into joyful music and the couples ran hand in hand from the stage. Justice, mercy, and love had triumphed, if only barely. Wakeman felt that the Chinese audience was fully aware of the serious issues of the play, and could sympathize with the predicament of Isabella when Angelo defied her to denounce him, or with Claudio's humiliation as he was paraded in the streets. These were experiences not unknown during the Cultural Revolution. The director had instructed his cast to play naturally, as if the characters were Chinese. Mr. Robertson has praised (private communication) Ying Ruo Cheng's outstanding contribution and the team spirit of the company.

The play has also been seen on TV. The BBC and *Time-Life* collaborated to produce the play on TV in 1979 as part of a complete Shakespeare on TV. The producer, Cedric Messina, has stated that the aim of the series was to make the plays available as entertainment for a potential audience of the very young who have probably no experience of the theater or of Shakespeare. The director was Desmond Davis. In the text of the production some lines rendered superfluous by the TV medium have been omitted; minor characters have been dropped or merged, and stage directions have been realigned. Most of the action takes place at sunset, night, or dawn, only the last scene being in sunshine. Many scenes are visually effective. For example, Angelo sits at a large desk in front of a throne with armorial bearings. While he appears large, Isabella in a corner looks tiny. The desk in the vast judgment hall constricts the movements of

those who come to see him. He himself sits at the other
end of the hall with its whole length behind him. Tim
Piggott-Smith has played him as an efficient, arrogant,
and overbearing bureaucrat. The antagonism between him
and Isabella is the center of this production. Isabella is
played by Kate Nelligan, who has declared that the school
of thought that considers Isabella a sexual neurotic and
the play a study in repressive sexuality is "absolute non-
sense." She has presented Isabella as a girl for whom
Heaven, Hell and eternal life are realities superior as
existential values to anything that this life has to offer.
The Duke (Kenneth Colley) is a recognizable human
being with just a touch of divinity about him and a certain
prankishness in his ways. The last scene is staged as a
show on an Elizabethan platform stage with the courtiers
and the people watching. The translation of a Shakespeare
play into the very different medium of television presents
some problems, but in this production they are imaginatively surmounted.

After this brief (and regrettably selective) survey of the
stage interpretations of *Measure for Measure*, certain general reflections may be offered. *Measure for Measure*
continues to be a controversial play, and there is no
prospect of its losing that status! But it is no longer an
unpopular or infrequently seen play. It has attracted full
and appreciative audiences and some very distinguished
and imaginatively gifted directors and players. It has
provoked as many interpretations on the stage as in the
study, perhaps more so. A stage interpretation can be
more varied, more subtle and nuanced, certainly more
immediate in its impact, with a longer life in one's imaginative memory than a critical book. Jonathan Miller has
declared that a text has no definitive or exhaustible meaning:

> I don't believe that any human utterances beyond
> engineering instructions have got that sort of quality.
> I think that every play which describes people talk-

ing to one another is very vague, very permissive, very noncommittal except in moments of very, very stringent commitment . . . . The greater the play, the more alternative and mutually contradictory versions are possible . . . all of which are at least minimally compatible with the text from which they spring. (*Shakespeare Quarterly*, Winter 1976, p. 12)

(He has reiterated this point of view in his interview with Ralph Berry, *On Directing Shakespeare* [1977] and presented it at length in his own book, *Subsequent Performances* [1986].) The limits of interpretation cannot be set in advance with theoretical precision. Tact and good sense are essential, but it must be remembered that these are virtues that hug the coastline, whereas the wild sea that Shakespeare represents requires a daring Columbus, an actor or director for whom Shakespeare is the natural element. Another fact that has emerged is that the director has become independent of the critic and the scholar. He consults them, but is no longer content to follow meekly in their footsteps. Some trends may of course be discerned—the recent human Duke, for instance—but the only safe generalization that one can make is that somehow *Measure for Measure* is felt to be a modern play —though there is little agreement on what constitutes modernity. Perhaps the chief value of the play and the use of its critical and theatrical history is that together they promote what Keats called "negative capability," when a man can remain in "uncertainties, mysteries, doubts without any irritable reaching after fact and reason." It may be that to take part in the drama of life we need some convictions and principles also, but their stability and worth will depend on a prior cultivation of negative capability. At any rate the study of *Measure for Measure* can help very considerably in understanding the art and vision of Shakespeare in the tragedies and the final plays.

Bibliographical Note: There is no book-length comprehensive study of the stage history of *Measure for Measure*, a surprisingly unfilled gap considering its very interesting stage fortunes. I have depended on the calendar of productions (up to 1977) given by Mark Eccles in his *New Variorum* edition, pages 467–477. Eccles also gives titles of books and articles that discuss the listed productions. For post-1977 productions I have depended chiefly on reviews in the daily and weekly press and the more detailed accounts in the learned periodicals. Excerpts from press reviews are generally available in the *London Theatre Record*. First-night reviews are often written in a hurry, and do not always agree with one another, but they are fresh and vivid. A performance may settle down after the first night and may even change in significant ways. Reviews in the learned journals, especially *Shakespeare Quarterly* and *Shakespeare Survey*, are written with greater deliberation and perhaps after more than one viewing. On William Poel's productions, see Robert Speaight's *William Poel and the Elizabethan Revival* (1954); on Peter Brook, see Ralph Berry's *On Directing Shakespeare* (1977); on John Gielgud, see Gielgud's *An Actor and His Time* (1979) and Ronald Hayman's *John Gielgud* (1971).

Suggested References

The number of possible references is vast and grows alarmingly. (The *Shakespeare Quarterly* devotes one issue each year to a list of the previous year's work, and *Shakespeare Survey*—an annual publication—includes a substantial review of recent scholarship, as well as an occasional essay surveying a few decades of scholarship on a chosen topic.) Though no works are indispensable, those listed below have been found especially helpful.

1. Shakespeare's Times

Byrne, M. St. Clare. *Elizabethan Life in Town and Country.* Rev. ed. New York: Barnes & Noble, 1961. Chapters on manners, beliefs, education, etc., with illustrations.

Joseph, B. L. *Shakespeare's Eden: The Commonwealth of England, 1558–1629.* New York: Barnes & Noble, 1971. An account of the social, political, economic, and cultural life of England.

Schoenbaum, S. *Shakespeare: The Globe and the World.* New York: Oxford University Press, 1979. A readable, handsomely illustrated book on the world of the Elizabethans.

Shakespeare's England. 2 vols. Oxford: Oxford University Press, 1916. A large collection of scholarly essays on a wide variety of topics (e.g. astrology, costume, gardening, horsemanship), with special attention to Shakespeare's references to these topics.

Stone, Lawrence. *The Crisis of the Aristocracy, 1558–1641,* abridged edition. London: Oxford University Press, 1967.

2. Shakespeare

Barnet, Sylvan. *A Short Guide to Shakespeare.* New York:

Harcourt Brace Jovanovich, 1974. An introduction to all of the works and to the dramatic traditions behind them.

Bentley, Gerald E. *Shakespeare: A Biographical Handbook.* New Haven, Conn.: Yale University Press, 1961. The facts about Shakespeare, with virtually no conjecture intermingled.

Bush, Geoffrey. *Shakespeare and the Natural Condition.* Cambridge, Mass.: Harvard University Press, 1956. A short, sensitive account of Shakespeare's view of "Nature," touching most of the works.

Chambers, E. K. *William Shakespeare: A Study of Facts and Problems.* 2 vols. London: Oxford University Press, 1930. An invaluable, detailed reference work; not for the casual reader.

Chute, Marchette. *Shakespeare of London.* New York: Dutton, 1949. A readable biography fused with portraits of Stratford and London life.

Clemen, Wolfgang H. *The Development of Shakespeare's Imagery.* Cambridge, Mass.: Harvard University Press, 1951. (Originally published in German, 1936.) A temperate account of a subject often abused.

Granville-Barker, Harley. *Prefaces to Shakespeare.* 2 vols. Princeton, N. J.: Princeton University Press, 1946–47. Essays on ten plays by a scholarly man of the theater.

Harbage, Alfred. *As They Liked It.* New York: Macmillan, 1947. A long, sensitive essay on Shakespeare, morality, and the audience's expectations.

Kernan, Alvin B., ed. *Modern Shakespearean Criticism: Essays on Style, Dramaturgy, and the Major Plays.* New York: Harcourt Brace Jovanovich, 1970. A collection of major formalist criticism.

————. "The Plays and the Playwrights." In *The Revels History of Drama in English,* general editors Clifford Leech and T. W. Craik. Vol. III. London: Methuen, 1975. A book-length essay surveying Elizabethan drama with substantial discussions of Shakespeare's plays.

Schoenbaum, S. *Shakespeare's Lives.* Oxford: Clarendon Press, 1970. A review of the evidence, and an examination of many biographies, including those by Baconians and other heretics.

————. *William Shakespeare: A Compact Documentary Life.* New York: Oxford University Press, 1977. A readable presentation of all that the documents tell us about Shakespeare.

Traversi, D. A. *An Approach to Shakespeare.* 3rd rev. ed. 2 vols. New York: Doubleday, 1968–69. An analysis of the plays beginning with words, images, and themes, rather than with characters.

Van Doren, Mark. *Shakespeare.* New York: Holt, 1939. Brief, perceptive readings of all of the plays.

3. Shakespeare's Theater

Beckerman, Bernard. *Shakespeare at the Globe, 1599–1609.* New York: Macmillan, 1962. On the playhouse and on Elizabethan dramaturgy, acting, and staging.

Chambers, E. K. *The Elizabethan Stage.* 4 vols. New York: Oxford University Press, 1945. A major reference work on theaters, theatrical companies, and staging at court.

Cook, Ann Jennalie. *The Privileged Playgoers of Shakespeare's London, 1576–1642.* Princeton, N. J.: Princeton University Press, 1981. Sees Shakespeare's audience as more middle-class and more intellectual than Harbage (below) does.

Gurr, Andrew. *The Shakespearean Stage: 1574–1642.* 2d edition. Cambridge: Cambridge University Press, 1981. On the acting companies, the actors, the playhouses, the stages, and the audiences.

Harbage, Alfred. *Shakespeare's Audience.* New York: Columbia University Press, 1941. A study of the size and nature of the theatrical public, emphasizing its representativeness.

Hodges, C. Walter. *The Globe Restored.* London: Ernest Benn, 1953. A well-illustrated and readable attempt to reconstruct the Globe Theatre.

Hosley, Richard. "The Playhouses." In *The Revels History of Drama in English,* general editors Clifford Leech and T. W. Craik. Vol. III. London: Methuen, 1975. An essay of one hundred pages on the physical aspects of the playhouses.

Kernodle, George R. *From Art to Theatre: Form and Convention in the Renaissance.* Chicago: University of Chicago

Press, 1944. Pioneering and stimulating work on the symbolic and cultural meaning of theater construction.

Nagler, A. M. *Shakespeare's Stage*. Trans. Ralph Manheim. New Haven, Conn.: Yale University Press, 1958. A very brief introduction to the physical aspects of the playhouse.

Slater, Ann Pasternak. *Shakespeare the Director*. Totowa, N. J.: Barnes & Noble, 1982. An analysis of theatrical effects (e.g., kissing, kneeling) in stage directions and dialogue.

Thomson, Peter. *Shakespeare Theatre*. London: Routledge & Kegan Paul, 1983. A discussion of how plays were staged in Shakespeare's time.

4. Miscellaneous Reference Works

Abbott, E. A. *A Shakespearean Grammar*. New Edition. New York: Macmillan, 1877. An examination of differences between Elizabethan and modern grammar.

Bevington, David. *Shakespeare*. Arlington Heights, Ill.: A. H. M. Publishing, 1978. A short guide to hundreds of important writings on the works.

Bullough, Geoffrey. *Narrative and Dramatic Sources of Shakespeare*. 8 vols. New York: Columbia University Press, 1957–75. A collection of many of the books Shakespeare drew upon, with judicious comments.

Campbell, Oscar James, and Edward G. Quinn. *The Reader's Encyclopedia of Shakespeare*. New York: Crowell, 1966. More than 2,600 entries, from a few sentences to a few pages, on everything related to Shakespeare.

Greg, W. W. *The Shakespeare First Folio*. New York: Oxford University Press, 1955. A detailed yet readable history of the first collection (1623) of Shakespeare's plays.

Kökeritz, Helge. *Shakespeare's Names*. New Haven, Conn.: Yale University Press, 1959. A guide to the pronunciation of some 1,800 names appearing in Shakespeare.

————. *Shakespeare's Pronunciation*. New Haven, Conn.: Yale University Press, 1953. Contains much information about puns and rhymes.

Muir, Kenneth. *The Sources of Shakespeare's Plays*. New Haven, Conn.: Yale University Press, 1978. An account of Shakespeare's use of his reading.

The Norton Facsimile: The First Folio of Shakespeare. Prepared by Charles Hinman. New York: Norton, 1968. A handsome and accurate facsimile of the first collection (1623) of Shakespeare's plays.

Onions, C. T. *A Shakespeare Glossary.* 2d ed., rev., with enlarged addenda. London: Oxford University Press, 1953. Definitions of words (or senses of words) now obsolete.

Partridge, Eric. *Shakespeare's Bawdy.* Rev. ed. New York: Dutton, 1955. A glossary of bawdy words and phrases.

Shakespeare Quarterly. See headnote to Suggested References.

Shakespeare Survey. See headnote to Suggested References.

Shakespeare's Plays in Quarto. A Facsimile Edition. Ed. Michael J. B. Allen and Kenneth Muir. Berkeley, Calif.: University of California Press, 1981. A book of nine hundred pages, containing facsimilies of twenty-two of the quarto editions of Shakespeare's plays. An invaluable complement to *The Norton Facsimile: The First Folio of Shakespeare* (see above).

Smith, Gordon Ross. *A Classified Shakespeare Bibliography 1936–1958.* University Park, Pa.: Pennsylvania State University Press, 1963. A list of some twenty thousand items on Shakespeare.

Spevack, Marvin. *The Harvard Concordance to Shakespeare.* Cambridge, Mass.: Harvard University Press, 1973. An index to Shakespeare's words.

Wells, Stanley, ed. *Shakespeare: Select Bibliographies.* London: Oxford University Press, 1973. Seventeen essays surveying scholarship and criticism of Shakespeare's life, work, and theater.

5. *Measure for Measure*

Bennett, Josephine Waters. *"Measure for Measure" as Royal Entertainment.* New York: Columbia University Press, 1966.

Berry, Ralph. *On Directing Shakespeare.* London: Croom Helm, 1977.

————. *Changing Styles in Shakespeare.* London: Allen and Unwin, 1981.

Bradbrook, M. C. "Authority, Truth and Justice in *Measure*

for Measure," *Review of English Studies*, 17 (1941), 385–99.

Chambers, R. W. *Man's Unconquerable Mind*. London: Jonathan Cape, 1952.

Eccles, Mark. *A New Variorum Edition of Shakespeare: Measure for Measure*. New York: The Modern Language Association of America, 1980.

Empson, William. *The Structure of Complex Words*. London: Chatto and Windus, 1951.

Foakes, R. A. *Shakespeare: The Dark Comedies to the Last Plays*. London: Routledge and Kegan Paul, 1971.

Frye, Northrop. *The Myth of Deliverance: Reflections on Shakespeare's Problem Comedies*. Toronto: University of Toronto Press, 1983.

Geckle, George L. (ed.) *Twentieth Century Interpretations of Measure for Measure*. Englewood Cliffs, New Jersey: Prentice-Hall, 1970.

Gless, Darryl J. *Measure for Measure, The Law and the Convent*. Princeton: Princeton University Press, 1979.

Hawkins, Harriet. *Measure for Measure*. Brighton: Harvester Press, 1987.

Hunter, Robert G. *Shakespeare and the Comedy of Forgiveness*. New York: Columbia University Press, 1965.

Jamieson, Michael. "The Problem Plays 1920–1970: A Retrospect," *Shakespeare Survey 25*, 1972, pages 1–10.

Knights, L. C. "The Ambiguity of *Measure for Measure*," *Scrutiny*, 10 (1942), 222–33.

Lawrence, W. W. *Shakespeare's Problem Comedies*. New York: Macmillan, 1931.

———. "*Measure for Measure* and Lucio," *Shakespeare Quarterly*, 9 (1958), 443–53.

Leavis, F. R. *The Common Pursuit*. London: Chatto and Windus, 1952.

Maxwell, J. C. "*Measure for Measure*: The Play and the Themes," *Procedings of the British Academy*, 60 (1974); London: Oxford University Press, 1975, pp. 199–218.

Miles, Rosalind. *The Problem of Measure for Measure: A Historical Investigation*. London: Vision Press, 1976.

Muir, Kenneth, and Stanley Wells. *Aspects of Shakespeare's*

Problem Plays. Cambridge: Cambridge University Press, 1982.

Nicholls, Graham. *Measure for Measure: Text and Performance*. London: Macmillan Education, 1986.

Ornstein, Robert (ed.) *Discussions of Shakespeare's Problem Comedies*. Boston: D. C. Heath, 1961.

Rabkin, Norman. *Shakespeare and the Common Understanding*. New York: Free Press, 1967; Chicago: University of Chicago Press, 1984.

Rossiter, A. P. *"Angel with Horns" and Other Shakespeare Lectures*, ed. Graham Storey. London: Longmans, Green and Co., 1961.

Schanzer, Ernest. *The Problem Plays of Shakespeare*. London: Routledge and Kegan Paul, 1963.

Shell, Marc. *The End of Kinship: Measure for Measure, Incest, and the Ideal of Universal Siblinghood*. Stanford: Stanford University Press, 1988.

Stead, C. K. (ed.) *Measure for Measure: A Casebook*. London: Macmillan, 1971.

Thomas, Vivian. *The Moral Universe of Shakespeare's Problem Plays*. London: Croom Helm, 1987.

Tillyard, E. M. W. *Shakespeare's Problem Plays*. London: Chatto and Windus, 1950.

Watts, Cedric. *Measure for Measure*. Harmondsworth: Penguin, 1986; New York: Viking, 1986.

 **SIGNET CLASSIC**

THE SIGNET CLASSIC
SHAKESPEARE

*Introducing the work of the world's
greatest dramatist in new combined volumes
edited by outstanding scholars:*

LOVE'S LABOR'S LOST, THE TWO GENTLEMEN OF VERONA, and THE MERRY WIVES OF WINDSOR: edited and with introductions by John Arthos, Bertrand Evans, and William Green.
(522877—$5.95)

HENRY VI, Parts I, II, & III; edited and with introductions by William H. Matchett and S. Schoenbaum.
(523121—$5.95)

KING JOHN and HENRY VIII: edited and with introductions by William H. Matchett and S. Schoenbaum.
(522990—$5.95)

TITUS ANDRONICUS and TIMON OF ATHENS: edited and with introductions by Sylvan Barnet and Maurice Charney.
(522699—$5.95)

PERICLES, CYMBELINE, and THE TWO NOBLE KINSMEN: edited and with introductions by Ernest Schanzer, Richard Hosley, and Clifford Leech.
(522656—$5.95)

THE SONNETS and NARRATIVE POEMS: THE COMPLETE NON-DRAMATIC POETRY: edited by William Burto, and with introductions by W. H. Auden and William Empson.
(523148—$5.95)

Prices slightly higher in Canada.

Buy them at your local bookstore or use this convenient coupon for ordering.

PENGUIN USA
P.O. Box 999 — Dept. #17109
Bergenfield, New Jersey 07621

Please send me the books I have checked above.
I am enclosing $_____ (please add $2.00 to cover postage and handling). Send check or money order (no cash or C.O.D.'s) or charge by Mastercard or VISA (with a $15.00 minimum). Prices and numbers are subject to change without notice.

Card #_____ Exp. Date _____
Signature_____
Name_____
Address_____
City _____ State _____ Zip Code _____

For faster service when ordering by credit card call **1-800-253-6476**

Allow a minimum of 4-6 weeks for delivery. This offer is subject to change without notice.